The
VENUS
Fly-Trap

Nick Stott

Published by 57th Parallel Publications

Acknowledgements

I am indebted to a tight band of reader/critics who read the proofs of this novel and made many clever and helpful comments whilst it was taking shape. In particular, Muriel McLean, Margaret Anderson and my friend and Scrabble opponent, Kate Pedelty.

Others who have given valiant additional help and support with criticisms and helpful suggestions are, Norman Burns, Grant and Mary Gordon, Ron Simpson, Stan Troup and my elder daughter Fiona, although I have had great encouragement from many other friends and family members. My cousin Jessie McIntosh has been of great assistance, as also have been my friends James M. Robertson and Gordon Hardie.

Again, to my friends from across the pond: Jack McAllister, Myron White and Carolyn Poole who gave me permission to use their real names and approximate situation in New York State, although I took great liberties creating imaginary thoughts expressed by them. They are real friends who have contributed some of the Americanisms in daily usage along with another American lady, Mikie Rossbach. I made use of other friend's Christian names, to all their great amusement and through their letters have introduced some pertinent points.

To all of them, I wish to say - Thank you.

Otherwise, the characters in the book are purely imaginary and any connection or similarity to people living or dead, is purely coincidental. The travel background and the factual detail is accurate, as far as I can ascertain through research and I have personally travelled the route.

The VENUS Fly-Trap

The cover illustration has been created by professional artist, Stephen B. Whatley, PO Box No. 2556, Enfield, London. EN2 8SE. He has become a personal friend and his works are in many private and public collections worldwide.

ISBN 0-9532852-1-9

Printed and bound in Great Britain by: Caledonian International Book Manufacturing, Bishopbriggs, Glasgow.

Other Publication by same author: 'Travel the World with Confidence', a safety guide and pocket-sized aide-memoire priced, £2.50 or $5.00.US.

ISBN 0-95-328520-0

Now discounted on direct sales to, £1.00 or $3.00.US inclusive of Post and Packaging.

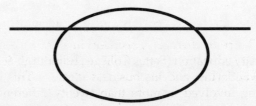

This novel has been published by 57th Parallel Publications and extra copies can be obtained by writing direct to them at 8 Rosebery Street, Aberdeen, Scotland, AB15 5LL. E-mail: fiftyseven@absco.fsnet.co.uk

Please enclose a cheque for the cover price that includes P.&P. For direct orders, allow 28 days delivery

Author's note

I have intentionally made use of the first and third person in the novel; purists of the English language will no doubt be appalled, but I wished my reader to feel closer at times to the sensations experienced by the characters. Where Americans were speaking or happened to be the only action character in a Chapter, I have used American phrases and spellings of many words. Again, to give the reader a flavour of Latin America, I have used a lot of Spanish and given the translation shortly thereafter. As I have edited and published this book personally, I do apologise for any mistakes that may have remained uncorrected. It is almost impossible to find a Literary Agent to represent your work and likewise to find a publisher who is willing to take a chance on a new writer. There are 100,000 books published annually and less than half of these actually make money.

I have endeavoured to research all facts quoted in the novel and believe them to be correct.

———————————————

Nick Stott was born in Aberdeen , Scotland in 1939.   An incomplete Public school and University education (Fettes College , Edinburgh & Aberdeen) was due to satisfying his wanderlust and his business ideas.   This led to being in 140 countries and being involved in more than twenty different business projects. He was thirteen years farming , ten years in car and commercial vehicle rental and chartered his own 67 foot , Ocean-going , luxury Motor Yacht in the Mediterranean among many other diverse business involvements.   He retired at 44 to build a luxury house that overlooked the Grampian mountains before selling-up once more to travel again ten years later.   As arthritis curtailed his outdoor pursuits , he started to write seriously two years ago when he returned to Scotland after three years of continuous travel.

List of Characters

Sobatsu operatives:
Kaitto Nomura, Chief executive.
Jorgé Philippe, Head of security.
Field soldiers:- Ramires - Sobatsu's cracksman, also
Señora Flores, Hauptmann, Parides, Juanito and Ramon Gutierez.

Law Agents:-
Jim Booth (murdered FBI agent)
CIA at Langley, Virginia:-
Nick Vyon (Head), Jim Turner (Senior field agent), Chuck Hanson,
and Joe & Hank, field agents.
Chief Inspector Thurlston of the British civil police.

Laurence C. Jefferson, CEO of Planet Ales, Inc. USA.
Ardeth - Jefferson's secretary - Captain André Schiffé of the yacht Venus.
Yussuf and Hossein - Emirati business friends and contacts of Jefferson in
Dubai, United Arab Emirates.

Bernard Martin of English Purity Chemicals, England.
Sally is Bernard's wife, Judy is Bernard's business secretary in England,
Fraser is the family lawyer

Friends of Martin:
Jack McAllister and girlfriend, Carolyn; also Myron White and his friend
Gerald, all in the Town of Penn Yan, New York State, USA

Juan Zambrano and Bismar in Managua, Nicaragua.

also Dr Holguer Holsh in Ecuador.

Murf and Claire from New Zealand

ATLANTIC OCEAN

PACIFIC OCEAN

CARIBBEAN SEA

ANTILLES

BRASIL

PERU

SURINAM
GUYANA
VENEZUELA
COLOMBIA
ECUADOR

TRINIDAD + TOBAGO

GULF OF MEXICO

MEXICO

MEXICO

UNITED STATES

BAHAMAS
CUBA

BELIZE
GUATEMALA
HONDURAS
NICARAGUA
EL SALVADOR
COSTA RICA
PANAMA

1 MIAMI
2 SAN PEDRO
3 BELIZE CITY
4 CANCUN
5 OAXACA
6 SAN PEDRO SULA
7 TEGUCIGALPA
8 MANAGUA
9 SAN JOSÉ
10 COLÓN
11 PANAMA CITY
12 SAN BLAS
13 CARTAGENA
14 BARRANQUILA
15 HAITI + DOM. REP.
16 ARUBA
17 BONAIRE
18 CURAÇAO
19 (ABC ISLANDS)
20 BUENAVENTURA

(NOT TO SCALE)

SCHEMATIC MAP
NOT TO SCALE.

1. HAVANA
2. CANCUN
3. CURAÇAO
4. BARRANQUILA
5. CARTAGENA
6. CARACAS
7. BOGOTÁ
8. BUENAVENTURA
9. QUITO
10. IQUITOS
11. MANAUS
12. BELÉM
13. LIMA
14. SUCRE
15. BRASILIA
16. RECIFÉ
17. SALVADOR
18. RIO de JANEIRO
19. MONTEVIDEO
20. BUENOS AIRES
21. ASCUNCIÓN
22. IQUIQUE
23. CALAMA
24. VALPARAISO
25. SANTIAGO
26. PUERTO MONTT

27. BARILOCHE
28. USHUAIA.

One

It was snowing, lightly at first, then with greater flurries and increasing tempo. I shivered and spooned another mouthful of 'sopa de zanohorrias' followed by some crusty bread. The dining room of Las Lengas Hotel was comfortably warm and I viewed the freezing scene outside with a high degree of self-satisfaction, being inside and enjoying carrot soup. It was almost as good as my wife's but lacked the teaspoonful of sugar that she included in all her soups, removing the slightly bitter taste. I was at the end of the world, in the southernmost city of Ushuaia, in Tierra del Fuego - Land of Fire, Argentina. It had been a long day getting here from Bariloche where I had enjoyed a few days skiing break prior to being advised by my office to meet a Señor Jorgé Philippe of Sobatsu Electronics, the world's largest electronics company, a branch of it being in Ushuaia.

Flying into the tiny airport between the craggy peaks of the rugged, snow capped volcanoes was a sensational experience soon to be dispensed with, as their International airport would be ready to receive wide-bodied, long-haul jets within another few months. The tiny plane had spiralled down between rock surfaces, so close, that you felt you could have reached out and touched them. It made up for what had been otherwise, a boring trip broken only by four short stops to drop off or take on passengers. It was the oil personnel of Argentina who made the air-route worthwhile. The huge tracts of Patagonia, a pock-marked land mostly water-filled, were interspersed with the nodding donkeys and flare-stacks of the oil industry. Offshore platforms and rigs could be seen along the coast as we crossed the Straits of Magellan to the Island of Tierra del Fuego which is shared with Chile, although it had been the volcanic activities, seen from great distances at sea that had prompted the early mariners to name it 'the land of fire'.

It was the beginning of winter and the warm soup spread comfort signals throughout my body as I allowed my mind to dwell on what Señor Philippe would be like to deal with at next morning's arranged meeting. A particularly good Argentinian Malbec of Finca El Retiro, although at twice the price of Chilean reds, contributed to my bonhomie and I was already anticipating my mushroom omelette to follow. My three fellow diners were of little interest, two mothers with well-behaved children, very obviously oil-linked and a blue-rinsed matriarch probably Chilean, treating herself to a winter break. The hotel was elevated on a hillside overlooking the Beagle Channel and the city itself. As I slowly turned my gaze from the orange street lights and my visual arc swung back over the black waters, my eyes finally focussed on the unmade road below the hotel restaurant.

I watched the careful approach of an American saloon car at the series of water filled, ice encrusted potholes and anticipated the inward draught of breath and body as a sole pedestrian was illuminated in the extra glare of headlights enhanced by the orange-yellow of an overhanging street lamp. In a split second the man was propelled through the dilapidated picket fence behind him as though thrown by a giant, unseen hand. The shot, while muffled, came to me a few milliseconds later. The car had gone, the snow fell, the incident was past, completely unheard and unrecognised by my fellow diners. More important matters of enjoyment were involving the children in the choice from the sweet trolley.

I sat stupefied, stunned by what I had seen, unsure if it had been real or imagined. I gazed at the gap in the picket fence. Two people were passing as I watched, but there was no reaction from either of them - perhaps I had imagined it. Should I mention it to anyone, or should I go down there to investigate before causing an unnecessary search and perhaps an embarrassing incident? I was a foreigner as well as a Brit on Argentinian soil and the Falklands War was hardly ten years into history. Many of the sailors of the Belgrano had come from this city and there was a large and moving memorial tribute to their loss just a few hundred yards from the hotel. I chose to investigate quietly first. Signing my bill I retreated to the security of my room where I collected a torch, gloves and suitable warm clothing to face outdoors.

It was easy to leave the hotel without arousing attention or comment as my room was one of four with a separate corridor that bypassed reception. I joined many other pedestrians who were heading towards the stepped hillside that took one to the lower street level. Swirling flurries of snow made me realise that it would be a heavy fall that night and that I had better hurry if anything was to be done. I approached the gap in the fence with caution not knowing what to expect.

The body shape could just be identified, although fast being covered with snow. Unsurprisingly, it was plain there was little that I could do, a large dark stain beneath the immobile form underlining the man's violent demise. My attention was then drawn to a flapping piece of cloth on the picket fence. I pulled it clear and found it to be a fabric covered folder stuffed with papers and without considering the implications shoved them into my parka and returned to the hotel as fast as conditions allowed. There had been no-one around that I'd seen to observe me and my tell-tale footprints would soon be covered. I decided to keep the knowledge of what I'd seen to myself, reckoned that I could be of little assistance to the authorities anyway and could only create greater difficulties for myself.

Back in the warmth of my room with the safety lock turned, I poured myself a large Scotch from a bottle that I always kept in my luggage; I both disliked paying the inflated prices of hotel bars and too often there would be others there, resulting in over-drinking and hangovers next day. I examined the folder and realised that I should have left it there, as it could be material evidence, but curiosity and the human magpie instinct had overcome sensible actions. As I tipped all the papers onto the bed, I could see most of the writings were in English or Spanish and easy to understand and were, it appeared, commercial in content with industrial diagrams; thank goodness they weren't state secrets! I glanced through the first few pages of detail which gave the names of ten multi-national companies, the Chief Executive Officer (CEO) in each and their mobile-phone numbers. The mainline telephone numbers followed these, also the names of their executive personal assistants whilst other long lists of global companies followed. Examining the diagrams, which had similarities to the micro-chips in my own industry, I realised that they were potential layouts for the dispensation of small quantities of chemicals. Two or three of these were printed on especially thick paper and on the rest of the paperwork were written explanations about innovative additions. Industrial espionage sprang to mind, but as there were no further areas of elucidation they might as well have been written in Greek. I returned the papers to the folder and put it into the zipped divider in my suitcase. As the man had been clearly dead, his papers probably of little use to the authorities anyway, I resolved to say nothing, but decided to buy the local newspaper and read the explanation.

A good night's rest and a cooked breakfast put me in the mood to meet Señor Jorgé Philippe. My taxi was waiting for me, having been booked before breakfast, and I was whisked off through the town centre and out to the industrial belt where televisions, washing machines, personal computers, mobile phones and music - centres by the thousand were assembled for sale in the Americas. All the main Japanese firms had representation, the names on the sides of the buildings, a veritable who's who of the electronics world.

My name is Bernard Martin, a highly-paid sales executive for an English chemical company specialising in chemicals for the laundry industry. The hotel and catering services are my field of expertise, companies that require fast and good clean laundry facilities for themselves and their customers. We had carved out a goodly, £50 million turnover business around the world, but as yet hadn't become large enough for the giants like Lever Bros. to buy us out nor to interfere with our markets. I had set-up a number of small chain hotels with our products and had hundreds of independent restaurants likewise utilising our services. Personal contacts, fast trouble shooting and just-in-time supplies at competitive prices kept the business growing steadily and my salary scale on a gentle upward climb with many perks. Most of the work was a milk-run, but occasionally I would be given the task of reorganising equipment and obtaining specialised machinery to tackle a unique cycle of ingredients for maximum output of the finally finished laundry. Like napkins and tablecloths for instance. The customer wanted to have them clean and returned for service within three days so as not to tie up too much capital on what was purely presentation for appearance. Various strengths of chemicals were used for speed in conjunction with cleanliness and colour dependency. The number of washes before replacement and the legal requirements of effluent disposal of the country using our chemicals being of prime importance. I visited mainly agents for our products, but would also deal directly with the end customer if requested to do so. Señor Philippe had to install specialised, industrial washing machines for a new account in the Far East obtained by one of the other three sales executives. My thirty years of experience with the company and being almost on the spot for full explanation of machinery requirements had given me this assignment. The job was now merely a dawdle, requiring little sales effort on my part; the products sold themselves on price alone and more commission could be earned by our agents gaining more customers. I was in charge of all our company's business in Latin America and had covered the isthmus and continent from end to end. Being a Spanish speaker had given me terrific advantage when dealing with the businesses in these parts and my company had rewarded my efforts with an excellent expenses account and top salary. I had to admit to having become used to staying in quality hotels as my company recognised both the business advantages of them, their extra security and at half of European prices.

I had a nice property in Hampshire, a wife who was five years younger than my fifty years and a son and daughter in their early twenties. At just over six feet, brown hair now greying at the temples, strong features and broad shoulders, I had little difficulty in meeting the opposite sex. I had too, a secretary of 35 years who'd had designs on me for five years, thankfully without complications, Judy made herself available at my convenience and was also completely loyal and devoted to her work. As she was a bit of a nymphomaniac, my own frequent travels allowed for batteries to recharge and my enjoyable, menage-a-trois lifestyle continued without difficulty. Travel and work for the firm allowed me to enjoy the company of many attractive ladies without compromising myself.

Sally, my other half, recognised Judy only as an indispensable support system to sustain our comfortable lifestyle. My hobbies were mainly confined to playing the occasional game of scrabble with the family, fishing when the opportunity arose and chess if I could find an opponent. The kids had practically been brought up by Sally and my little family unit lived in spurts between foreign excursions.

Señor Jorgé Philippe was not the person that I expected to meet. He was smartly dressed and well groomed, his tie and matching silk handkerchief underlined a meticulous attitude that combined with balance. His office walls were covered with engineering and electronics certificates and highly complex diagrams, under the heading, work in hand. This was someone whose obvious mental capabilities were in the Mensa bracket. A dapper, little man with long thin side-burns and a sallow complexion, but with dark piercing eyes that seemed to penetrate your very soul. There was something about him that gave me an uneasy feeling, his handshake had been cold, damp and unwelcoming, although his manner was super-efficient. His searching questions about the equipment required took him less than ten minutes to ascertain all that he needed to know. His questioning then took a different tack as he asked about my trip, my hotel and whether I had known about the hit-and-run accident that was front-page news in the Ushuaia Noticias. I felt myself reddening as I said that I'd retired early and that I was unaware of any accident. His look of complete disbelief discomfited me still further and I was glad to return to the business of delivery, costs, etc. I declined his offer of lunch (out of character, as a free lunch was always welcome) and obtained a taxi back to Las Lengas. A strong black coffee settled my nerves as I read the news report about the 'hit-and-run'.

An American tourist, by name Jim Booth, had been killed outright. There was no mention of murder nor of the tourist having been shot, but the reward of $50,000 offered by Señor Philippe's company for any information was a veritable blow between the eyes. Why hadn't he mentioned their interest? What did he know? It was an enormous reward under the circumstances; and who would shoot a tourist and not stop to rob him? Again why were the police not releasing the truth? I was too anxious to eat anything and, pouring myself a stiff whisky, I hung the 'Do not Disturb' sign on the outside door handle then locked and bolted myself in.

After drawing the curtains, I checked that there had been no clandestine entry to my case before retrieving the documents, the combination figures remained exactly as I had set them. I spread all fourteen sheets of paper on the bed and examined the folder to see if I had missed anything, then picked up each page in turn and read the content. The lists of companies were fascinating, a thousand or so of the largest, most powerful and economically strongest of their type around the world. The detail concerning micro-chips was complicated and beyond my comprehension, other than recognising that some of the circuits were for dispensing amounts of chemical, like we used in our washing machines. Perhaps these were industrial secrets and Philippe's company hadn't got around to patenting the system yet?

The three thicker pages caught my attention again; they appeared bulky as though they doubled as envelopes! That was it! They were cleverly camouflaged envelopes! I examined one of them very carefully and retrieved a scalpel from my toilet bag and a small magnifying glass from my odds and sods repair kit. As I use an electric rechargeable razor, I find a scalpel with a handle very handy for removing callouses, rag-nails or the occasional blister. The seal was almost invisible and required a very steady sliding motion of the scalpel to open the envelope. The re-sealable plastic faces were difficult to separate; inside were three closely typed, wafer-thin sheets of paper. The other two envelopes were identical in their contents, but not the script. Each set of papers was entitled Transcription of taped conversation of the meeting of The Millennium Club, followed by the date, place and other details. The second was entitled Century and the third had Top Ten replacing the word Millennium. Their contents were vastly different.

As I read, my skin crawled, beads of perspiration forming on my forehead and upper lip. It took me the best part of an hour to read it all. I felt absolutely stunned, somewhat frightened and more than just a little panic stricken. Human rights would no longer be of importance if these companies succeeded. This stuff was dynamite! No wonder the carrier had been killed - he must have been an agent. But for whom? M.I.6? FBI? Mossad? Interpol? It could be any of the world's secret services or criminal investigation departments. What should I do? They'd already killed one man. If they suspected me I could be next.

I returned the papers exactly the way that I'd found them and re-sealed the envelopes, but put all the papers amongst my own office records which was mixed with the advertising blurb of our products. I would dump the cloth folder; somewhere that it couldn't be linked to myself. I was shaking and poured yet another large Scotch, recognising that I shouldn't, but requiring its comfort and the Dutch courage that it sustained. I had to work out what I was going to do and tackle the task logically without arousing suspicions in those who might be observing me.

Definitely Sobatsu Electronics was involved in this right up to their necks. Their name had been on all three lists -1,000, 100, and the Top 10! So, Señor Philippe had to be avoided, but where was I going to get rid of these transcripts? And the sooner the better. It wouldn't take them long to figure out that the only safe way of making certain such news wouldn't be in the hands of law-enforcers would be to remove permanently all the possible directions that these vital papers could have taken. I daren't risk going to the authorities as most of the Latin American nations were recent young democracies and corruption still existed within the ranks of their law enforcement agencies. I daren't take any chances. I had to organise tonight, now in fact! But first, plan my escape and stay alive. Think! I wrote out a list of objectives, I can organise myself best that way.

1. To whom should I deliver this information?

2. Where would it be best hidden until delivery?

3. Should I photocopy it and have a secondary backup?

4. Who could I contact to keep the photocopies safe?

5. How do I get all of the previous four steps completed safely?

6. Do I disappear, as Sobatsu Electronics would shortly recognise that I could be implicated in the disappearance of these papers?

7. How to effect such a disappearance and get to my first objective?

8. Computers would track flights, ships sailing and border crossings and any credit card transactions.

9. Fast moves with constant changes should just keep me out in front.

10. Routing would be all important, with alternatives!

11. Cash withdrawals from ATM's just prior to a change of direction and only if strictly necessary.

12. My route had to avoid blind alleys or dead ends!!!!

I scribbled various routes on successive pages of the telephone notepad, aware that the first steps were the most important. Being at the end of the South American continent, there were only two major routes out and the first 600 miles or so of travel would be easily followed. Think!

It was 1900 hours and the phone was ringing. Reception was asking if I wished dinner in my room as with so few guests the dining room would be closing at eight. I said that I'd be right down.

"Buenos tardes Señor Martin".

My heart almost stopped and with tremendous control I turned and said, "Buenos tardes Señor Philippe", then instantly recognised the complete dishonesty of his next words as he introduced me to his two companions.

"This is my technical director Señor Parides and my personal secretary and chauffeur Señor Hauptmann. Gentlemen, Señor Martin of English Purity Chemicals".

The two henchmen who bore these names had more to do with the technicalities of torture and hit-men, I thought, making a supreme effort to control my facial expression and to sound genuinely pleased to meet them. Shaking hands I said,

"How about joining me for a drink and dinner gentlemen. I would enjoy the company, but perhaps you came here on other business, Señor Philippe?"

"No Señor, we'd be delighted to have a drink with you, but cannot stay for dinner. There was just one small point that we'd like clarification upon in case you were flying back to England shortly."

We entered the small lounge bar, drinks ordered and delivered as we sat around a table and Señor Parides rolled out a large technical diagram. I relaxed a little. It was about business, my imagination and nerves were a little overstretched. I put on my spectacles and for the second time that evening my heart skipped a beat - it was the same diagram of the micro-chip that was among my papers in my room! I said easily,

"Is this the chemicals-dispensing control you've designed for our washing machine? I'm afraid that this is out-with my expertise, but we have technical engineers in England who can help if there's any difficulties with the exact calculations that you may require."

"No Señor, we have it fully under control I assure you", Philippe replied, nodding to Parides whose heavily-set frame was more attuned to all-in wrestling than executive company documentation. He rolled up the diagram and slid it back into its sleeve roll.

Philippe continued, "I felt that you might be able to understand that the costs we discussed this morning could be exceeded by a few extra requirements involved in the micro technology needed for calibration, but that any extra cost will not exceed another three per cent, if this is acceptable".

"Completely acceptable gentlemen and I in turn, can give you full assurances that your costs will be covered by my company." I could feel small trickles of cold perspiration running down my chest but my mind was racing ahead as Philippe changed tack.

"When are you returning to the UK?"

I laughed, "I was interrupted with an attractive, red-headed piece of business on the ski-slopes of Bariloche when the job of meeting you for this specialist washing machine was given to me. I was on a week's vacation and relaxation break prior to returning to home duties, but now feel that I'll finish the business with my red-head before going home. I was going to phone Lupitá tonight to let her know that I'll take the first available flight back to Bariloche."

"Ah!, then let me assist you in your arrangements", Philippe said, "I'll fax your hotel and book your flight and have Hauptmann drive you to the airport tomorrow".

With that he stood up leaving his drink untouched, only Parides and Hauptmann having downed theirs. Mine was only half finished.

"I'll bid you a good night's rest and safe journey, be careful with the red-head", Philippe laughed. "It's been a pleasure to do business with you Señor Martin".

We stood and shook hands, the cold clamminess of his grasp again impacting upon me, but already Parides and Hauptmann were out in the hall joining a third man waiting there. I sank back into my chair, my legs a little weak. Although my appetite had vanished I ordered the menu and wine list. Safe for the moment I thought. Thank God I'd dumped the cloth covered folder in the cleaner's trash bag at the end of the corridor and had set the combination locks on my suitcase. I had to force my food and wine down and appear relaxed.

It was my overactive imagination that made me feel the blue-rinsed matriarch was examining me closely, but couldn't catch her observing me.

It was a relief to gain once more the security of my room. I bolted the door and put on the safety chain and examined the window fastenings before I checked my case. The combination locks had been tampered with; the eighth turn off-centre of, both central figures, were now fully aligned. My shakiness returned and feverishly I laid my case on the bed and opened it. Nothing was out of place, everything was exactly as I had re-packed it, my business paperwork in their correct order, the secret papers still there. Think! My belongings had been checked, that much was clear. The fourth man had been an expert, but had missed the vital papers, or had he? I got out my personal organiser and retrieved my hotel telephone notes from my body-belt where I kept $10,000 in Traveller's cheques and a similar amount in cash. These were for emergencies and the undeclared fun extras of my foreign trips. Telephoning Lupitá in Bariloche I said that I'd be on the first flight back to Bariloche and that I'd be staying at the same hotel for a few days more, she was delighted and said that she'd be waiting, her husky tones full of sexual undertones and meaning. At that moment it was the last thing I had on my mind, but Bariloche gave me avenues for escape and I was glad of my knowledge of the South American continent, collected on the many previous, business trips. I faxed the company with details of the successful meeting with Philippe, adding a small postscript of sexual innuendo to Judy that would confirm my infidelity and ordinariness to any prying eyes.

I had little alternative, but to assume that my innocence of any involvement in the previous night's murder was fully accepted by Philippe and would continue to behave in that context until Bariloche. Ye gods! Twenty four hours had hardly passed and I was behaving like James Bond! Sally used to tease me about my Passport number which began with the figures 007, that amusement had now evaporated. I referred to my notes and the varied routes that I'd jotted down. With luck I'd reach Bariloche unmolested and intact, but I'd better move fast from that point on! Time was running out and I tried to anticipate my opposition's thinking if they were in the slightest suspicious. What were their alternatives as to where the missing papers might be? Or did they know already and were choosing their time for retrieval? Perhaps my chauffeur driven trip to the airport tomorrow could be my last? I shivered involuntarily. How stupid could I get? I was always telling others not to look for trouble in foreign countries! And yet here I was up to my neck in the worst forms of International intrigue with world domination by ten of the most powerful multi-national companies existing in the world today! What were my chances of survival let alone success? I gulped the rest of my whisky, said a heartfelt prayer for help to God, took a couple of paracetamol to aid the sleep process and switched out the light. Tomorrow would tell!, this particular, laundry -chemicals salesman recognised that there was no going back, it was in the hands of mightier forces than mine. I found it difficult to relax, sleeping fitfully, plagued by nightmares and wracked by guilty thoughts of all my previous infidelities. Sally and the children seemed a long way off. I vowed to turn over a new leaf and become, if given the chance, a loving father and husband to my family as finally sleep overtook me.

At the telephone's first half-ring I was instantly awake, it was 0830 am. Years of travel, of catching flights and attending out-of-the blue meetings, had honed my reactions to be fast and to get my brain in gear.

"Buenos dias", Philippe almost purred down the phone. "Your flight leaves at 1030 a.m. and your hotel reservations made for four days, Hauptmann will collect you in an hour with your air-ticket, the airport has been advised of your last minute arrival. Have a safe journey Señor Martin, I hope we'll meet again."

I thanked him effusively, but the conversation had finished, a double click suggesting two connections. I was definitely being checked out very carefully, but they were still unsure of my involvement. My shaving was less careful that morning and I examined my face in the mirror to see if it betrayed my thoughts.

A strong, grey eyed man looked back, whose temples of silver and the slightly thickening neck and fullness of cheeks betrayed his age and the enjoyment of the good life.

Dressing quickly, I was organised, had paid my bill by AMEX platinum credit card and even had time for a couple of rolls and coffee before a black Mercedes 350 saloon arrived and Hauptmann was opening the trunk for my suitcase.

"Buenos dias Señor", he greeted me and held the door open.

"Buenos dias Señor Hauptmann", I replied and sank back into the rear seat. So far so good I was thinking. I should never have received such courtesy if anything was about to happen here and in a very few minutes we were arriving at the small building that served as an air terminal.

Take-off was swift and with immense relief I said a mental prayer of thanks. As our plane soared above the new runways of their new International airport, now almost completed, it described a long, sweeping, but climbing arc across the Beagle Channel and set course northwards. My six foot frame, broad shoulders and now-thickening midriff felt decidedly uncomfortable on this return journey. I examined my fellow passengers carefully, there were none who paid any attention to myself and all appeared to be oil personnel or businessmen. I relaxed. Safe until Bariloche, I slept through nervous exhaustion.

Two

Changing aircraft at Rio Gallegas and again at Commodero Rivadavia was part of this disjointed flight, but I instantly fell asleep after each takeoff. Having woken at the pilot's warning of imminent arrival ten minutes before touchdown at Esquel, I'd spent the remaining minutes mentally running through my escape plans and hopefully, my vanishing trick. As the Rapide taxied towards the small airport terminal at Esquel, a thirty five minute taxi-ride from Bariloche, I could see Lupitá's flaming red-hair at one of the terminal's windows. How the hell did she know when I'd be arriving? But of course, it wasn't exactly a scheduled bus route and there wouldn't be more than two flights from Ushuaia in a day. This was highly inconvenient to my plans, but I daren't take a chance on trusting Lupitá who was in truth little more than a high-class hooker who preferred expensive presents and a good time to money.

I'd already decided that it would be wise to draw as many cash dollars that I could get here. Thankfully, in an International ski-resort the Banks wouldn't consider it an unreasonable request from a Brit on business and pleasure and would undoubtedly carry large stocks of notes. The South American countries being among the favourite areas, along with the off-shore Island Banking scene, where drug-money, counterfeit and the criminal earnings of the world's serious nasties could be laundered. Half of the world's top criminals have luxury, multi-million dollar palatial villas in neighbouring Uruguay, a superb country with great people, but whose previous Governments had turned a blind eye to the super-rich fraternity that enabled their own citizens escape the poverty trap. Montevideo, the capital of Uruguay, owed its night-life, the proliferation of numerous excellent restaurants and some of the finest bronzes that I had ever seen, to the shadowy world of the criminal fraternity whose expensive estates made up a large suburb. Many of the super-rich come to San Carlos de Bariloche to ski, the snows being of comparable quality as to anywhere in the Austrian or Swiss Alps. Bariloche was, in essence, a little piece of Switzerland; the architectural styling, the chocolate-box scenery and even their famous chocolate-making, now relocated to this spot. Every second shop sold hand-made chocolates, the smell of cocoa emanating from a hundred sources and permeating the atmosphere.

Lupitá was all over me. As she'd arranged a taxi I forgave the intrusion and quickly collected my suitcase and a half-hour later was checking into the Hotel Nevada for the second time in a week. Her affected "Dahling, Dahling" was somewhat grating now, I thought somewhat ungraciously, although it had been welcomed and thoroughly enjoyed less than a week ago. Again I was thrown a little as Lupitá continued.

"Dahling, I've booked the Llão Llão for dinner tonight, in your name for 8p.m. You did promise to take me there when you returned, is that O.K.?"

"Sure", I replied, recognising a terrific convenience for my plans; that luxury, five-star hotel had a business centre with good photo-copying facilities and it was open around the clock. It would post any letters with complete integrity of the contents fully assured. That left three hours to organise before dinner and I said sweetly to Lupitá.

"I didn't sleep en route and if you want me to go dancing afterwards I'd better grab a few Z's before going out. Where are you staying tonight Lupitá?"

"I managed to get a room here on the first floor Dahling", she breathed sexily.

Thankfully I had previously warned her about sharing a room with a snoring bear and evinced the reply. "I'll see you later Dahling, at about 7.30, O.K.?"

"Esta es perfecto para mi Carina", I replied and entered the lift with the hotel porter, blowing her a kiss as the doors closed.

This hotel had a peculiar system of lifts and corridors to gain access to the various floors and I think it had been reconstructed from a number of individual dwelling houses, but was ideal from my point of view. It meant even greater privacy for me, easier routes to take in avoiding people that I didn't wish to meet and a couple of exits that couldn't be easily observed. I needed forty-eight hours free from interruption or pursuit to succeed in making myself disappear. During that time I had to visit a bank and withdraw cash, lay a false trail for three days time from now, hoping that a flight booking that was paid for to Buenos Aires, then booking a Lufthansa flight to Charles de Gaulle airport in Paris, might lull the opposition into thinking that all was normal if I was being checked upon. Lupitá might be a problem.

I needed to somehow incapacitate her for a day without raising alarms or making the hotel have doubts that could have devastating effects on my disappearing act. I had deliberately paid for my four-night stay in advance when I had signed in again and now asked, if they'd be able to cope with a last-minute extension of stay.

"Pero no es un problema Señor, es muy bueno te tener un huésped respeto otra vez". To be valued as a wealthy, good paying, good-tipping dependable guest was exactly what I wanted. Now to make my comings and goings more flexible and accepted by the hotel reception. Lupitá would be luxuriating in her bath by now, with a gin and tonic prior to her usual hour's make-up session, if I knew her. I should have no interruptions from that direction for two hours at least. Reception made little comment in response to my enquiries as to where the best snow was at the high resorts and said that they would keep my room for me if I stayed

~ 12 ~

overnight at one of them and there would be no need to call. The skiing season was in full swing they said and I might have difficulty locating a bed or beds (smiling).

That would be "No problema" I said, reinforcing my ability to organise by tucking another twenty-dollar note in his pocket. It would also help him not to be so receptive to any later enquiries by others and earn me more time. I had time to check with one of the local travel agencies that opened late, catering for the many foreign tourists who flooded their town at this time. A quick shower, a fresh shirt and with the papers that I wished to have photocopied in a convenient tube, that previously had contained the complete details of the piste, runs and chair-lifts of the upper resorts; I was ready.

I telephoned Lupitá's room and said that I'd ordered a taxi in thirty minutes time and would meet her in the lobby. It was now 1845, dinner would be taken before eight, my planning was on target. Admittedly, Lupitá was a stunner, her five foot eight inches exaggerated in heels and the blue velvet dress drawing attention to eyes of the same hue. My resolve of saying "Adios" finally that night, weakened a little, then was immediately reinforced by the sight of the large single sapphire on a thin strand of platinum at her throat with a matching one supported by two more single-carat diamonds on her right hand. She'd prepared for war, but she was also expecting an additional trophy to add to her collection. An hour and twenty minutes later we were in the sumptuous surroundings of the Llão Llão hotel, a hang-out of the seriously rich. Those people could spend, $10,000 a day and not even miss it, let alone bother to count the cost. I knew that dinner would cost the better part of $500 with a bottle of Krug, drinks and coffee.

We sat down to large drinks in the bar lounge and I excused myself during the second round on the tab, taking my tube of ski-routes for photocopying. "Won't be more than ten minutes Cariña, must get some cigars and check-out the little boy's room, order us both another round and look at the menu". Lupitá wouldn't be lonely, I'd recognised at least a couple of self-styled Romeos who'd been eying her cleavage and well formed legs. Ten minutes could stretch into thirty if necessary, but I'd better bring my fly-swatter back with me; I smiled inwardly, it was exactly as I required. Hurrying along to the business centre, I was relieved to see none but a male manager and a secretary, both chatting to pass the time. I had already decided to photocopy only the fourteen pages and not the nine in their envelopes and had written three notes to addresses in the US and UK. The missing other nine I decided, might lull my pursuers into thinking that I wasn't party to their grand designs yet and could buy me a little more time if these faxes were intercepted. My requests were speedily seen to and the three A4 envelopes addressed by the efficient secretary who had nothing but her boss on her mind, this being reinforced by her continuous glances at him, but she was super-efficient at her job. The sleight of hand addition of my hand-written note to each envelope was simple and covered by my own ministrations of help. A twenty dollar note to each would ensure their lips were sealed against questions. Dictating three faxes to the same addresses took but a few minutes more and I rewarded the secretary with another $20.

Returning to Lupitá, I found that one of the young bucks had been a very fast worker and that Lupitá was showing interest to an alarming degree. I chose to go-with-the-flow and invited the young man to dinner. He might after all prove himself an asset. As I'd entered the bar I noticed a man leaving by a side-door, his bulky figure and badly fitted tuxedo had resembled the shape of Parides. It wasn't possible! He couldn't be here that quickly, as I had checked the arrival time of the next flight from Ushuaia when meeting Lupitá. Another hour would pass before he could arrive on the next scheduled flight. Unless?, I dismissed the thought. There were more than sufficient if's, but's and maybe's.

Help! and I needed it!!! And an awful lot of luck, but I was still playing the part of innocent playboy (when out of sight of the cat, mice will party); even the photocopying and faxes had been carefully thought out from this angle. Lupitá and Romeo got to their feet and followed me to the dining-room, both giggling, sometimes uncontrollably, and I realised that this might be what the doctor ordered or manna from heaven to enable my scheming to succeed.

I'd often recognised the inability of many females to cope with alcoholic drinks and had taken advantage of this physical defect of women in the past, to end or duck out of a relationship. Here, this budding gigolo was doing the job for me and had obviously plied her with a few extra rounds during my absence, but on my tab. Champagne with the Beluga caviar and Lobster thermidor, an excellent Chilean bottle of Santa Carolina and an Amoretto with her choice of crêpes Suzette; there was hardly any need for the coup de grace of the coffee liqueur. Amazingly, she was as always after prodigious drinking, still able to function; her testiness and open defiance to myself, now in favour of lover-boy and openly proclaimed. She to coin a phrase, had changed horses and would be dancing 'till dawn with the upstart. I feigned disappointment and slight jealousy, recognising that with a little luck, a few more drinks and final rejection through disgust by her newly acquired consort, that this would help my plans. Lupitá wouldn't be facing any of her public again until a goodly thirty-six hours had passed. It was perfect.

I left in what appeared to be high dudgeon and caught a taxi back to San Carlos de Bariloche, the few drinks and recovered confidence had made my spirits soar. Again the meal had been great, although with the cost of faxes, taxis, tips, drinks, including Lupitá's newly acquired devotee; I'd spent close to $1,000, albeit using my credit card. Dear Lord this had better work, but then again if it didn't, I wouldn't need the money! Attaining my room on the fourth floor, I worked back from my required deadlines and booked an alarm call at 0730 hours, having first re-packed, no interference with the locks! -great, and having sneaked out the back way to have a chat with a taxi-driver I finally went to bed with a larger dram, a true Scots measure, to aid sleep. Tomorrow, I should either live or die; at least in the immediacy of my thinking. Luck was the vital ingredient, completely out-with my control! Dear Lord I'll reform! Oddly enough I slept, deeply and well.

The alarm-call was almost un-necessary as I'd wakened five minutes before it rang. After shaving, a fast shower and final packing, I was ready for a hearty breakfast. It had nothing to do with the adage about the fate of the condemned, I was absolutely ravenous.

Unfortunately, the banks didn't open until ten and my taxi trip to my coach on the outside limits of town would require a fast piece of driving if I was to catch up with it. I'd booked a tourist ticket through the high passes of the Andes and across their scenic lakes to Puerto Montt on the Chilean side. I made a show of discussing weather prospects at the high resorts with the receptionists and clarified my previously-made arrangements to retain my rooms here, leaving a hand-written note for Lupitá.

My taxi-driver was waiting at the door and loaded my suitcase into the trunk and had me outside the bank just as the doors opened. There I obtained another $10,000 in $100 bills. Then we were off through the town, but very carefully, so as not to attract undue attention. My heart was racing and I thought with amused cynicism that at least there was nothing wrong with it, as lead poisoning or worse could be my fate.

My driver caught up with the coach after an hour's fast driving, it having left the terminal at 1030 a.m The coach driver had left on time, but had been forewarned of such a connection by the travel agency because of my own requirement to visit a bank. Only a few stares by the other passengers greeted this interruption and I sank gratefully into a rear seat, my suitcase stashed in the stowage and in turn, scrutinised my fellow passengers. It was off-season for this usually fully-booked, tourist trail that connected Argentina with Chile.

Highly popular in spring, through summer and autumn, there were only seven other passengers, four young people in their early twenties and three around my own age (a couple and a single woman). These last three, I took to be locals returning to the other side of the lakes with presents for their families, four or five paper parcels on the racks above them proclaiming this. I wondered how long it would take before Sobatsu would be checking on where I was? I was now convinced that it had been Parides that I'd seen briefly in the bar at the Llão Llão. They were keeping me on a very short lead until they'd established my guilt or innocence. Just a little more time please Lord, I silently prayed.

Three and a half hours after boarding the coach we arrived at Puerto Pañuelo or translated, Port Handkerchief. I remembered being highly amused when I'd first come through in the opposite direction from Puerto Frias or the Port of Colds! We had crossed Lakes Liao Liao and Nahuel Huapi in a large launch that could cope with 100 passengers, the crossing taking a little more than an hour. At Puerto Frias, both Chilean and Argentinian Customs and Immigration controls were a cursory feature, the officials more interested in dealing with the locals and catching up with their news.

Another coach, this time Chilean, climbed into the high passes, gears and differential grinding as very low-gear work proved necessary. Five hours later with spectacular glimpses of hair-raising views, we had crossed the mid-point of the Andean range and hurtled down into yet another valley. We pulled into the courtyard of an old-fashioned hotel, that nestled in the lee of the towering volcanoes. Peulla Hotel belied its interior as it had a somewhat threatening and unprepossessing outward appearance, giving it a gloomy effect, due to being in almost perpetual shadow. Enormous log fires greeted the visitor in every public room and the main lobby, the rooms were fitted with old-fashioned cast-iron radiators, blistering to the touch and huge, thick duvets covered the beds. The double-glazing being of the simple attached variety, not 100 per cent effective, but hardly necessary.

I relaxed and enjoyed an excellent German-style meal complete with sausage, pickled red cabbage and black bread, our hosts being German immigrants of the third generation. My fellow travellers were pleasant enough and I'd given myself a completely false identity, having hung back at Customs precisely for this purpose. The young folk were out for fun on their holidays and invited me to join them as they'd been skiing in Bariloche, but I declined their invitation and left them to their carousing. The hotel and travel-agency, coaches and fellow travellers would only know that a Mr Bierman from Holland whose work involved the tourist industry was pleasant enough company and had paid cash for everything in dollars and had also almost missed the coach.

It had been relatively easy to secure my Customs and Immigration inspections out of any hearing of curious ears and so far everything was going nicely. Don't tempt fate!, I thought. Think out the next steps and some alternative ones, just in case the opposition was waiting for me in Puerto Montt. It was beautiful sunshine as we boarded the coach, having enjoyed a breakfast that a woodcutter would have appreciated. Unfortunately, I had managed to break a tooth on eating sausage of all things! Blast and Damn!, I would have to plan a visit to the dentist in Santiago, although remembering an excellent one I'd previously used in another emergency, but he was right in the city centre.

It was a short trip to the waiting launch at Lake Llanquichue ('Lost' in the Amyrin, Indian language). I hoped that it would prove prophetic from Sobatsu's point of view. The snow-capped volcanoes of Osorno and Calbuco were uplifting sights, their reflections on the mill-pond conditions making it more so and the four hour crossing of the lake passed very quickly. The launch being almost empty added to the sensation of natural wilderness.

Another coach awaited beside a large hotel and restaurant complex, it would leave in an hour and a half, allowing the passengers to enjoy an expensively priced lunch if desired. Tourists and locals had already disgorged from the coach that was now awaiting its return load. The locals who'd joined us were eating sandwiches and drinking from flasks, sitting at the tables outside and thoroughly enjoying the brilliant sunshine. I chose to sit outside also and forgo lunch, in another six hours I'd be in Puerto Montt and my tooth was niggling. My stomach was beginning to churn a little anyway, nerves increasing the acidity as we neared the next danger area. I chewed a mint and was greatly relieved when the coach finally started up.

A stop at beautiful falls, Los Saltos del Rio, had our guide/driver telling us about the great white-water rafting available there. The huge gouts of turquoise and white rimmed water echoed this blatant piece of advertising and I'd duly joined the tourist numbers trooping along the paths and walkways to the falls while the locals sat patiently aboard the coach and waited for our return. It was also a convenient loo-stop, the necessary conveniences being next the car/coach park.

The final thirty miles of descent from the mountains required a detour to avoid a massive land slippage where the driver cheerfully announced that two cars had plummeted to the bottom of the gorge the night previously, killing all four occupants. It had been the third vehicle that had been travelling more slowly that had raised the alarm and avoided a similar fate.

The view of Fruitillar, another town at the end of another large lake reminded me that in another hour we would arrive in Puerto Montt. The scenery that we were passing through in the foothills of the Andes was a duplication of the area that my father had been born into, Cluny in Aberdeenshire Scotland. It was odd how many areas of the world were so similar in climate and appearance. The fiord country of southern Chile matched New Zealand's and lent greater credence to the understanding of continental drift and that of Gondwanaland.

I shook myself out of these reveries! Concentrate and organise! The coach was now approaching the main square and final stop in the centre of Puerto Montt. I'd grab a taxi and go straight to the airport, risking a lengthy wait for the next flight to Santiago de Chile. I knew that airports, rail and bus stations would be the most dangerous areas for me and requested my taxi-driver to take me to a pharmacy first. Here I purchased a black hair-dye, scissors, a safety razor and a pair of tinted glasses. The hour's wait for the next flight was excruciating and I spent half of it in the male toilet and on emergence I couldn't see anyone around that I recognised or who even appeared to be looking for anyone else. My nerves settled and re-awakened the hunger-pangs, but I would wait until Santiago.

The flight was uneventful and I avoided chatting by burying myself in a copy of the Santiago Telegráfo. Collecting my suitcase from the carousel, I made a mental note to buy another in the city and leave my own conspicuous one. Mine had various quick-identifying marks on it for easy retrieval at airports and to describe to airline officials if lost in transit. It was very definitely, a liability for me now, even with some of my markers removed. A cab whisked me into the city-centre where I checked into the Gallerias hotel and I paid for two-nights accommodation in advance. I realised that my name on their register and computerised booking system was going to attract the opposition's attention, but by that time I intended being elsewhere.

I'd done it! I had managed to drop out of sight, now to confuse my trail even more and make it impossible for them to follow. However, I was feeling much happier and my confidence had fully returned, although my radar was screwed-up to maximum. I had to keep my wits about me and anticipate problems that might be my undoing. This broken tooth was an unforseen inconvenience that had to be attended to. It was now driving me crazy, the rough edges lacerating my tongue.

Dr. Machiavelli's surgery was on the third floor of the adjoining shopping mall or galleries. His name had disconcerted me on the first occasion that I'd attended his surgery, but he was excellent and had been trained at St. Andrews College for dentistry in Scotland. I hoped to get an immediate appointment and left to call on him first before I bought another suitcase. An appointment for early the next morning was suitable and a perfect suitcase found and purchased. I put to one side all my shirts that I'd worn in Philippe's company and any other clothes that looked English in style. Transferring everything that I was keeping to my new key-operated, four-wheeled, hard plastic suitcase. Having combination locks also, made it ideal. My lovely expensive designer ties were dumped. I'd get rid of my old case in the left-luggage lockers of the International airport when I left. My dental appointment went without problems, Dr. Machiavelli appearing genuinely pleased to see me and assured me that his repair job would be there when I departed this life. I hoped that my inner anxieties on this particular subject were not obvious!

Returning to my hotel room I spent a careful hour over my toilet, cutting my sideburns at a forward and tapered slanting angle. With my hair now black, I re-touched eye-brows and eye-lashes with the aid of my tooth brush, I had now completely changed my appearance. I hadn't considered my eye-brows at first, until the mirror made me look like some police identikit picture, but now suitably darkened and with a fresh open necked T- shirt of a designer name, I looked Italian or of Mediterranean descent. There were many tourists from Italy throughout the continent. Señor Barolo from Firenze in the northern part of Italy now peered at his visage in the mirror. O.K.!! I'd already decided to move again and long before lunchtime was heading once more to the airport.

My driver dropped me off at the International terminal as requested. Recently built, it was the last word in modernity and had sufficient left-luggage lockers just inside the main lower hall. Pulling both suitcases, I passed through the automatic doors and headed for the lockers. Groups of Japanese tourists, obviously en route to Easter Island before returning to their own native land, hindered my passage. I became instantly aware of the intense scrutiny by a man who was just inside the entrance. He stared hard at my green suitcase and then at me! Making an immediate decision, I pushed both suitcases into the large locker I'd chosen, removing the key as the coinage dropped for a twenty-four hour period. Damn! I'd been too clever, but I raced out of the entrance/exit and headed towards the car-parks.

I caught sight of my observer following, my peripheral vision picking up his black suit. This was what I'd hoped for, I had to get rid of him and permanently, but how? I'd never killed anyone in my life, hadn't even thought about such a thing But this was either my life or his; he could describe me to others and all my efforts to disappear would come to naught. I knew just how long that I'd last in their hands. Snowballs in hell came briefly to mind. I was now running fast, forcing my pursuer to thrust his mobile-phone into his jacket and increase his pace to keep up with me. Communication with others was the last thing I wanted and I was intentionally threading an erratic course through the parked vehicles. I cleared a perimeter hedge in Olympic style; yesterday I shouldn't even have attempted it. Fear was pumping adrenalin round my body and adding strength to previously unknown physical ability. I crossed the lines of traffic on the dual carriageways of both incoming and outgoing vehicles, the many horns blaring and brakes squealing emphasising the fact that I had missed being run-over by inches. An enormous crash made me turn as I reached the far side; my pursuer hadn't been so lucky. He'd tried to emulate my crazy crossing of the fast traffic and had mis-judged an incoming truck's speed as it overtook a coach. I didn't hang around, fate had given me another chance and with luck, that guy wouldn't be pursuing anyone in future. Certainly he'd now have rather vague memories about me.

Returning cautiously to the terminal I noticed three men at the entrance, examining closely, all the people entering. I walked confidently past them and was approaching the lockers when my heart skipped a beat. It was the blue-rinse that caught my eye, she was talking to a knot of men and women in the hall and pointing to the lockers that spread around three of the sides. I almost ran to the locker to retrieve the black case and as I turned was almost knocked down by the matriarch and one of her cronies. There was no recognition from her, she was concentrating on giving out her instructions. I overheard in Spanish, "The green suitcase is in one of the large lockers, find out which one and post a watch over it, but send the case to the factory for examination". I had been heading for the lifts to the upper deck from where the Departures left and I continued back out across the walkway, then back down below again. The old International air terminal was only a few hundred yards away, now used solely for domestic flights and I forced myself to stop, light a cigar, then walk slowly, enjoying it and the sunshine. Any observer would have paid little attention to me, my disguise would have fooled my own mother. Entering the domestic terminal I noticed a number of watchers scanning all the people who were entering the hall. There must have been twenty or thirty of them that I spotted. This wasn't a game! They had huge numbers of personnel to call upon. Fortunately, the domestic traffic was reasonably numerous with many miners for the north mixed with tourists from both Europe and the Americas. I put out my cigar and bought a newspaper and checked the departure board with the flight times.

I knew exactly where I wanted to go, but a last minute booking could be of life and death value to myself. My flight to Calama, in the north of Chile, left at 1355 hours. My nerves were now under control, my racing pulse now slowing to normal and as I paid for my ticket I was told to hurry to the departure gate as the flight was being called. My suitcase was being trolleyed through to the aircraft by an airport porter. I joined the last two people on the access stairs and was relieved to see my suitcase being loaded into the hold. It would be amongst the first to be unloaded and come onto the carousel at the other end. I shook from reaction, prompting a matronly Chilean lady beside me to ask if I was alright. Assuring her that I was, I forced myself into a self-controlled mode for the trip. Feigning sleep, the final roar of the throttles and pressure in my ears told me that we were airborne.

An excellent lunch and a couple of free whiskies, courtesy of Ladeco, one of Chile's two, first-class airlines, put me in much better fettle. I had to have the next stages of my trip carefully thought out. I had almost disappeared, although it had been a close call in Santiago. Certainly, from Sobatsu's point of view, my trail should now go very cold indeed. All was dependent on my not making a mistake during the next few days. No-one would be able to work out my route then! Over confidence was my enemy, I had to retain my concentration.

The four-hour flight passed reasonably quickly, my suitcase retrieved and a taxi trip to the nearby mining town of Calama obtained. The Hosterias or local hostelry of the same name was my stopping place, for hopefully, just one or at most two nights prior to the next move.

I was beginning to feel much safer. With luck, in another forty-eight hours my trail would be impossible to follow. My disguise and false name should leave few clues as to my exact whereabouts in Chile. My green suitcase would yield nothing but possibilities in different directions, but would be insufficient to either discard or reduce the possible permutations.

James Bond would have been proud of my thinking and actions, although luck had replaced his gadgetry and licence to kill.

Having ascertained from the reception staff an address nearby of a free-lance guide for the area, I walked along the main street in search of him. The pepper corns of the shade-giving trees that lined the sidewalk scrunched noisily underfoot. Fortunately, that night I located both the guide and a driver whose new four-wheel drive pick-up truck had an extra rear seat. This would be my sight-seeing trip to San Pedro de Atacama before taking the train into Peru, an essential train-journey of note for the world's eccentric travellers. I would stay at San Pedro for a few days before heading north to Peru and would only require a one-way trip. Extra cash easily overcame this difficulty and my companions were organised for an early start the following morning.

It was a beautiful day with not a breath of wind and the dust cloud that hung almost permanently above Chuquicamata copper mine hove into sight, the final miles to it now a well-surfaced dual carriageway. Chuquicamata is the largest mine of its kind in the world, three miles long and almost two miles wide. Conditions there, although exceptionally well paid in Chilean terms for its 8,000 labour force, were in reality a death sentence, as few saw their late sixties and died from silicosis or other lung and heart diseases.

The volcanoes, Peter and Paul and The Lion were the backdrop to this feverish site of activity, as we narrowly avoided a monster 100 plus-ton, dump-truck as it barrelled its way towards the crushing plant with its load of ore. It was a site of furious activity requiring many water-spraying trucks to keep the permanent dust-cloud to even a reasonable level.

There followed two hundred kilometres of arid desert, the driest in the world, with an occasional oasis and pictographs carved on the odd rock giving information for the llama trains of the past. The four-wheel drive truck might have been built for this sort of torture, but my frame wasn't and I bounced up and down in this cocktail shaker as every one of the ribbed, graded, road surface bumps transmitted its presence to myself. Wilson, my driver, said that to go slower would be only to increase the torture, but I detected a degree of masochism as well as sadism in his smiling acknowledgement to the guide.

It was a shattered, dusty and thirsty Señor Barolo who quite literally fell out of the pick-up when we pulled into the courtyard of San Pedro de Atacama's one and only hostelry. Half a dozen separate cabins and the same number of rooms were available in the hostel. I was pleased to learn that the town had been cleared of the hippies and drug-addicts who had been present in large numbers there the last time that I'd visited. It was a pretty Indian village with many friendly mestizos, the people of mixed blood who made their living from the tourist trade. It had much to offer with desert sunsets being of unimaginable splendour, old Indian pukaras (forts), salt workings and a first-class museum that defied belief. Its contents are an unexpected addition to the area's incredible sights. The museum contained not only artifacts and a comprehensive, historical record of the Inca tribes of the area, but also a vault like the one for the Crown Jewels in the Tower of London (slightly smaller), containing the gold regalia of the Incas. As in the Gobi desert of China, there were many mummified bodies thousands of years old on display.

The fact that San Pedro was at the back of beyond was the final building block in my disappearing trick. Although I'd made many references to my driver and guide about taking the northern railway into Peru, this was yet another false trail, as I had another route in another direction planned out. I had come here for a week's break many years ago to see the flamingoes on the nearby Salar de Atacama or salt flats and had enjoyed many of the sights in the area. Staying at the hostelry one day, having a lazy time doing little, I was amazed when four obviously brand-new and the latest model cars swept into the yard in convoy. Covered in dust, they'd very definitely come a long way and were refuelling at the one and only petrol pump for hundreds of kilometres. I had chatted to the drivers, to find that this was the delivery route for new vehicles that were unloaded in Iquique, a Port in the far North Their final destination for delivery was the land-locked country of Paraguay, over a high pass in the Andes where there were no Customs or Immigration officials.

These little convoys swept through San Pedro on a once weekly basis. My idea was that they would carry a passenger this time, knowing that a couple of hundred dollars would ensure their silence and enable me to vanish entirely from Chile. There would be no documentation to follow nor exit stamps required and as I'd had previous experience of missing out on stamps in my passport from other South American officials, I wasn't too bothered about future reactions. All I had to do was await the next convoy, although I didn't wish to attract attention by asking when it was due. I would feign a tummy-bug as to my reason for hanging around the hostel or at least nearby where I wouldn't miss their arrival.

They had just refuelled, eaten some food, paid their bill and departed within an hour on the last occasion that I'd observed them. I would have to be prepared to move quickly and at the same time not show my anxieties to the community. I was taking no chances in missing them and the long boring hours of oppressive heat were difficult to fill, the feelings of tension increasing with every passing hour. I daren't ask anyone, but perhaps they were using an alternative route or had employed another method of delivery. At least the beers that I drank supported the excuse of a tummy-bug with my frequent trips to the lavatory. The heat combined with the alcohol and I fell into a semi-soporific state.

Three

"What the bloody hell do you mean Jorgé?, you've lost him?"

Laurence Caldicott Jefferson the third, CEO and MD. of Planet Ales Inc., registered and selling varieties of non-alcoholic drinks in over 200 countries, thundered down the phone.

"A so-called bloody amateur you say. Then you tell me that you've lost him? Hell's teeth man. If those papers get to be public knowledge, we'll all be locked away for life do you realise that? You and your company were in total charge of security in São Paulo and you assured the rest of us that an ant couldn't get into any of our meetings without detection, yet here we are in this mess! The others are looking for your head my friend and I'm seriously considering their request. Where the hell do you think this guy Martin is now? And convince me that he doesn't belong to one of the security agencies and why I shouldn't be packing for an incognito life in Brasil or suchlike country! Jesus Christ man, pull your finger out and get him! I don't care if you have to shoot half of South America, but stop him dead!'

Philippe was perspiring profusely as he listened to the tirade over the phone, he was glad of the scrambler devices that all ten companies had installed for secure communication with one another. He continued to enlarge on his explanation of an earlier call that he'd made to Jefferson.

"Hauptmann and Parides only learnt that Booth must have had the papers with him after Ramires searched his room in Ushuaia. It took some time to trace where Booth had been staying, but by then Martin was in Bariloche. He was never considered to be a threat until he ran. We're 100% certain that he's in Chile, probably Santiago, and while you denigrate Parides and Hauptmann; they're not stupid and have great expertise in obtaining local help. We've thirty people covering the International airport around the clock on three shifts and tomorrow Parides has said that he'll have fifty of the local hoods bought, paid for and instructed as extra pairs of eye. We have many photos of him to distribute and a full description of him, his clothes and his suitcase. He'll be spotted when he surfaces. Parides and Hauptmann will check out all the hotels systematically from the airports outwards. He won't stray far from them as his fastest escape routes. Yes, he had laid a false trail from Bariloche and due to the thirty-six hour delay in receiving the border crossing details; we were not advised that he'd crossed into Chile through the passes. Parides had kept a close watch upon him at the Nevada, but assumed that his non-appearance was more to do with the red-head, than flight. We do know that he's not an agent, this being confirmed by the sending of the photocopies of our meetings in São Paulo, the short Faxes he'd dictated and sent to two addresses in the UK. and the one to New York State, that you've undertaken to check-out. The fourteen pages sent to all three addresses contain only the names of our companies, a few diagrams of our micro-chips but no explanation of our activities".

"Just backgrounds of the thousand most powerful companies in the world, their commercial activities and all the names of their top personnel with full communication details, that's all!", Jefferson interrupted. As we've now gained a copy of the original transcriptions of all of the pages that Booth had the audio-typist in Ushuaia type for him, this being his own personal undoing".

Philippe tried to take the seriousness out of the known problem.

"We do know that Martin hasn't found or doesn't possess the others. Martin either doesn't have the tapes that Booth smuggled out, can't make sense of them or hasn't found any of the vital transcripts other than the lists. And we're only assuming that such transcripts exist. The audio -typist didn't make any, although she heard some of the content of one of the meetings before Booth curtailed her work."

"Listen Philippe!", Jefferson almost made his name sound like a bad word, "Booth didn't run all that way down to Ushuaia for no reason. He recognised that his cover was blown and that it was just a matter of time before your guys nailed him. I've thought a lot about why he went south instead of flying directly back to the States and obtain more back-up from his buddies to deal with your hired hoods. I reckon that the tape-recorder was in the epidiascope that we used at all three meetings, supplied by Sobatsu, but cunningly altered by Booth. I have established through my contacts in the FBI that he was an electronics major at college".

Jefferson was in full flood, recognising that his own constructive thinking was making Sobatsu's security chief squirm and would act as a goad. He continued "Again, I think that he was in Ushuaia to recover the tapes for transcription when your Señora Flores spotted him. That second-hand typewriter that he bought down there wasn't as a present for back home. See what she says to my theories? Where is she now, by the way?"

"In Santiago, she's heading the first shift of watchers at the International airport from six a.m. to noon. I'll have her call you then. Do you wish me to have the three sets of photocopies recovered in the meantime?", Philippe queried.

"No, there's nothing incriminating in them, even if they might make people curious and the diagrams could be anything without further explanation" Jefferson replied. "It's better not to arouse any extra suspicions in other areas if Martin continues to be lost permanently" The final two words were heavily emphasised and needed no further explanation. "You could however, ask your

English branch to covertly, check on Mr & Mrs Martin, their credentials, etc and also that of English Purity Chemicals. It might prove useful to us", and with that Jefferson disconnected.

Philippe mopped the perspiration from his brow and buzzed for his executive secretary. There was a lot to organise and put in motion and it needed to be all completed yesterday! Jefferson wouldn't tolerate any more mishaps. Any future bad luck was likely to be duplicated by his own! He would mobilise his whole organisation around the Americas and the British branch of the company. He buzzed his secretary again, "But first get a hold of Ramires", Sobatsu's expert thief, locksmith and photographer, "And tell him to bring all the blow-ups of Martin's personal organiser". Ramires had taken insufficient time to fully check on the contents of Martin's case, but had found nothing that was incriminating to make a complete investigation at the time necessary.

Mierda! That damn epidiascope! Nobody thought of checking it. Parides had delivered it to São Paulo, personally. Ah!, but little sand-martin I'll see that your wings are well and truly clipped, you won't fly much farther!, Philippe thought. I'll post men at every contact that you have on the South American continent, then we will see if you can escape my net.

Philippe controlled almost 2,000 men and women worldwide, just for security reasons to protect the Top Ten, although they could be employed for internal investigations by any one of the companies. Two hundred of these 'soldiers' were awaiting new instructions in São Paulo, having been kicking their heels for ten days when the tracking southwards of Booth began. He would concentrate their fire-power at the major International airports on the South American continent. Martin had to go through one of them. He told his secretary to place immediate calls to the mobiles of Hauptmann, Parides, and then Flores asking them to call in. ASAP.

On the other side of the world, other conversations were taking place.

"Judy, I've just had a fax from Bernard, asking you to check your mail and faxes over the weekends for the duration, is there any problem?" Sally was concerned. Bernard usually contacted Judy himself, he never asked her to do anything concerning the business. Rather he resented any intrusion. This request was completely out of character.

"No there's no problem Mrs Martin, it will be just emergency supplies that will be required. Some of our chemicals have obviously not been delivered and our policy of just-in-time supply factors has come unstuck I expect. Judy was adept at facile explanations and the soothing of clients, but also she recognised the code the she had Bernard make years ago, for a holiday break together in the Caribbean. She had been manoeuvring Bernard into taking her on a Caribbean trip for some time. There were now plans to follow that would give Bernard extra time to be away and she would organise her own, long overdue, holidays.

In legal offices of Hallstaff, Ferret & Wheesel, yet another discussion was taking place. Only young Hallstaff survived the original partners' names, the firm of twenty partners, all now exceeding his own seniority.

"This is a damn funny fax that Bernie's sent", the senior partner James Henderson was saying to the assembled meeting What do you make of it? It says that the documentation which will follow has extreme value to the companies listed and should be carefully preserved and that if anything happens to him that they are passed onto the appropriate authorities".

"Should we not hand it over to M.I.5 or whatever, or GCHQ., that telecommunications place that looks after the nation's security when his letter finally arrives?", another of the partners" queried.

"A sound suggestion, Fraser. See to it."

The meeting went onto more important sources of income. A memo was noted by Fraser to get his secretary to send it to the Intelligence people with a short explanation about their client Martin. What had he been up to?

Back in New York, Jefferson's personal secretary, Ardeth, was trying to find out exactly where Penn Yan in NY. State was, and the most convenient method for her boss to visit it and at the same time answer a series of telephone calls, from mobile-phones in Chile of all places. There was a panic on, that much she was aware of, but the detail had yet to be given to her. Experience had taught her that she'd be informed when it was necessary and to do her job in her usual fast efficient manner. Larry could be more than just cutting when it served him, he could also be very cruel. Especially in the bedroom. Although nine times out of ten, that area was usually pleasurable in the extreme and an expensive present would undoubtedly follow. Larry's imposing height of six foot three gave him an even more commanding presence, his ability in business, physique, plus a needle-sharp intellect, made him a force to be reckoned with.

Another call brought her back to earth.

"I'm connecting you now Señora Flores" and buzzed the intercom, informing her boss of the next call.

"Yes Señora, I hope that you have some better news for me?", boomed Jefferson into the mouthpiece remembering that this call wouldn't be secure.

"Just give me the outlines, so that any other ears can't understand, have you got that Señora?"

"Si Señor", Señora Flores proceeded to give him a briefing of the lost parcel and the prospects of finding it, as well as an opinion on his theories about Ushuaia "Esta es muy possible Señor", before the connection was instantly severed.

Jefferson buzzed his intercom, "Well how the hell do I get to Penn Yan then? Book us a nice hotel in the area, I'd better be there for tomorrow."

"Yes Laurence", said Ardeth, using her boss's Sunday Christian name while looking at her reflection in her vanity mirror. This could be a fun trip after all, she thought.

Meantime, thousands of miles north of Chile, Jack McAllister sat and puzzled over Bernard's fax, it sounded mysterious. What had the guy gotten himself into?

Read the letter that's following very carefully Jack, and put your thinking-cap on, I may need your help and will contact you when it's safe to do so.

Regards to yourself and Carolyn,

Bernard.

Frustrated, Jack tossed the fax to Carolyn, "What do you make of it?"

"Woman trouble again. You know what a charmer Bernie can be with the ladies, huh Jack," Carolyn replied. Remember that you promised Myron that we would join him for dinner tonight. We can't be late. He's got some people booked in from New York for tomorrow, a big hitter in world terms according to Myron and his computer. They'd booked him through his internet advertising. He'll have some way of extending his hotel advertising that he wishes your opinion upon!'

Jack smiled, it was true about his sailing buddy, he was an opportunist when it came to advertising. The number of entries that ended on the Internet, "for further information, contact Myron White of the Red Fox Inn, Penn Yan NY. State". One of these days, he would come unstuck with that little ploy, but so far, none of the bureaucratic or official tourist information guides that carried his 'offers of extra help' had complained. Myron's ability with a computer had increased his own knowledge immensely about what they could do and his own, hobby businesses had benefited immeasurably. He cuddled Carolyn thinking that, Yes this could be the one Bernie, saying only.

"Right let's get going, your car or mine?" His British pal had said that he had recognised the chains being wrought into place. Bernie was a character and aloud, "I think that I'll stop work at the hospital early for the next few days, just to see what Bernie's letter contains." Jack was a consultant on respiratory diseases, causes and defects and was on call by his local hospital for three days and also for the main hospital in Syracuse, just an hour and a half's drive away. He stuffed the fax in his pocket to show Myron for later discussion at dinner.

"It could be that he's found yet another environmental disaster in the making and wishes our opinion Carolyn. You know Bernie's hobby-horse".

In New York City, Ardeth was making flight bookings for her boss and herself to the same city of Syracuse. They would be in Penn Yan, the tourist town of the Finger Lakes in the State of New York, a cute little Inn booked for two nights that she had found very highly recommended on the Internet with no less than a dozen different recommendations. She'd heard of this beautiful area many times from friends who'd visited there. As there was a fairly early flight to catch, she left early, having heard Larry lock-up and shout "Good-night, see you at the airport" five minutes previously and she had yet to pack. There was also some new lingerie to purchase on the way home. As she locked her office, the fax-machine was spitting out names and addresses of Martin's contacts in the States. It was four-thirty p.m.

Back in Ushuaia, Jorgé Philippe was making other arrangements to move his main headquarters for security to Rio de Janeiro, it was a central location and he could exercise better control of his troops from a large hub airport. As practically all of the world's airlines flew into it, there was also the slight chance that Martin would use it as an escape route.

With so many flights leaving it daily, there wouldn't be a lot of time to fully check-out the passenger lists before some of them landed at their destinations. This pursuit was now on a personal level, Jefferson's comments had done more than just sting. He was aware that if he failed, then he could pay the ultimate penalty. The inner circle of the top ten had laid down a code that would be adhered to and Jefferson, being the main man, had a known penchant for physical cruelty.

Philippe buzzed once more for his secretary saying, "Send all the names and addresses of Martin's contacts in the America's to Jefferson in New York as soon as you have them typed-up from Ramires' photographs". He cursed again, the fact that the final X, Y, & Z pages hadn't been included. Ramires could so easily have taken more time. After all, Martin had been about to go into dinner and another half-hour's privacy in Martin's room had been assured. But he sighed, he couldn't expect to have it both ways. After his own remonstrations with Ramires on that point, Ramires had then taken Booth's room apart with a fine toothcomb when they'd ultimately discovered where he'd been staying. That long search had resulted in Martin making good his escape. He looked over the notes that he'd taken from a rather distraught Señora Flores, should he include a reference to them to Jefferson? He decided against it. The knowledge that Martin had eluded the whole team of watchers at Santiago and that he'd dumped the identifying suitcase and was probably disguised would send Jefferson ballistic. He would fly to Santiago first and examine the suitcase personally, before going onto Rio. Martin's clever he thought, but he'll make a mistake somewhere.

As an afterthought, he dialled the Research and Development's direct number in Japan, recognising that he might just catch someone through the time differences.

"Hai, research and development speaking. How may I help?"

"Philippe here of Sobatsu, Ushuaia, Argentina. Tell me how close are we to producing that voice recognition bug you're working upon?"

Four

A steady drizzle at La Guardia airport New York, didn't improve Laurence C. Jefferson's temper and Ardeth's solicitous attitude was beginning to annoy him.

"Well tell me about this hotel you've booked for us then", he asked testily and immediately silenced any reply by adding, "It had better be all that you say it is".

"Oh God!, Ardeth thought, hopefully this bad start signalled a better ending. She'd bought his favourite cigars and some new, sexy lingerie and with Larry having enjoyed a cigar with a large brandy after dinner, then she could make him into a pleasant lover. Were all the presents really worth these times when he behaved like a pig! But she had a very high salary, a good $5 to $10,000 per annum above the rate that she'd get in comparable positions and some of these travel destinations could be fun and interesting. It all depended on Larry being reasonable and in good humour. Whatever the hell it was, this problem was very worrying for him indeed.

The previous evening in Penn Yan.

"Hi Myron, what culinary delicacy have you prepared for me and Carolyn tonight?" Jack had the question asked, half-way up the steps to the back door of the Red Fox Inn, the smell wafting towards him in a tantalising manner. Myron, deeply concentrating on the multitude of pans on the stove replied,

"Actually this is for tomorrow Jack, as I've a booking from some high-powered guy from the New York. I'm taking you out for Tex Mex tonight. But first, have a glass of wine with me while I add the finishing touches to these dishes".

"Had a very odd fax from Bernie this morning", Jack said, continuing, "Take a look at it and see what you think; I don't think it's woman trouble as Carolyn suggests, he's too wily an expert for that problem."

Myron accepted the fax while stirring one of his pots and giving Carolyn a peck on the cheek with,

"Hi babe, why don't you get rid of that old bore and come stay with me?" Laughter followed, as all knew too well that Myron's sexual preferences lay in a different direction, but he was a charming and highly intelligent man whose friendship was valued by all those who knew him.

"Hmm", he said, scanning the fax, "Bernie definitely has more on his mind than just women. He may have been tempted to take some photos of something he shouldn't, and I don't mean military, he's not that stupid, but you know what he's like about the environment".

"Yeah", Jack replied, "He's even had me agreeing with his forecasted problems for this next century and that the advanced nations will have to do something to avert an impending catastrophe for humanity. Somehow I don't think it's that. I'm going to come home from work early for the next few days until I get his letter, check your e-mail too, he knows both of our addresses".

Carolyn interrupted, "I still think it's a woman that he's got out of his depth with and he's looking for extrication prior to going back to the family".

Jack and Myron replied as one. "You don't know Bernie!"

Jack continuing, "He wouldn't jeopardise his nice little set-up in England, not for any woman. That's why he keeps his affairs thousands of miles away".

"Here's to Bernie anyway !", said Myron, raising his glass. "He's a great guy, good company and throws a different slant on life".

All agreed to this observation and re-filled their glasses. The topic switched to the arrival of the city-slicker next day.

"It'll be just a sexy week-end with his secretary", Carolyn volunteered.

"Have a feeling that it's more than that", said Myron. "His secretary asked me to obtain a town-map and have it upon their arrival. A map of the town, not the Finger lakes".

Their plane having touched down at Syracuse, the driver of the limousine had collected their luggage and was standing beside the car with the door open for them. At least Larry's importance and money made airports into more human places, Ardeth thought. There was never any waiting if the plane schedules were adhered to. Even then, delays in that sector were always less painful with the champagne and canapes and their superior sitting areas, together with all the facilities that Airports kept for their V.I.P.'s. Although the company's private jet was even better, but was seldom used for short domestic flights, being generally held in reserve for important trips.

The two-hour trip to Penn Yan passed painlessly, due mainly to the liberal amounts of brandy dispensed from the cocktail cabinet. Larry was much calmer now and was back in full control of himself. I wonder what the problem is, she thought. The beautiful countryside through which they were passing, received hardly a second glance from him, he was preoccupied with whatever this backwater contained. Time would tell. The limo swept up the short driveway of the Red Fox Inn, the colonnaded front giving it a much superior appearance to the rest of the surrounding dwellings and even the public buildings. The front door was opening as they climbed the steps and the owner, Myron White, was introducing himself and welcoming them into a large sitting-room, a roaring log fire adding to the feelings of bonhomie. The frown had gone completely from Larry's face Ardeth noted, and they both accepted a brandy as the limo driver delivered their luggage to their room. The smells coming from beyond an attractively set table in an open-plan dining area suggested that even in this hinterland, the finer points of life were upheld. Larry was saying,

"Myron do you have a street plan for me? I'd like it as soon as possible".

"Yes Mr Jefferson, I'll get it", and Myron departed to his office beyond the kitchen to fetch it.

"Well Ardeth I must admit that your hotel appears to be all that you claim, but you'd better check out our room before I'm fully satisfied". Ardeth hurried off to check as the limo hadn't been dismissed and the chauffeur would be finding other quarters nearby in the town and was to be on instant call.

"Here's the town-plan", Myron grinned, waving a long brown tube and continued. "This bit of paper's worth at least a bottle of Scotch, I had to hock the Chevy to get this copy from City Hall". Another waft of delicious smells emanated from the kitchen as he entered. Myron had played the game well in the past. What were these guys after?

"Let me show you the main watering holes and places of interest".

"No that's all right", Jefferson replied and added as Ardeth entered once more, "We're here essentially for a week-end break, but had told a friend in the city that we'd say hello to his nephew who lives in the area; a guy named Jack McAllister, do you know him?" Myron presented an easy smile and poker-faced said,

"Yes, Jack's a good friend of mine, we sail together. I'll give him a call and he'll join you after dinner if you'd like; he's only a mile or two away".

"That'll be great, Myron", Jefferson agreed. "It will allow Ardeth and myself to see some of this beautiful area before we fly back to the city on Sunday".

Jefferson could already see that this was going to be much easier than he'd thought and that he could curtail a third night away and still have his fun week-end with Ardeth. This was much better; he accepted yet another brandy. Dinner would be served in thirty minutes and Ardeth slipped up to the room to change, leaving Larry relaxing in front of the fire with his cigar and brandy. He was now enjoying himself hugely, the brandy having its effect, as generally he would have stuck to his favourite tipple of Bacardi and cola. However, he couldn't resist the quality Armagnac that Myron had laid on for his guest, Larry recognising that shows of careless wealth would impress. His previously worried demeanour had been replaced with one of supreme confidence and relaxation. His mood swings were difficult to interpret, but somehow the emergency had vanished whatever it had been and her new teddy was once again in vogue.

In Santiago de Chile, Philippe was being updated by Señora Flores, his own worries were increasing, as he listened to her full accounting of Martin's movements.

"He's vanished completely", Señora Flores abjectly admitted. "Parides and Hauptmann tracked down that he'd stayed at one of the central hotels for some unknown reason and not in one closer to the airport. It takes a little time to check them all out and they missed him by a few hours. There has been no taxi-cab that could confirm having taken him to the airport but we know he arrived there, it was unfortunate that our hired watcher met with a fatal accident when chasing him. The garbled phone message that he sent whilst chasing Martin only mentioned the suitcase and the lockers".

"What about the suitcase?", Philippe queried. "Any leads there?".

"No Jorgé, immediately adding, "Señor Philippe", as Jorgé bristled at her familiarity. "Only confirmation that he's discarded all his English clothes and other things that would identify him easily to our watchers. I think he's disguised himself and the papers that he'd left in the case are probably red herrings to make us look for him in anywhere but where he's actually going. There were leaflets on Valparaiso and Viña del Mar, also Peru, the Atacama desert and La Isla del Pascua (Easter Island) with flight details to New Zealand, but he couldn't board an International flight without showing his Passport. There's no trace of him having flown out of the main international terminal, so he's taken a domestic flight".

"Hmm!, probably north maybe heading for Peru", Philippe considered. "Send a team up there to cover all the towns and cities, and check on all the visitors to the local hostelries in the area. You sent Jefferson all the details on his North American contacts?"

"Si Señor, he would have had them before his office closed", the Señora replied.

"Bueno, then I'm off to Sobatsu HQ in São Paulo first, I'll be there for thirty-six hours before I fly to Rio where I'll establish co-ordination between our teams. Have all of the information sent by scrambler phone to me personally as soon as you get it, give me an indication on my mobile -phone and I'll give you a secure number for any updates. Leave a few men here just in case he tries to double back. He's a slippery fish, but also very lucky, although I've another technological miracle arriving at Rio in a few days that could just eliminate his luck".

Philippe smiled grimly as he recalled the Japanese R & D's guarantee to have one hundred voice-recognition bugs ready for collection in Rio within seventy-two hours. Without the use of international flights, Martin would be extremely hard put to cover the vast continent of South America before he'd installed these tracking devices. It was a little unfortunate that all the satellites for full coverage hadn't been launched, but he'd content himself with the fact that Martin could be traced with, almost pinpoint accuracy, as long as he spoke to someone. All of his business meetings were taped as standard practice and so Martin's voice print had been easy to extrapolate for the boffins in Research and Development. Surely between his teams of watchers, the spy in the sky and all the computerised information now being collated hourly from the world's airlines, border points, ports and banking facilities; it was only a matter of time. Where the hell are you hiding now my little sand martin?, he thought Abruptly, he strode off to the International lounge for a quick drink prior to catching his flight to São Paulo, leaving a worried Señora Flores to contact her own ground troops and carry out his orders.

Meantime, Jack was puzzling over Myron's e-mail, informing him of Jefferson's arrival and wish to meet him. He didn't have an uncle in New York, not that he was aware of anyway. Together with Bernie's odd fax, life was becoming mysterious. O.K., he'd go, although Carolyn declined to accompany him. Too much boring business talk, booze and cigars; it wasn't her forté and she'd hear about this uncle later.

"Told you Jack, it's just an excuse for Jefferson to have a sexy week-end with his secretary as I said. By the way when are you taking me on the next one?".

Men were all the same in that department, she thought, although Jack wasn't a strayer. She was glad of that, too many were like Bernie, although she admitted to herself he was good fun. Jack thought the world of him anyway and with Jack's finances under strain with so many future, commercial interests just about to take-off, maybe there was an opportunity through Jefferson to ease that situation.

Kissing him lightly and saying, "Have fun darling, I'll probably be asleep when you return, but I do see that there could be another aspect of finance through Jefferson for your ceramic catalyser. Don't drink too much".

After an exceptionally good meal with quality wines, Colombian coffee and another large Armagnac, Larry felt in an expansive mood as he lit one of the cigars that Ardeth had fetched for him. She had her good points, he decided. Turning to Myron, whose company he'd requested and asking him to put his own brandy on the tab, he said.

"Now fill me in a little on Jack and how you two teamed up sailing together. What exactly does he do? His uncle wasn't very informative".

Myron had just completed a little potted history on his friend, when Jack appeared via the kitchen, immediately accepting the proffered brandy and cigar after introductions and handshake. Jefferson's sketchy detail on his mystery uncle was superfluous when faced with the man's powerful charisma and the easy manner when he talked in billions of dollars. All other thoughts were dispelled as Jack recognised a definite source of funding for his project and as Larry told Myron to bring another full bottle of Armagnac and put it on his bill; it was obvious that Myron was prepared to allow his wealthy guest complete freedom from any awkward questions. Opportunity knocks only so many times in life and both Jack and Myron's tongues were loosened over their boating, their foreign holidays and their friends. The twin influences of a great brandy and immense wealth in the same room as themselves were having the desired effect.

Larry thought how easy it was to get information from these country boys, small town inhabitants were easy to get on your team. He steered the conversation to Bernie Martin with a needling,

"Brits are generally stupid at business and only think they're sophisticated because of their history".

This evoked the expected defence of their friend and he learned more about Martin than he'd dare hope, why the hell had he not been informed by Philippe about this long-term friendship? He must be aware of it. He'd have some stronger language to underline that the man wasn't on top of his job. How the hell did an amateur like Martin manage to run rings around Philippe's organisation? Jefferson allowed the thoughts to creep into his mind, Jack was on a boring explanation about his new ceramic catalyser that he and an inventor friend of his were trying to market. Corning, one of the neighbouring towns, was the centre for production of catalytic converters for all the US motor industry and half of the rest of the world's. As Jefferson had already decided to finance the project, he allowed Jack to prattle on about the technicalities. Not that he was interested in this small deal, even if it was as good as Jack said it would only be worth a few tens of millions. Small beer as far as he, Laurence C. Jefferson was concerned, but it would make certain that all possible contacts with Martin would be in his own domain. He'd already established that there was a letter following. If he couldn't intercept it, then at least he would know its contents. Larry was suddenly glad that he'd had the lists of all the company names placed in alphabetical order. Even if Martin had had time to study them, it was unlikely that he'd place any emphasis on the name of one CEO in a particular company, although it was on all three lists. Jefferson's train of thought was broken by the mention of Martin's name yet again. It appeared that Martin had encouraged Jack to pursue the idea to the hilt, but the project was undercapitalised. It was another opportunity to elicit greater detail and asking Myron to top up their glasses, he said easily,

"Where did you guys actually meet, somewhere in central America I gather?".

Unwittingly, Jack and Myron, filled in the account of their friend's travels and Myron even fetched a few postcards from him that had arrived from strange places. Jefferson decided to cut his weekend short and get back to the city where he could organise the right people to intercept mail and photograph letters and postcard's that could help in the destruction of Martin. To keep Jack and Myron onside, he said conversationally.

"You know Jack, I have a great friend who's in New York at this moment, but who will be returning to Detroit probably on Monday. He's the main purchaser for G.M.'s (General Motors). I think it might be sensible for me to talk to him about your new ceramic before he leaves, I'll take a rain-check on this week-end and return to New York tomorrow". These hicks were so easy to corrupt through an opportunity. They couldn't even organise themselves, thought Jefferson. Jack was ecstatic, Myron very drunk, having heard all about these ceramics many times before and had copiously topped up his own glass at Jefferson's expense. After all, Jefferson's bill in the morning, though large by his own standards wouldn't even be looked at, let alone be checked. In this assessment Myron was right, as Larry had little time for Ardeth's sexy underwear, although she'd wakened at his entry to their room. They were leaving for the office in the morning. There was something very odd about Penn Yan and this guy Jack McAllister, she thought. She resolved to keep an eye open for an explanation to this particular mystery as it had her boss behaving most erratically.

At least another expensive present had been assured as Larry appeared very satisfied with his trip and had even given her a peck on the cheek before falling asleep. All in all, Ardeth considered, this trip had been decidedly unsatisfactory from her point of view, although she was pleased to note that Larry's worries had somehow magically evaporated. The return drive and following flight would at least be pleasant.

Five

A roar of engines and a following dust cloud heralded the arrival of six cars into the Hosteria's yard in San Pedro, drawing up in line to obtain a refill of fuel. Two Mercedes, two Audi's and two BMW's were the team's deliveries this time. I recalled that the famed Volkswagen beetle was now produced in Brasil and so, only the luxury German models would have to be imported via this route. I studied the small group of drivers, finally selecting their leader and the man in charge. This had to work and I approached the ginger-headed, heavy featured and dark complexioned young man whom I estimated to be in his early thirties. Chatting, I offered cigarettes all round, they and I completely oblivious of the possible fire risk. They were thirsty and hungry and I offered to buy them all a beer in the hostelry if they could give me a lift to one of the neighbouring towns that I knew they'd be passing through. "No problemas Señor", a few beers being an open sesame for lifts just about anywhere in the world.

My case was stowed and we trooped into the hostel for a couple of beers. Paying my bill, I let my host know that I was moving on and would get a lift to the next town where I could get a bus to the north.

Once in the Mercedes 250 CE, I chatted to José the lead driver and asked if he'd have any real objection to my accompanying him all the way to Asunción and that I'd be happy to pay $100 for the trip. He was amazed that I was happy to undertake such an uncomfortable trip, but when I told him that I was saving almost $800 by not returning to Santiago first and that seldom were immigration stamps ever enforced in their continent, he laughed and agreed; provided I paid another $100, "after all business was business and he'd his other drivers with whom to share the extras involved". As I knew they were carrying all sorts of contraband and the doubling of my fee was both anticipated and expected, I was more than happy. With another four and a half days drive and a week to return, it would be old news to anyone on my trail and practically worthless. If I had offered more, they would have been more suspicious of my reasons. As it was, everyone liked to save money if their expenses were a set figure like mine and corners could be cut. After all, the companies made the largest profit.

Paraguay here I come I thought, by way of that other land-locked country, Bolivia. Those initial 400 miles were the most uncomfortable of the whole trip, the first 150 miles being the western Cordillera (Range) of the Andes. The boring trip through the foothills was broken only by the sight of two Rheas (South American ostriches) and a number of small herds of Vicuña (wild llama), that had been seriously under threat of extinction through hunting, but were now recovering in numbers.

As the drivers didn't wish to stop at the higher altitudes where snow and ice prevailed and temperatures dropped to minus 10 degrees C., we crossed the pass after midnight. The car heaters preserved us from the elements. The stars were beautiful and as we approached the highest point my heart missed a beat as an enormous searchlight shone through the pass. Immediately I realised that it was Venus, then corrected myself again as I remembered the latitude; it was Mars with the crescent moon lying on its back beneath. Fortunately my panic hadn't transmitted itself to my driver who had hardly ceased his questions about Europe.

Shortly after, we were descending to the Gran Chaco, an agricultural and grass savannah, which like its counterpart in Paraguay was almost totally uninhabited after Tarija, our final fuel stop. Small farms here and there run by Indian farmers supplied us with good plain meals. As all slept in the cars with the doors locked, this protected both the cars and us. Border crossings from Chile to Bolivia and thence into Paraguay were recognised only by cairns of stones and the official signposts of the countries concerned. I had another busier border crossing in mind further on, where the immigration officials checked only one in a hundred and then, only if they hadn't paid the going bribe; I knew that these remote border crossings would be unmanned.

The final seven hundred miles to Asunción was boring and used up the cigarettes and gum that I'd bought to keep the drivers happy. I was glad to see the city and bade farewell to my compadres in one of the main squares. Looking at the departing cars, I felt that the new owners were definitely being cheated, 2,000 miles wouldn't appear on the odometers after their outsides were washed and polished and all traces of the previous week's thrashing had been removed.

I found a pleasant three-star hotel not far from the centre and decided that I could afford to rest for a couple of days and plan the next steps in my journey. I would also write a few more letters, hopefully to give me greater security nearer to journey's end. I daren't risk telephones or use fax machines. I knew that I should have to appear as a tourist but avoid all the places where passports were necessary or where I should be forced to use my proper name, Señor Barolo from Italy suited me just fine.

I hoped too, that I might be able to avoid other Italian tourists who would quickly penetrate my disguise.

Asunción was an enjoyable break, its busy and bustling streets with friendly people wishing to increase their tourism added to my well-being. I was in an upbeat frame of mind when I left the Continental hotel, having planned the stages of my journey up to the northernmost point of the continent and all of it without needing to produce my passport. I was hoping that I could then bribe some of the Colombians to smuggle me into Panama from where I could get a flight up to Mexico, the shorter flight time wouldn't allow my pursuers sufficient time to catch-up with me. There were still too many if's, but's and maybe's and I put that section of the journey out of my mind. I had sufficient on my plate right now. I was fully rested and mentally alert and had re-touched my hair where it was necessary, although pleased to see that the colour had toned down sufficiently to make my tanned complexion look completely natural. It had been slightly suggestive of hair-colouring previously.

My taxi to the airport was driven by a lunatic, who drove like a bat out of hell despite my protestations, using his horn as a noisy broom. I caught a plane, a small Jetstream 31, to the Foz de Iguassu, the Paraguayan tourist township near to the beautiful falls of the same name. These falls were shared by the three countries of Brasil, Argentina and Paraguay, although in reality they were one quarter Brazilian and three quarters Argentinian. Paraguay, being much cheaper for the tourist by almost half, in comparison to either of its larger neighbours, made its own tourist town an attractive, alternative jumping-off point for both the falls and the nearby Itaipú Dam. I intended to cross the Friendship Bridge into Brasil whose dependence on the Dam's electricity had made it enter into an agreement with Paraguay to construct the largest Dam and hydro-electric facility in the world. Although this dam would soon be eclipsed by yet another larger one in Venezuela and an even mightier one on the Yangtze at the Three Gorges. More ecological disasters in the making I thought, my kids and grandchildren would have to sort it all out. However, if Philippe and his Top Ten succeeded, those problems were academic.

I caught a taxi at the airport into town, stopping at a restaurant for a beer and bite to eat before hailing another for the crossing of the Friendship Bridge. As always, it looked like an evacuation from war or pestilence. The queues on both sides stretched miles with those on the Paraguayan side being lined with traders on each side of the road. Thousands of Brazilians and Argentinians crossed this bridge every day, to buy goods at half the cost by avoiding the duties in their own countries. I had learnt when visiting the area before, that many traders made anything up to ten separate daily trips each, in open defiance of enormous notices proclaiming a $200 purchase maximum per day with suitably heavy fines for any contravention. Mini-buses, cars, lorries and many tens of thousands of bicycles groaned under the loads of contraband goods being transported from Paraguay to the other countries.

Customs and immigration officials had enough on their hands making sure that they received their correct bribes. Passports were a nuisance.

My taxi-driver was content to see me enter the office near the lavatories, then he drove me to a superb four-star hotel overlooking the famous falls. They are truly breathtaking, the finest in the world with 276 cataracts of all sizes and volumes of water. They beat the other world contenders of Niagara and Victoria into second and third place. I booked a tour of the Itaipú Dam and a late dinner when paying in advance for a night's stay, asking reception to book my flight also to Manaus via São Paulo and Brasilia next day. It was a common enough request and excited no comment.

I couldn't resist another walk down the sturdy system of viewing platforms that the Brazilians had created for their tourists. The falls are best viewed from this side, the numerous toucans in the trees, monkeys, racoons and the myriads of butterflies and stick insects were an added bonus to this visual feast. For an hour or so I forgot my troubles and lost myself to this wonder of the world, almost missing the coach tour of the dam.

Forty thousand men had laboured for seventeen years in its construction, shifting almost nine times the rock and earth moved to construct the Channel tunnel. Its German made generators now produced 12.6 million megawatts. If it had been an oil-fired electricity plant, it would have required 420,000 barrels of oil per day to generate the same amount. The guided tour enabled me to establish my credentials as a bona fidé tourist and I enjoyed a superb dinner and good night's sleep. I knew that I'd lost my pursuers for the time being and my disguise was sufficient cover for the moment.

It was the time it was taking to cover this enormous continent that worried me most and I hoped that my decision to mail photocopies of the full pages of transcription (including those in the envelopes), to the FBI, c/o. J. Edgar Hoover Building in Washington DC, had been a wise one.

These companies on the lists, let alone the final ten of them, controlled the world or at least its finances. Why not the Federal Bureau of Investigation?

I felt very small and very alone and I daren't phone my family for fear of prejudicing their safety, as well as my own. Oh God, I definitely need your help, another silent prayer was made as sleep overtook me.

I had time for a quick breakfast before my taxi took me to the airport, catching a Varig flight to Brasilia via the hub airport of São Paulo. It was a long diversion, but would not be thought unusual as it was half of the cost of a direct flight. I was aware of many watchers at São Paulo and steeled myself to the time-wasting exploits of a normal tourist who was filling in time awaiting his flight. Three hours dragged past, but at least there was sufficient of interest in that enormous hub airport so as not to invite closer inspection. I had to force my gaze away from the numerous watchers. The flight-call, when it came, was a blessed relief and having been given a window seat by the airline clerk, I enjoyed the view of the city as we swept over the skyscrapers. Few people outside Brasil knew that São Paulo had around a hundred times as many skyscrapers as there were in New York. It was a long flight with a half-hour stop in Brasilia's futuristically styled airport that matched the sci-fi concepts of its designer. As we took off once more, I could see the city's layout in the shape of a Bow with notched arrow, that appears in the form of an aircraft to others. Superb hotels at prices to suit all pockets made it a tourist must, but I'd been there before as I said to my fellow passenger and was short of time to catch my river-boat to Belém. I made him laugh by designating Brasilia as the city of the quick and the dead as a pedestrian tourist in that city, which had been specifically built for the motor-car, if you weren't quick enough on crossing the carriageways you were most assuredly dead!

I took no chances even with complete strangers and gave them misleading information just in case. I found myself becoming an expert liar. I dozed for part of the second leg, looking out of the window to avoid my fellow passenger's requirement for conversation. Manaus lay almost 1,500 miles up the Amazon where the two major tributaries join to form the mightiest river on our planet. As we came into land I could see the black waters of the Rio Negro running alongside the yellowish water of the Rio Solimões. It's a fascinating sight that is best seen from the air, the bi-coloured waters flowing side by side for two miles before they gradually combine. I loved this continent. I loved my job and I fiercely loved my family.

I prayed inwardly once again that I would live to enjoy more of them all. But this next stage was untried and untested and the unknown could prove to be more difficult. Brazilians, of course, were Portuguese speakers, but thankfully most of them were either bi-lingual or could understand my Spanish; the difficulties arose when trying to understand what other people said to oneself. Safety being paramount, I would stay at a quality hotel where all the staff would speak Spanish as well as other languages. I had thought of going down river to Belém, but reckoned that if my pursuers found that I'd been in Manaus, then they too would think I'd used that route. It did have a lot of merit with an easy short flight to Guyane and direct flights to France, as Guyane (also known as French Guyana) was a province of France. But I anticipated watchers in both places. It could prove to be a French cul-de-sac. The alternative was far longer and more difficult, but with many options in case of flight. I stayed in a four-star hotel, a Novotel, well outside the city and risked a couple of phone calls to a friend in Ecuador and one to Judy. Dr. Holguer Holsh, with whose sister's family I had lived, many years ago when I'd attended one of the best teaching schools for Spanish in Quito, the Capital. He answered immediately and after the usual inquiries about family, work and travels; he alerted me to other queries.

"I've had a friend of yours asking for you Bernard", Holguer said continuing, "A Señor Silver."

I replied that I didn't know anyone of that name and could he describe him. It was Parides, they must have details of all my contacts in South America. These devils were thorough. Thanking Holguer, I asked him to give the family my love and best wishes saying only,

"I could be seeing you shortly".

Ecuador was out, that much was apparent. The country would be ring fenced as my pursuers were fully aware of my involvements there. They must have noted my addresses in my personal organiser. Damn!, my options had seriously reduced as I'd contemplated using one of the family as a courier for the documents. I would have trusted them, an honest and intelligent, first-class family. My second call was to Judy's flat in Chichester Sussex. I had to use her and not let her know about my devious intentions, but I had fewer options and part of me recognised that it was for her safety, as well as my own, hence the reason for my duplicity. I would make it up to her later, financially if not physically. She took ages to answer and I apologised for wakening her, having temporarily forgotten the time differences in my concentration over my plans.

"Sorry darling, but I didn't want the office to know anything about our holiday together", I lied smoothly. "Are you ready to join me for a ten days in the sun. Do you fancy a tour of the ABC Islands and some scuba diving? Bonaire has a great coral reef and Aruba is also a fun island. KLM flies direct to Curaçao from Gatwick and I'll join you there ten days from now. Can you organise your break to suit?"

"Yes Bernie, I've been waiting for your call and already informed the boss that I'm taking a well earned break and will organise a temp. to cover. Are you alright?, there's been some officials here to see the boss asking lots of questions about you. You're not in any trouble are you? Sally's been on the phone also, having had police officers making routine inquiries as to your exact whereabouts. Maybe you should drop the office a fax and put everyone's mind at rest, OK?"

"Certainly sweetheart, I'll do just that", I replied. "I can assure you that it's nothing to worry about, see you on the twenty-fifth. Book in at the Princess Beach hotel, they have superb facilities, Bye!"

I disconnected before Judy could ask any more. She's going to be furious when she realises the truth, I thought. Hell hath no fury like ——.

There were more immediate worries, survival being foremost. I'd better move out tomorrow. I wondered how long it would take them to find out that I had been in Manaus. Could they trace these calls? Surely not immediately, but take no chances - keep moving. I had still thousands of miles to cover, but at least hotel and transport costs were reasonably easy to contain, being half what one would pay in the Western countries and sometimes only a third.

I used one of my traveller's cheques to pay my hotel bill in the morning, yet another giveaway, and cashed the others at a poor rate into dollars at one of the major banks. Recognising that I was already compromised and this location would be old news in a few days time. I intended being far away by that time.

At the docks next morning I found a small cargo/passenger vessel that was destined for Ilha Grande at the headwaters of the Negro and paid for a tiny berth in a double cabin. Heading back into town I found a small barber's shop, the owner radically changing the colour and style of my hair. With my deeply bronzed tan and a locally bought shirt and jacket, I could pass as an inhabitant of any of the neighbouring countries, deciding that Señor Barolo had now served his purpose and that another identity would be more suitable for Colombia, for that was my next destination. I returned to the docks and obtained a passage on one of the cargo boats destined for Iquitos in Peru where I reckoned I could get a light aircraft to take me illicitly to Pasto or Tulcan in southern Colombia. The headwaters of the Amazon spread into no less than five other countries and access to all of them without a passport was child's play. No wonder the authorities had such a problem in stemming the flood of drugs. I'd been in Bogotá a few years ago and had visited their fabulous Gold Museum, it was a mind experience that I would never forget. In their recorded history of the Indian tribes, I'd learnt that because of the exceptionally high altitudes in their country and because they had no beasts of burden, not even llamas until after the Conquistadores vanquished the Incas. Cocaine was a necessity to allow work to be done, overcoming fatigue, pain and the lack of oxygen. There was no stigma attached to the drug within the tribal societies. Now that the major multi-nationals had cornered the market in cereal production and much of the other agrarian produce, many of the tribes now grew coca and exported death, in preference to dying of hunger themselves. The drug-barons, often European or American, had seized upon this convenience and increased their hold upon simple communities by casting themselves in the 'Robin Hood' mould of aiding the poor. With the jungle covered borders extending over thousands of square miles, two oceanic shores, one to the Atlantic and the other to the Pacific, both with thousands of offshore islands, policing it was a complete nightmare. Such is the country of Colombia. Otherwise it's a veritable garden of Eden with flowers almost everywhere including all trees and bushes; the backdrop of the three snow-capped Cordilleras giving it an enlarged Swiss effect. It is a beautiful country, but dangerous for the unwary and those who do not care about their safety. However, it was ideal from my point of view and tourism had no part in my plans from this point on. I had made great use of the tourist hotels and the cover of being just one of thousands of numerous Europeans of Mediterranean extraction had served me well. It was now time to alter my identity completely. My Spanish was impeccable and I fitted into the local scene, becoming just another trader in search of new markets.

The cargo/passenger boat up the Negro would be calling at four ports before reaching Ilha Grande, without the passenger Señor Barolo who was on its manifest. In many ways I wished that this had been my actual route, as the acid waters of the Negro didn't allow mosquitoes to breed along its banks while those of the Solimões were a different matter, although the necessary prophylactic tablets had now being taken and a liberal quantity of repellant obtained.

My vessel would take a week to complete its journey, with four ports of call en route, but with no real communications with the outside world. The hammocks on the cargo vessel's after deck were the only attempt at provision of a degree of comfort for passengers, facilities were rather basic to say the least. I was gambling on all of the other choice of routes being more worthy of investigation first, or at least Colombia being discounted as my destination.

I had sent letters to Jack and my lawyers, enclosing all of the photocopied papers, and a reassuring fax to my company. God alone knew what they thought I was up to. This would be their first indication that I was travelling to the north, but for what reason? In view of the fact that I was meant to be working and asking for further orders. I daren't elucidate in my fax. The next seven days were far from pleasant, the trip being more of a youthful enthusiast's form of travel I thought, applying yet another coat of repellant on my exposed skin. The mosquitoes of the

Solimões required it as an appetiser, I thought miserably. At least the food, although boring, was palatable. The variety of fruit however, did make a pleasant change; Brasil has 215 different types of fruit. I would definitely lose some weight at least!

Sleeping a lot, I conserved my energies and paid little attention to the dozens of dug-out canoes that hailed the ship from both sides. The tribes of the Amazon had recognised that they could obtain handouts from any tourists who were taking passage on the larger vessels. The locals, and I, ignored them. Tribal dwellings dotted both sides of the river and small patches of corn and greenery denoted their meagre forms of agriculture that, together with fishing and hunting, made up their way of life. At the larger ports our cooks took aboard some fascinating specimens of fish, Pirhaña by the dozen and very tasty too, even served with their teeth intact. It was the enormous river fish, the Piraruçu that was truly amazing, growing up-to 450lbs and more in size, but they are air breathing and with forward facing eyes, this making them somewhat human in their facial appearance. Their flesh however, was somewhat bland and needed the spices that the cooks added. Amazonia was an amazing place with more than 80% of its flora still to be investigated or even named. However, I had other things to consider and these mysteries were put on hold. My fellow inhabitants of the hammocks were noisier than myself with their snores and I took to sleeping early and having afternoon siestas, so as to be fully rested and ready for the next section of my journey.

With Tefé and Fonté Boa behind us, finally São Paulo de Oliveca foretold that we were on the last stretch of navigable river and would dock in Iquitos next morning. It wasn't a moment too soon, my patience and skin through mozzie bites, having worn more than a little thin. I scanned the docks for obvious watchers, there were none that I could detect, and I wasted no time in obtaining a very rickety taxi to what passed for an airport, finding the ubiquitous drinking place of the bush pilots nearby.

During the rainy season, when the gold mining in the Mato Grosso had reduced, many of these light aircraft pilots moved to various other areas, so as to supplement their precarious income. Questions were seldom asked, borders conveniently overlooked, papers not necessary, as long as the correct cash (in dollars or gold) was proffered. The five men sitting round a table covered with empty bottles and smoking hand-rolled cigarettes were definitely representative of their breed and all I noted could have done with a bath, most of them being unshaven with a few days' stubble on their faces. A very unreliable lot I thought, but there was little choice. I'd dumped my suitcase in Manaus in preference for a largish, woven cloth bag. I looked like many of the Indian traders that bought artifacts from the tribes to sell in the large cities. As I had deliberately not shaved on the boat nor used any lotions, even my own body odour fitted the part. Washing and hygiene were unnecessary luxuries in these remote parts. I found myself entering into the persona of an Indian trader.

"Anyone of you doing the Colombian route?", I queried, as I bought a beer at the table which passed for a bar counter.

No answer. A truculent lot of pilots I decided, but was aware of their own calculating, assessing stares. I would let them come to me now. Eagerness in business was not the Spanish way; it was up to them to open negotiations. I hadn't to appear in a hurry. Eventually, one of them stood and joined me at the bar, awaiting a beer before he even acknowledged my presence.

"Where exactly would you like to go Señor ? Colombia is a large country".

As he smiled, he revealed a mouthful of gold teeth. Definitely a radiant smile, I thought.

"As close to one of the small, southern airports as you can, say Tulcan or Pasto for instance", I replied and watched as the pilot took another swig of beer and thought about it. "O.K.", he belched loudly, "but it will cost $500, it's about five hours flying time to get there". Golden smile, slowly pared a finger nail with a large knife and awaited an answer.

I nodded and bought another round for the two of us.

"When do we leave?"

"After siesta time Señor. It helps to cross borders in darkness. No?"

"Si, esta es perfecto", I replied and left my bag with the barman so that I could kill the waiting hours more comfortably in town and knowing that any search of its contents would establish my recently chosen credentials.

As I climbed into the still-waiting taxi, a six-seater Cessna was touching down, its Ecuadorian markings proclaiming its country of origin. There were neither Customs nor Immigration officials at this Peruvian field who cared to inspect the new arrivals and I watched two Doberman dogs bounding for joy as they escaped from the plane. Rabies was endemic anyway I thought, quarantine would be superfluous. I had an excellent lunch at a Mexican style restaurant, chilli with plenty of tortillas to mop up the gravy and five Jalapeños, the large green pickled peppers that can blow the heads off those who're not used to them. They're a great excuse for those few extra beers that aided my siesta in the noonday sun.

The rickety taxi hadn't moved from where I'd left it, its driver apparently hadn't moved either. How some of these guys managed to survive beat me, although they were all first class mechanics. They had to be. Many lorries, buses and especially taxis were antiques of thirty, forty and more years old. Their odometers had long since ceased to function, an unnecessary luxury in any case. Most of the roads in these wilderness areas were never designed for speed and nobody cared about distances or the time taken to get there. My first trip to the Latin American countries had been to Mexico and when the plane's passengers broke out in a round of applause when it touched down safely; I had grave doubts about both the pilots and the aircraft. After dozens of flights and coach trips I was used to it and the sight of someone praying fervently prior to take-off or even the bus leaving, I now took as normal. Mind you, in the Andes there were too many crosses adorning hairpin bends and sheer drops, not to join them in a few personal prayers too. Today, I joined in all applause.

Another twenty minute jolting ride had me back at the airport bar. Golden smile, my pilot, was chatting to a swarthy Indian at whose feet lay the Dobermans that I'd observed earlier.

Six

Philippe was incredulous,

"Where is he?", he demanded. "The voice bug has pin -pointed him to where? Ecuador? He's there then. O.K., it's only that he's contacted a friend there. So give me some definite facts that might be useful, not possibilities!'

Parides knew that his boss wasn't in the mood for just possibilities, replying,

"It's due to the satellite delay Señor. I wasn't aware that he'd phoned his friend until more than twenty-four hours had passed and even after questioning Holguer Holsh; we aren't much further on. I know only that he's close by in a neighbouring country and could be making for Quito. I'm having Holsh's telephone connections checked and we'll know shortly where Martin was when he phoned. No you can rest assured, he wasn't hiding anything and he will not be telling any others."

Philippe studied a large schematic wall-map of the upper half of the South American continent. Where are you my little sand martin, he wondered. You are an opponent worthy of greater thought. Abruptly, he disconnected the call and called Japan.

"Research and development please. When are we due to launch other satellites for the voice identification bugs so that we can get immediate land sources of their emanation?" He cut the excuses short, recognising that it would be too late for any effective coverage. His next call was to Hauptmann in Brasilia, ordering him to transfer to Belém. Martin or whatever he now called himself, was nearing the top of the continent; something that he'd been willing to bet against just a few days ago. This was an amateur after all and he, without any shadow of doubt, should have been in the net two weeks ago. Martin had ability, there was no question of that, and he was aware of his own powerful connections for tracking him down. There was also no doubt that he was heading for the States, but was he? There were still many escape avenues that he could use, via The Guyanas for example. That was it! It would be impossible to cross the Darien jungle and gain access to Panama, his only other route to the safety of the US. Martin couldn't risk an international flight of more than two hours duration, he would be aware that computers would have assimilated complete details of his whereabouts in that time, allowing others to intercept him. Once in Panama, his apprehension would be more difficult. He could country hop easily up to the States and there were too many international airports to cover, although Panama itself and San Salvador were both large hub airports for Central America. It was too big a risk, they had to stop him before then. Too many of the free Press would be at his disposal. He'd better call Jefferson, accept the onslaught of his appalling temper and hope that he'd see the logic of his request. He shuddered involuntarily. Jefferson didn't realise how wily this little bird was. Philippe cursed himself again about that damned epidiascope! He should have had it examined. He knew it and Jefferson knew it. The initial mistake was his and if Martin blew the whistle on them, he'd little doubt about his own fate. The Top Ten wouldn't tolerate mistakes! Another call had Señora Flores and her team on their way to Manaus. Yet another from watchers in Brasilia gave little comfort. You know your continent my clever friend, he mused, but you will have to show yourself shortly. His overseas line was flashing and he picked up the handset, pushing the scrambler as he did so.

"Yes, what information have you for me", trying to keep his voice from showing his extreme concern.

"Mr Philippe, this is Sobatsu, England. We have ascertained all the details that you wished".

Philippe listened intently as these details were transmitted. He cut short a potted history of Mr and Mrs Martin with an explosive,

"Cut to the basics hombre", not realising that he'd mixed Spanish with English. His agitation hadn't gone unnoticed and simple facts then followed. Martin's wife knew nothing, she was an ordinary housewife, but Martin's secretary had booked a flight with KLM. to Curaçao. The office of English Purity Chemicals was furious about Martin's shenanigans. All the office staff were aware of Martin's little affair and the boss would have his guts for garters when he had the gall to show face again. A fax to the office showed little to be concerned about. Martin was not about to involve his family in this affair. At least that was something he could be thankful for, thought Philippe. The problem was confined to and contained in the Americas! Before phoning Jefferson, he wrote down all the points that he could be certain of, then re-read them carefully. This next call would be either game, set and match to him or result in his own permanent retirement.

Scanning the wall chart for inspiration, he watched the clock tick steadily and inexorably towards the hour of his expected call to Jefferson. At one minute to the hour, his extended hand stopped in mid-dial; he dialled Parides' mobile instead.

"Parides here", his lieutenant answered immediately.

"Yes Parides, where are you right now?", asked Philippe.

"At Quito airport, heading to Bogotá, Boss", replied Parides. "I've organised a team of watchers here around the clock".

"Have we anyone reliable there in Ecuador that you could dispatch to Iquitos, as soon as possible?", Philippe queried.

"Si Señor, an old Indian friend, but he's a tracker with dogs, not a watcher", Parides replied.

"That's perfect Parides, and would you have anything that smells of Martin to give his dogs a scent?"

"Si Señor, I'm wearing one of his ties".

"Right, dispatch your tracker and dogs to Iquitos immediately, hire a plane if necessary, O.K.?"

"Si Señor".

Philippe disconnected. Now all your routes are covered my little sand martin! He smiled and proceeded to dial Jefferson's private number. Another glance at his map had a glow of self-satisfaction spreading throughout him. If only Jefferson would agree to the final solution, then Martin was as good as dead.

"Jefferson here, where's Martin then, you're a minute late with your call. Bring me up to speed with your information".

Philippe outlined all the known detail of Martin's movements and the five or six optional routes that he might have taken. Although not completely comprehensive, they covered most of the alternates.

"He's very well informed about South America then", interrupted Jefferson.

"Yes sir, but I'm pretty certain that he's heading for a meeting with his mistress in Curaçao, he'll be using her as his courier for the transport of the transcripts to the authorities. I have men on their way there right now and we're covering all other possible exits. We do know that he was in Manaus, his telephone call to his friend Dr. Holguer Holsh in Quito, Ecuador, confirmed that it was made from the Novotel Hotel, along with a fax to his office. That fax has also been checked out and contained nothing detrimental to us, Martin wishes to protect his family. There was a booking in the name that he was using, a Señor Barolo, an Italian, at the Novotel in Manaus and we have a full description. I have men checking all the passenger lists of all the river boats and ferries, both east and west. We're not far behind him and his alternatives are being reduced, he doesn't have too many options left".

"You're a damn fool, Philippe", snarled Jefferson. "This guy's got more balls and know-how than the rest of you put together, I'll believe it when you bring me his corpse. I've found out that he's sent all the material, and I mean all of the material to the FBI. Thankfully, my man there intercepted it before any damage was done. There's no doubt now, this guy's got to be eliminated and the sooner the better. Capiche?", using an old Mafia term.

"Si Señor, yo comprendo", Philippe replied. "Perhaps I could suggest that we put some of the planned operation for the reduction of unwanted purchasers in Central America into action then the demise of Senor Martin will be certain. I've already ascertained that his taste in soft drinks is exclusively your's in the UK. from our operatives over there".

~ 48 ~

"I'll think about that Philippe, the timing's a little awkward and I don't wish to prejudice our greater plan at present, but I'll instruct my factories to add the second ingredient to our brew meantime".

Disconnection.

Philippe mopped his brow and replaced his receiver, unsurprised to see that his fingers had turned white through the pressure of holding it. It took a full twenty minutes of studying his wall map before he could relax sufficiently to pour himself a tequila. At least Jefferson was now considering the ultimate sanction as a possibility. Martin would never escape that! He shuddered. What a damn nuisance this man Martin, or whatever name he'd now assumed, was. He telephoned Señora Flores on her mobile. He'd saturate Venezuela, Colombia, the ABC Islands, Guyane and Panama with more watchers just in case. Martin could island-hop through the Caribbean, but they'd easily track his movements through them. Just try it hombre!, he thought. No, his own gut feeling and personal betting was via the ABC Islands, the main island Curaçao had direct flights to Europe, but with a flight from there to somewhere in central America would be just over two hours. After Señora Flores had organised her team in Manaus, he'd dispatch her post haste to Curaçao and send more of his soldiers from São Paulo to help her. If they had all the boarding names just after the flight left, then an intercept in Central America was assured. He doubted that Martin would risk a long-haul flight to Europe, it would be his last. He couldn't see any loopholes that were uncovered. It must just be a question of time!

"Ah! Señora Flores, when you've covered all the points that's needed in Manaus, I wish you to go to Curaçao. If you call in at Belém en route, you can use the secure telephone there to phone me for instructions. As Hauptmann is already there, you can compare notes and give me a full update on all the possibilities. "Adios por el momento".

He recognised that she would be Jefferson's choice if a replacement for the Sobatsu security services should be needed. He wondered about the possibility of shifting the blame, she had after all been at the São Paulo meeting. Unfortunately it had been his man, Parides, who'd taken the epidiascope up to the meeting. He'd have to give that area more thought sometime Niggling doubt assailed his myriad thoughts. There was something that he couldn't identify.

In New York, Jefferson's thoughts were on Philippe's suggestion and he called the two major bottling plants and canneries that distributed their soft-drinks in Mexico and Central America. "That minor additive you're storing, the number two that we sent to you last month, our chemists here wish you to add it to the recipe. Yes, it will make it almost impossible for our competitors to crack the formula with this addition, but they're still working on yet another ingredient that will confuse the issue even more. When it becomes available we'll send it down for immediate inclusion".

There had been no curiosity on the part of his general managers at both plants, formulae for successful soft drinks manufacture had been a target for their competitors for years and he'd made all aware of head-office's chemists wish to make theirs impossible to break down. It was somewhat previous though, to what the other nine companies had agreed. He would update them only if the other ingredient became necessary. Philippe did appear to have most of Martin's escape routes well covered and there were no other leaks to be plugged. He'd decided against having McAllister's mailbox raided, it would only complicate things and he did have an answer ready about his company's inclusion on all of the three lists. But he'd made doubly certain of keeping tabs on what happened in the sticks by having two of Sobatsu's operatives posing as a couple taking an out of season break at the Red Fox Inn. If there appeared to be problems, they had instructions to organise a bad accident the next time the buddies went ice-boating on the Finger lakes.

Myron asked his computer if he had incoming mail, a recorded voice confirming the existence of an e-mail; Jack was on his way over. Help, dawn had hardly broken, there must be a panic about something. The kettle had just boiled when the fly-screen was banging and the kitchen door opened.

"Morning Jack, coffee? What's all the hustle for? Let's have breakfast first, my brain doesn't work on empty".

Myron busied himself with ham, eggs and tomatoes and extracted a dish of hash browns from the fridge as Jack said.

"I received that letter from Bernie yesterday and it really doesn't make sense, it's only lists of companies. Although, there's one odd thing about them, they're divided into 1,000, then 100 and finally 10, with Planet Ales Incorporated and Jefferson as CEO and Managing Director, and also his secretary Ardeth are named. What do you make of it?"

The bacon now grilling, eggs frying and the hash browns in the microwave, Myron took the proffered lists and skimmed through them.

"Let's eat first Jack, I need the injection", and in a couple of minutes they were tucking into an American breakfast; eggs over-easy, hash-browns with lashings of coffee, toast, preserves and orange juice. The pages were spread between the dishes on the table for discussion.

"What's Bernie's letter say about them? Does he give an explanation?", Myron asked between mouthfuls.

"Yeah, he wants me to pass them to the FBI and says that a full explanation will follow later, but that he didn't want to compromise me at this time. He says that apart from you, I was not to discuss it with anyone, as the company he's underlined, Sobatsu, are killers and out to stop him from passing the full info. to the FBI. He's given this guy's name, Jim Booth, and thinks that he was an American agent that the Sobatsu mobsters' shot".

"Do you think Bernie's losing it?" Jack asked, mopping up the last shreds of the hash browns and egg with a piece of toast. "It's a damn funny letter, and what about Jefferson and his company being on all three lists?"

The dining-room door opened and Myron's latest guests entered, with a bright-

"Good morning everyone". Jack scooped up the papers as Myron prepared their breakfast, saying that he'd have it on the table in fifteen minutes. They were a nice couple, up from the Big Apple. A winter break from all the hassle of the city.

"Want us to give them both a boat trip on the ice if it's not too much trouble Jack", Myron mused aloud. "We'll discuss that letter later, right now buddy I have to earn a living and so do you". With a cheerful,

"See ya later", Jack headed for the hospital in Syracuse, the vital papers under his auspices and care. As he drove, he decided that he'd make three sets of photocopies and send a set to the CIA as well as the FBI, retaining the third for discussion. Whatever Bernie had stumbled upon, Planet Ales must be a part of it he reasoned. The first list of a thousand companies were of the largest companies in the world. Shit, he even had shares in some of them! It must be some form of price-fixing cartel and completely against the anti-trust laws of the US. He wondered if this would jeopardise his financing from Jefferson? Damn it Bernie, this has come at a highly inconvenient moment, he thought and then, perhaps it's too much of an inconvenience or coincidence? He must discuss all this in depth with Myron. Right now there were patient's charts to check and assess, x-rays to see and reports made out for all the surgeons and other specialists. "You'll have to wait Bernie- buddy!", he said aloud as he parked the car.

Across the pond, in Hallstaff, Ferret & Wheesel's office, Fraser was reading their client Martin's letter with it's enclosures. He'd just taken a rather distressing call from Mrs Martin. She'd been seriously upset by a police visit and all the questions they had asked about her husband. However, on phoning the local police station, they had no record of such a visit, nor of the Chief Inspector's name that Mrs Martin had recalled. The police had said that they'd make further inquiries on the matter.

He dictated a letter about Martin and included all the detail that he thought could be relevant. Buzzing for his secretary, he asked her to find out the addresses of MI5/6., he could never remember which was the section that dealt with domestic and which was foreign, also the address for GCHQ.

"When you've done that you'll get the letter that's already on my printer", the firm having invested in the latest machines that now made typists and their errors a thing of the past.

Sally had been comforted by Fraser's words and the assurance that he would check everything out with the police. But it was worrying and now that Judy had taken a holiday in the Caribbean of all places, that was even more worrying. Sally had never before considered Judy's existence to be any threat to her comfortable life. Judy was after all just an oversexed, pretty little plaything for Bernard, but although an efficient and loyal secretary she was considered to be a bimbo otherwise. That had been his precise summation of her and Sally's instincts echoed the truth of this statement. But there was something odd going on now; the police weren't checking without reason. She fetched Bernard's latest post-card and re-read it. It was his usual, mainly details of good wines that he'd come across and dishes that he found appetisingly different in his travels. The police had made notes about it though and even used a magnifying glass on the Paraguayan postmark. Something was very, very odd indeed. Her mind jumped from point to point, it was difficult to concentrate. She had unburdened herself to Fraser, their lawyer. He would know what to do and take the appropriate actions. Now I wonder where I could get that last recipe that Bernard wrote about?, she pondered.

Jefferson came to a decision. It could be anything up to ten days before a new batch of soft-drinks would be in circulation in the areas chosen and Martin was, at the very least, only three weeks away from gaining access to the Isthmus of Central America, into Mexico and thence to the US. A quick call was made to his chemists, ordering them to dispatch the third ingredient to the two bottling plants, but advise them to hold off adding the final addition until Jefferson contacted the general managers personally. He buzzed Ardeth and asked her to contact his fellow CEO's of the other eight companies, asking for an emergency meeting to be held in Dubai in the United Arab Emirates. It was a convenient meeting-place for all of them, and as it was a totally-controlled society, it would be completely secure and had the latest communications. It had also all of the little diversions that appealed to his fellow directors' peccadilloes. He asked Ardeth to place a secure call to the Vice president of the Chamber of Commerce in the UAE and as an afterthought added,

"And let the eight other companies know that Sobatsu won't be attending this meeting and to retain this information only for themselves".

While waiting for his call, he recalled that it was on a previous visit to the UAE many years ago, that he'd seen the way forward to have complete control over the world's business and politicians. These Arabs had their own area of influence completely tied up; he'd learnt from their methods when discussing business with some of their top influential people. They knew how to do things and how to keep all the strings in their own hands, but they were only interested in retaining control in the Arab world and apart from perhaps, the Islamic religious countries, wouldn't interfere with his Top Ten's plans for the future. He buzzed Ardeth again, "And inform the eight to take their personal communicators with them".

Sobatsu were top-dogs when it came to systems, he thought, but they'll have to await the outcome of the Dubai meeting before being informed of any other decisions. Doodling on the list of Top Ten companies, he pencilled in their approximate worth beside the German, French, Swiss, English, his own and two other American companies, a Korean and a Japanese company. Sobatsu, the other Japanese company, completed the list.

He added up his rough totals, one hundred and eighty trillion dollars, even without Sobatsu, they controlled almost a third of the world's wealth! Extending his flight of fancy, he added first an approximate figure of half that amount again for the 100 companies and a further eighth more when including the 1,000. The phone rang.

"Hello Yussuf my old friend, how's your buddy Hossein, I'm intending visiting your city for a business conference soon and wish to have you both as guests for dinner at the Sheraton's best restaurant or wherever else that you'd recommend. My business colleagues would enjoy a round or two of golf while we're there also, I'll have my secretary fax you the exact dates and times of arrival when everything's confirmed. If that's O.K. with you?".

"Perfectly Larry", replied Yussuf, I'll arrange everything that you need".

They neither waste time nor words thought Jefferson, as the phone went dead. He smiled at the thought of his first meeting with Yussuf. Yussuf had been in the city of Cancun en route to Havana for a spot of gambling and fun. As he had been there personally to meet his own wife for a five day cruise, he'd asked Yussuf where his other half was.

"Do you take sandwiches with you when you go to a restaurant?", had been the Arab's sharp retort.

These guys really know how to live and organise themselves and their women. This would be an expensive jaunt for all of the nine. When it came to business or having their favours returned, the Gulf Arabs were unbeatable.

"Ardeth, organise my golf-clubs and let my wife and valet know that I'll need my tropical gear packed for the Middle east, O.K?"

"Yes Laurence", Ardeth found it odd that she would not be accompanying her boss on this trip, as practically all his foreign tours had included her company when Mrs Jefferson didn't accompany him. Again the strict instruction that neither Sobatsu's security arm, nor the company, had to be informed about either the meeting or the whereabouts of Jefferson should Philippe call when he was attending it; that was in itself very odd. Something highly peculiar was definitely going on. However, all calls would have to be re-routed to wherever Larry was. Larry's Lear-jet had all the necessary scrambler devices aboard for completely secure communications. Meantime, there were all these instructions that had to be carried out to the letter, on top of all the other tasks she'd yet to complete. Another call was put through to her boss, the guy from Sobatsu that Larry had sent up to Penn Yan was now on the phone.

Her puzzlement increased, but remembering the diamond-studded Rolex that now adorned her wrist, she stroked it, thinking only, keep your little secrets then Larry. Just a few more of these presents and I'll be able to afford more pleasant work elsewhere. Curiosity too, had a price! Damned men. They think they own the world and everything and everyone in it as well. Ardeth's femininity had taken a severe knock lately, there were no more quickie feels up her dress from Larry any more or gentle pats on her ass and even fewer requests to stay late for the, up until Penn Yan, the regular session against or atop Larry's executive desk. She studied her face in her vanity mirror. An attractive reflection with perfect make-up peered back. A rétroucé nose and dimpled cheeks with a mop of dark curls lent strength to her confidence. It's not me then, she decided.

The first of the international calls to the other CEO's secretaries demanded her attention. Efficiency took the place of wistfulness.

Jefferson lifted his phone again.

"Yes I've got that", he replied to his operative who was calling from a coin box in the neighbouring town of Gorham near to Penn Yan.

"I'll have our man in the bureau intercept everything from upstate during the next few weeks. How many pages did you reckon there were? Fourteen, and a letter? O.K., but the sooner you and your wife learn all about ice-boating the better. I think that it would be best to tie-up these loose ends, we've learnt all that we'll ever learn from that source. Organise it and then take that long holiday in Hawaii I promised you. If I'm away on a trip, see Ardeth about your tickets and some spending money when you return to New York".

That will stop all leaks from that direction, he thought, pressing the disconnect button on his hands-free phone. Buzzing Ardeth once more, he confirmed that there was sufficient cash in the contingency account that she'd access to, to cover these extras. Agreement on the timing for the addition of the third chemical would be all important now. After that, he could go back to the overall plan that the Top Ten had devised. Philippe would have to be replaced, but not until after the meeting in Dubai, he didn't foresee any difficulties explaining his demise nor Sobatsu's exclusion from such a gathering. After all, the Japanese had a similar, pragmatic sense of duty and loyalty that the French had. What was that phrase they used, that emulated our aphorism, of having to break a number of eggs to make a really good omelette?

Seven

Once more my heart was giving palpitations as I saw the contents of my bag strewn over the floor behind the table that passed for a bar counter. I could hardly tear my gaze from my tie that adorned the Indian's belt and in a slightly strangulated voice I forced out.

"What the hell's going on here?"

My brain was moving at supersonic speed. Thankfully, I'd sewn the papers and my passport into the lining of my jacket and replaced the shoulder pads with wads of dollars, first wrapped in pieces of canvas. My other cash and written notes were safely out of sight in my body belt. There was nothing to incriminate me in my bag, in fact any search of it would help to prevent a more personal one, or so I had hoped. I'd dumped all my convenient items, such as my toilet-bag, electric razor and after-shave in the Solimões at the beginning of the seven day voyage. The bag contained no identifying articles and would only yield innocuous materials, clothing suited to the jungle mostly, as would befit a trader in Indian artifacts. Even my personal organiser now lay at the bottom of the river, having already taken a copy of some necessary numbers and sewn them too, into my jacket. I became aware that Golden Smile was speaking and mentally shook myself.

"I told this Indian that you weren't a European, there hasn't been one through here for weeks", he said, pointing to my bag and clothes and continuing apologetically,

"That was his idea, not mine".

The barman agreed, although I gave him a dirty look over his perfidy. I stiffened involuntarily as the two dogs stretched, then ambled over to me, sniffing at my trousers and hands. The Indian who was inspecting me closely, abruptly asked.

"Were there any Europeans on the ship that you came in with?"

"No", I replied, now recognising that my tie would have smelt more of after-shave and cologne than of me, my own body odour having taken on the taint of the hot spicy flavours of the food I had been consuming lately. The dogs had been happy to confirm my innocence of any suspicious odours..

Turning to Golden smile I said.

"Well are we leaving or what?", continuing to the Indian.

"And you can buy us another beer for rubbishing my clothes". This suggestion clearly met with the pilot's and barman's approval, the flashing smile greeting a begrudged "O.K." from the Indian.

I relaxed for the wasted thirty minutes that it took to re-pack my clothes, drink my beer and follow Golden smile to his battered Cessna. It wouldn't do to appear in too much of a hurry to depart and the last I saw of the Indian was of him and his dogs boarding the same rickety taxi for a trip into town to gather information about other vessels that were due. The plane's engine sounded as sweet as a nut anyway and I climbed into the rear seat to stretch out, having stowed my bag in the fuselage locker. To my query of,

"What's the other parcels", I received a shrug of the shoulders and the reply.

"One's got to live Señor and your $500 is insufficient for such a long trip".

There was little point in my having scruples about what they contained. My own clandestine crossing of the border would only be compromised, I thought. We were soon winging our way westwards and into the setting sun. My thoughts drifted poetically, as we climbed through the clouds; they were incredibly beautiful with surging shapes that frothed and boiled. Ethereal, misty, cotton-wool lumps and cotton puffs were alternated by striated threads, then soaring cliffs of purity lay above an azure blue sky that rapidly darkened to a deep violet. Flying westwards we retained these images for many minutes. Tiny flashes of light in the south spoke of a faraway storm. Nature now dropped its final curtain, obliterating the spectacle and my friends, the clouds, left me to sleep.

I woke with a bone-jarring thud as the tiny plane was buffeted by high winds and torrential rain, lightning lit up the cockpit interior and I glimpsed that our heading was still westwards. My pilot was, quite literally, wrestling with the aircraft as it skittered and bucked in the thunderstorm. He shouted that he was unable to climb above it and as it had come in from the south, he'd had little alternative, but to fight it out. The smile had been replaced by a determined grimace and I knew enough about light aircraft to recognise that we could be in trouble. An air-pocket caused us to drop a hundred or more feet and our plane was struck by a bolt of lightning, leaving me with a tingling sensation all over my body.

Then our engine stopped, we were going down! The lightning must have hit some vital part. My pilot shouted to me to prepare for a crash landing and briefly, in the illumination of another sheet of lightning, I saw the jungle canopy rushing at us. Screeching metal, a scream, then driving rain and lumps of foliage hit me, another almighty bang and all went black.

Wood-smoke assailed my nostrils and as I struggled back to consciousness, I made out the open fire within the interior of a native hut; I felt that I'd gone through a mixing machine. I retched and movement from the other side of the hut turned out to be a young native woman who gave me a drink of water. Slowly and gingerly I explored my body, I was naked apart from my shorts and a native type duvet covering me appeared to be made of woven sisal and dried moss, it was warm and comforting. My whole body was tender to the touch and I realised that I was one large mass of bruises, but apart from some form of moss and bark bandage on my left thigh, that was very painful, I appeared intact.

I asked my 'nurse' if my pilot was nearby. As she then gabbled back in a language that I took to be Amyrin, I could see that neither understood the other. Our voices had the effect of bringing another two Indian men into the hut and as they threw more wood on the fire, I could see more of the hut's interior. I was deep in the jungle, there was nothing that denoted the twentieth century and with a start I saw that what I'd taken for coconuts, hanging from the beam in their plantains larder, were in fact shrunken heads. The two Indians spoke briefly to the girl, then left as abruptly as they'd arrived. I examined my plight as logically as I could. I was being looked after, my thigh wound had been bandaged and I'd been put to bed. My nurse even smiled at me, none of this suggested that I was at risk or about to become another trophy. I had also vague memories of being fed with gruel or soup and had drifted in and out of consciousness many times.

Another swallow of cool water made me feel better and I scratched my face, realising immediately that my beard was almost an inch long. It had been just a stubble when we left that airfield in Peru! I must have been here for a week or more. I checked for my body belt, it had gone, but almost immediately I saw it hanging on the wall beside my jacket. My digital, quartz watch had also vanished, but that was all and I sat up with some difficulty as my nurse brought me one of my shirts, obviously my bag of clothes remained intact. The first few days of recuperation were confined to watching the village women at their chores of making flour, pressing cane sugar and preparing the main evening meal. The Indian diet of manioc flour, rice and pulses flavoured with herbs and insects was not to my taste, although I supplemented my diet with berries gathered on walks in the jungle with the youngsters of the village. It was a mouth-watering treat to be invited to a village feast of a tapir, roasted whole over an open fire. Around twenty adults and half as many children made up the numbers in the village. I had been accepted by the tribe and was free to do as I pleased, but with no other method of communication than sign language; I didn't know a lot about my surroundings.

I gathered that my pilot was dead and that I'd been thrown out of the plane, the numerous lianas that I'd been entangled in, breaking my fall. My thigh wound I'd sustained I guessed, as I'd been ejected from the plane. It was now healing well and I sat down with three of the headmen to draw some pictures in the dried mud near the fire.

I was in Colombia, that much became clear. These men understood my lines representing borders and stick-figures of men with rifles. Distance from a town or area of civilisation was more complex to ascertain, but eventually I reckoned that I was only fifty miles west of Tulcan. The three major ranges of Colombia (Cordilleras), being landmarks that all understood. Four days travel to Tulcan was explained by a rising sun and four strokes in the mud beside it. They agreed to take me there. I had repaired well and after the roasted flesh and a bowlful of fermented fruit juice, I retired early.

Lying there, I became aware of my nurse crawling under the cover and a tightening sensation in my loins. She wasn't a full blooded Indian, more of a mulatta. Her coffee, cream-coloured skin shone making her pert breasts even more appealing and I'd forced myself to put all ideas of sexual encounters out of my mind during these past few days. She had other ideas that night and expert hands and lips overcame my willpower. It hadn't been thoughts of infidelity that had stopped me, rather the wish not to invoke anger in any of the males of the tribe. I had no wish to become another decoration and had seen the many gruesome additions that adorned all the huts. There were a number of bones amongst those of monkeys and tapirs, that looked decidedly human to me and those coconuts in the plantain larder didn't have the appearance of antiques. I had also become aware that it was probably the pilot's gold teeth that now dangled on a wire necklace of the headman's, but hoped that this was only a case of the waste not-want not philosophy of jungle living. I was hoping that the tribe's friendliness was open and real and that they would assist me in reaching Tulcan. They didn't appear to have any covert or unfriendly intentions that I could detect, but realised that there was no alternative to placing my full trust in them. My trek to Tulcan would begin tomorrow; the warmth of my sleeping partner's body was again, arousing more basic and carnal desires. What the hell! - my future, if there was one, now lay with the tribe!

I had taken regular baths in one of the small streams during my stay and kept myself reasonably clean. My shorts were now in an shocking state and the money belt was rotting and I hoped that the dollars were in better shape, having placed them into a sealed polythene bag in Manaus. The polythene however, had contributed to my own sweat rotting the money belt's cloth. I should have to do something about clothes and another money belt, when and if I reached the first town. I had already decided to donate all my other clothes and a few of the dollars in my belt to the Indians and retained only a pair of trousers and a shirt for myself to enter the western world once more.

My reflection in the waters of the stream showed an uncouth wild man, but I'd regained my physical strength, my thigh was completely healed and I had become fitter than I had been before, having shed thirty pounds or so. I took my leave of the tribe's kids who had been my constant companions in my walks in the jungle and who'd taught me a lot about its dangers.

My coffee-cream nurse stroked my beard in a grave gesture of farewell as I set off behind three of the elders towards civilisation. I had a fleeting horrible thought that perhaps one of those shrunken heads in the pantry had originally belonged to her father. Jungle existence, is more a matter of survival and one has to make use of all opportunity and advantage. Altogether, I'd been their guest for almost three weeks and they willingly accepted the dollars together with my clothes, razor, scissors and bits and bobs as payment. I was fully aware that they could have so easily just taken them.

These Indians, like so many tribes that I'd come across, were happy with very little. They laughed, played Andean pipes and chanted songs at their fireside and got uproariously drunk on their own form of alcohol.

As we approached civilisation on the third day's march, I felt a high degree of respect for these men of the jungle. They had wished me no harm. Roast monkey and steamed snake flesh, flavoured with herbs had been our diet during the trek and these senior members of the tribe appreciated my own appreciation of their culinary efforts. I would re-organise in Tulcan and decided to remain disguised as a trader with the Indians. I would take buses to the north of Colombia and avoid any of the watchers around major airports, although I knew that I'd blended with the South American inhabitants and would be taken for one. I reasoned that the longer I remained invisible to any of the opposition, the better were my chances if something did go wrong.

On the third day's trek, the paths were taking on a better defined outline and were fairly obviously in use and the fourth morning revealed a large town spreading throughout the valley. My three companions squatted in a circle and yabbered away to one another then each in turn, stood upright, held up his hand in a form of salute and trotted back into the jungle. I was left with my bag to find my own way down to the town below.

Without the aid of the well worn path I could easily have lost my way but eventually reached the shanty houses on the periphery. I could smell them first and mentally compared the filth and degradation that this poorest section of so-called civilised society with the freedoms expressed by the jungle tribe that I'd just left. Neither sector had much in the way of facility, but at least the tribe had been clean and had sufficient food. The distended stomachs of the shanty town's children and the running, open sewers at the side of the tin and cardboard huts told a different story.

Nobody paid any attention to me and, on my asking where the nearest store was, a woman directed me to what passed for their local supermarket. A couple of new shirts and trousers, soap and other toiletries purchased allowed me sufficient improvement, appearance wise, to find a hairdresser's. It had been imperative to have a haircut and have my beard tidied, the colouring that I'd applied to my hair was now growing out. The colour, together with my straggly beard had given me a wild and rather unstable appearance that had to be rectified so as not to attract attention in the next stages of my journey.

An hour later, a tidy and clean Indian-trader bought a ticket to Cali at the main bus station. It felt good to be one's own boss again and no longer dependent on others. If I could make this next section work I was pretty definitely free of my pursuers, certainly until New York at any rate. Even then I reasoned, I should be able to get help or some form of assistance from the authorities once I reached the US. Getting through the Central American countries should be reasonably easy as I wouldn't take any flight that lasted more than a couple of hours. They'd need that length of time anyway before tracing my passport number and flight details before trying to intercept me. I'd be long gone and had no intention of making logical moves with flight connections that could be worked out. Mexico would require care, but the worst was almost behind me. If the Colombians in Barranquilla would play ball, for that's where I was heading, although I would stay in nearby Cartagena for greater safety until I'd tracked down the next transport; I should be safe until Panama. Meanwhile I'd sleep the long boring hours away of traversing this country by bus. As many mestizos and Indians used this form of transport, you could even have a pig, goat or cage of chickens as your travelling companion.

South American buses are definitely amongst the noisiest forms of transport in the world, comparable only to those on the sub-continent of India. They are certainly the most colourful with bright, hand painted decoration, all originals and unique. The countryside was lush and green in the valleys, the estancias or ranches grew impressive crops of wheat, maize, potatoes, etc. Small farms or fincas supplied free labour to the larger ranches and estates in return for this form of share cropping. Large haciendas on the hilltops, denoted the powerful and wealthy classes who had control of the country and as we approached the bus depot in Cali, our bus was stopped by a cavalcade of expensive American cars We had to wait while twelve armed men disgorged from three of the cars and stood at vantage points on the street, then a single figure exited from another and entered the bank to conduct his business. It is a common enough occurrence in Colombian cities, the drug-barons with their private armies, armed to the teeth, well almost or so it appeared. Their high-walled properties with fortified and very impressive security had commanding views of the surrounding countryside so that none could approach without being fully identified. I wondered if Sobatsu had contacts within some of their organisations and decided against it, but they might hire expertise from them. My own disguise now, was more from deceiving this new area of help, than continuing to outwit Philippe's men. I couldn't take any chances and would have to accept slower progress as the price for improved security. I saw no watchers at either of the bus parks and had soon purchased another ticket to Medellin. A rather large lady with three howling kids, who each received another slap whenever one fell silent, made this section of the trip less than just boring, but whose presence deflected any interest in me. I decided to stay a couple of nights in the city to catch up on lost sleep and renew my spirits.

Medellin is the home of the South American variety of black pudding and very good it is, rice being the main carrier for the blood. Its reputation locally even outshone that of their local hero, a drug-baron of world notoriety, Pablo Escobar, who bestrode the area like a Colossus until finally brought to book by the authorities. Because Medellìn is in a very deep valley and like all cities suffers from serious traffic congestion, there is a constant stink of exhaust fumes and unburnt petrol. In spite of this it is a vibrant, modern city with all entertainments, shopping facilities and a range of reasonably priced hotels, right up to the luxury with stratospheric prices. The profits from drugs had built the latter and probably drug barons owned them, but many of their guests came from both sides of the line. The DEA or drug enforcement agency bosses being regular visitors to the city due to their constant war against drug smuggling. I chose a much quieter hotel in the city centre. The Hotel Laureles was perfectly situated and it accepted two days in advance payment without fuss or comment.

My first morning was a little upsetting as the hotel was shaken by an earth tremor; I found out later that an earthquake had destroyed a town 150 miles away. As I been trimming my beard, the temblor caused the mirror to fly off the wall and I hadn't been able to believe my eyes when the wall appeared to liquify for a couple of milli-seconds before solidifying again. I had to touch it to verify that it was indeed solid. Next day's newspapers gave the details of the 6.4 temblor on the Richter scale that had killed forty in Pereira. I reflected that this small quake probably wouldn't get a mention on the west's news media, such small quakes weren't newsworthy to us. As always, it was the poorest people who lost their lives in 'El sismo'. Their mud, adobe built houses had collapsed on top of the inhabitants.

I headed for the city centre, hailing one of the buses going in my direction. Movement throughout this city was by one of three classes of owner-operated buses who vied for business with one another. Taxis or the nearly completed and highly-modern, German constructed Metro were alternatives. The buses were very cheap, the cheapest being a quarter of the fastest, more luxurious ones. There were no bus-stops as prices were displayed on the front window and on the sides. You flagged down the one you wished and paid a single price, whatever the distance, entering via turnstiles at the open door.

Cheap restaurants were everywhere and I chose one of the 'Asados La Ochenta, Numero dos' chain to enjoy a fried egg, fried green plataños and fried sweet bananas, together with an enormous ladle-full of huge red beans in tomato sauce; I was in need of a few meals like these after my jungle cuisine. I'd also forgotten how luxurious a shower could be and to experience a real bed again.

Two days later, a new man, fully rejuvenated, caught a coach for the longer coach trip to Cartagena. That city was the Caribbean/Atlantic tourist, seaport of sun, sea and sand for Colombians and the tourists from many of their neighbouring countries. Its counterpart on the Pacific coast, the city of Buenaventura, was equally well patronised by those from further south. I found a quiet Bed and Breakfast in the old city, avoiding the hotel belt, as I wished to visit a number of the less salubrious areas for information on how best to continue my journey from Barranquilla.

Years previously, I'd accompanied Jack and Myron on a visit to the San Blas Archipelago, a string of islands just offshore from the Darien jungle of Panama. We had watched the black Colombian traders offloading bananas, sugar and coffee to the Kuna Indians and loading coconuts, dried fish, crustaceans and artifacts for sale back in Colombia. Talking to these traders at that time, I'd elicited the information that regular trading trips were made from Barranquilla. As there were no authorities to oversee the small coastal vessels, these quite often carried other clandestine cargo.

This route was my way into Panama as all international flights from Colombia were routed via Bogotá, the Capital, and were of more than four hours duration. A journey of more than two would spell disaster for me as watchers would have me quickly identified and scooped up. My intention was to avoid any of these high-risk areas and take a more tortuous route.

Cartagena is a fascinating city. La Popa, the old fortress stood watch over the older part, its now defunct cannon still in place and facing mainly seawards against the predations of the early English buccaneers and pirates who raided their shipping and coasts in the fifteenth and sixteenth centuries. A bronze statue to their 'half-man' hero stood in the lee of the fort, his one-arm and missing leg bearing witness to his courageous stand against the pirates. Another imposing bronze of an Indian princess was striking in her naked beauty. The black community of Barranquilla were descendants of the many slaves that had been imported to work the sugar and banana plantations prior to abolition of slavery. The use of indentured labour from India then became the alternative source of cheap labour for the plantations and these mixed peoples now populate many of the islands in the Caribbean. I knew that I'd have to tread very warily in seeking a safe passage and in obtaining help from the black community, although there was less animosity to the Hispanics than there was to the Europeans.

The true story about one boatload of slaves being shipped to the Caribbean on the ship, Amistad, from Sierra Leone about which Stephen Spielberg was making a film. This, and many similar voyages, were still indelible memories and not easily forgiven nor forgotten.

I toured the bars and eateries in the old town and around the dock area until I found an old salt whose loquacity increased with liberal quantities of rum. He supplied me with the necessary information. There were two captains of small coasters that he could vouch for, although their crews might be a different matter. I posed as an Indian-trader wishing to purchase numbers of shrunken heads from the tribes of the Darien, a trade banned by law in Colombia, but still flourishing and commanding big prices from wealthy drug-barons and opulent Americans. My cover story was acceptable, but safety would be better guaranteed with the promise of a large payment to be made on return with my spoils. I recognised the inference that was contained in this piece of advice and carefully rehearsed my plans before I visited either of the nominated Captains.

An hour's bus trip to Barranquilla allowed me to look at both of their vessels and their crews, as they were both in port to offload their trading goods of the last trips and to restock for the next. One was due to leave in two days and the other a day later. There was little to choose between them and so I chose to speak to the captain who would be leaving first.

Captain M'mboya was a tall, handsome guy with many scars on his arms and chest; the results I guessed over crew problems or trade disputes. I asked to speak to him over a rum or two at one of the dozens of nearby bars. He readily accepted when I told him that I hoped to trade with the Darien Indians and wished to take passage with him. Four rounds of rum later we shook hands on the deal, the five hundred mile voyage would take just over three days to get there but four days to return because of currents. He guaranteed my safety and those of my goods in both directions. I would pay a nominal sum on the outward journey and a much larger balance to be released upon both our signatures at a local bank.

As the goods to be traded with the tribes were quality knives, small hatchets and leather mocassin of superior hide; I agreed to the supply of a new knife to each of his six crew members on the outward journey as part of the deal. I'd already bought four boxes of these trade goods in Cartagena for the express purpose of supporting my reason for visiting Panama via the back door. I would have them transported and be there at his vessel a few hours before she left port.

Papers for myself and Customs weren't necessary, they paid little heed to these coastal traders. All the major contraband like drugs were shipped in much faster craft, of which Colombia had a surfeit. Here, as in Cartagena, there were thousands of the latest high powered speed-boats and launches that could outrun most of the law enforcement vessels. With the immense number of islands and all the interconnecting rivers and canals, the authorities had far more to worry about than a bit of rum smuggling and the rest. The Americans, whose navy and coastguard cutters were far from uncommon visitors, kept the Colombian police forces on their toes due to their omniscient satellites and their encircling, AWACS, radar-platforms. All knew that it was an unwinnable war and that it wasn't even being contained. Until the poor farmers were either paid not to grow the stuff or could grow crops with a reasonable resale value to make a living; it would never be eradicated. Colombia's climate allowed three harvests per annum and their fruit and vegetables were second to none. I had seen peaches the size of grapefruit and avocados that were little smaller than a football. But the American, multi-national, fruit-growing combines with their total control of the canneries, kept prices and all supplies in their own hands. The small farmers were isolated from the major markets and had to be content with local sales at low prices.

I hired a van and driver to take me to the docks in Barranquilla. My bag now contained not only my clothes, but also eight of the finest Bowie knives that I could get, plus a box of fifty Dominican cigars. These, together with my four boxes of trade goods, were soon loaded aboard the high-prowed, wooden coaster and we left on a suitable early tide. The San Blas Archipelago that connected with the Archipelago de las Mulattoes, depending on whether you were Panamanian or Colombian, had me thinking about the names of rivers, stretches of water, strings of Islands like the Spratleys in the China Sea, that all caused so much strife around the world. Even La Manche, or the English Channel, still evoked irritation amongst some of the French and also the English. The Falklands or Las Malvinas and Gibraltar could just be a different matter, but there were many areas around the world where equal rights of others were not considered, if only in the different names. It's a funny old world I reflected, as I watched the crew gambling on deck. They had appeared very happy with their knives and paid little attention to me. The Captain regularly appeared for a chat with me and as all ate their meals topside on this fifty foot coaster with its wide beam of twenty feet, conditions were cosy to say the least.

I slept in a hammock on deck as I didn't fancy the black hole of the men's quarters. Also, I felt much safer with the tiller being manned at all times. The odd shower of rain or driven spray was a minor inconvenience. The stars were another reason to sleep in the open, many of the Southern constellations still just visible from this latitude. This barque was built to take as much cargo as it possibly could within a short hull, the broad beam made it wallow a bit, but its high prow made it cope with difficult weather conditions when necessary. A steady nine or ten knots was maintained with the current providing three or four of this speed for northerly assistance. The main Island of Achitupu, was off our port bow as dawn broke on the third day; we'd made exceptional time and Captain M'mboya was delighted. The crew likewise were pleased as they would have more leisure and trading time.

I lost little time in thanking the captain, saying that I would be returning in approximately two months and that I'd be staying in the tourist huts on a small atoll nearby. I would head there first and make arrangements for immediate accommodation, obtaining the use of a fisherman and his dugout canoe for the short trip. My trade goods, bag and myself were soon aboard and the Kuna fisherman swiftly paddled across to the other island.

The grandly entitled Lodge consisted of four huts with very basic facilities, although there were beds set upon the concrete floors I required the proprietrix to book a flight for me via her radio link with the Capital. Flights being infrequent to this area, it could be several days before I obtained one. I now remembered that the palm roofed cabins had bamboo walls and shuttered windows with washing and lavatory facilities in an adjoining building. The shower had only cold water and artificial lighting had been supplied by kerosene lamps or candles. The short sea crossing was quite choppy and I felt queasy and light-headed, something that I'd never suffered from before, sea-sickness never having bothered me.

Mariella helped me out on the other side and plainly didn't recognise me from my visit of four years previous. I was now shivering and shaking and Mariella didn't need my observation that,

"I've a bout of malaria coming on, can I stay here for a few days".

I was helped to one of the huts and into bed, Mariella shouting to her helpers to bring an extra duvet and to organise some hot soup. I was in the full grip of the fever and was soon delirious. Bright, whizzing lights alternated with brown faces and I slipped into deep unconsciousness.

Eight

Philippe was incredulous, Martin couldn't have disappeared again! He was listening to Parides who was now in Bogotá. Parides said also that he might have another lead but would confirm its validity later. Earlier, Philippe had similar calls from Señora Flores, also Hauptmann and their team leaders that they in turn had organised in Manaus, Belém, Ilha Grande and Guyane.

Martin must have gone to ground he thought, or had the wily fox reversed his route and made for an International airport back south? No, he wouldn't be that stupid as he'd recognise that Sobatsu security would scoop him up as soon as he landed, whichever country he headed for. There would have to be better news for Jefferson before he spoke to him; he wouldn't accept the fact that his own security people couldn't find him. Time was running out, excuses would not be tolerated. Help!, he'd almost nine hundred people involved in the search, not including dozens of computer operators in five of Sobatsu's offices. He made the decision to move yet again. He'd move his centre of administration and operations to Sobatsu in Caracas Venezuela. Martin had to be in Colombia, Venezuela or The Guyanas. Philippe would know immediately if he arrived in Curaçao, one of Señora Flores' young men was on friendly terms already with Martin's mistress there, and was teaching her to scuba-dive amongst other duties. Philippe had absolutely nothing positive to report to Jefferson, who puzzled him still further, when there was no tongue-lashing. Even the news that he was moving his HQ to Caracas evinced nothing more than a brief acknowledgement of the fact. Jefferson seemed preoccupied with other thoughts and Philippe was glad when the call was finally terminated with just, "Let me know immediately he's spotted again".

Jefferson called Señora Flores' mobile and asked her to phone him from a secure line. He wouldn't await the Dubai meeting for the full agreement of the other eight men; there had been too many mistakes on Philippe's part for him to have many wishing to champion his position. It was time for his retirement and replacement.

"Ah Señora Flores", Jefferson almost purred down the phone.

"And how are things in Belém? Give me the overall picture as you see it", inviting her views on more than just her own areas of search.

Neither the tone nor the line of questioning was lost upon her. She thought rapidly, sensing that there was an opportunity in this for her. Philippe had fouled-up, she thought and added.

" I had eight teams cover all of the river-boat traffic, from the largest to the smallest, Señor Jefferson. Hauptmann and I, with another fifty people, have scoured Belém for any signs or information about him. We're both certain that he didn't come down-river and therefore, Guyane couldn't possibly be one of his alternate destinations. Hauptmann and I have, during intense discussions and referring to a large-scale map, decided that Martin must have headed to either Colombia or Venezuela. He could be planning to join his mistress in Curaçao or utilise her as a courier, but I personally, think that this is another false trail and that he'll try to get through to the Isthmus of Panama by boat from either Cartagena or Barranquilla. I've made arrangements for a convenient accident to occur to her anyway".

"O.K. Señora, and what had Philippe to say about the theory about Martin exiting from Barranquilla", asked Larry, recognising that his instincts about both Philippe and Flores had been correct.

"They were not acceptable Señor Jefferson, Jorgé didn't think that Martin could organise himself with a boat across to Panama as both Colón and Panama City were controlled by the Americans and their Immigration rules would be strictly observed. This would in turn, make a passage without a passport an impossibility, according to his thinking".

"And what are your own thoughts on that Señora", Jefferson asked, now doodling on his desk-pad. He should have promoted Flores long ago he thought, as he listened to her various theories on what Martin would do and what options there were.

"Would you be averse to taking over Philippe's position as from now Señora?", he asked.

"Con satisfacione grande Señor Jefferson", Flores replied.

"And you're prepared to have Philippe retired permanently and immediately Señora?" Jefferson was amused to see that he'd subconsciously drawn a gibbet with a tiny stick-figure dangling from it. He wrote Philippe's name beneath it as Flores told him that only Parides would miss him and even he knew that final power was way above Sobatsu's present head of security. She would have Hauptmann visit Philippe in Caracas with the correct, final and permanent retirement notice; she could fully depend on him.

"Señora, if Hauptmann could make it appear as another accident, that would soothe any ruffled feelings", Jefferson suggested.

"Exactamente Señor Jefferson, esta es perfecto. Yo comprendo muy bien". Jefferson smiled as he disconnected, drawing a line through the stick-figure. There would shortly be a new head of security for Sobatsu and one that he could fully depend upon. If it hadn't been for Philippe's supporters within the other nine, he'd have had him replaced long ago. Perhaps it wasn't too late to track down Martin and de-fuse the situation. He daren't take any more risks about the guy any more, he thought, and buzzed the intercom again.

"Get me the general managers" of Planet Ales canneries in Mexico and Panama, Ardeth", and clicked off.

Flores lost no time in briefing Hauptmann and asked his opinion about Parides.

"Do you think that we might have to retire him too?", she asked. "We can't have a vendetta on our hands and Parides is closest to Jorgé after all".

Hauptmann considered this last point deeply before replying.

"No Señora and especially if it is an unfortunate accident that occurs in Caracas. Just make certain that I've a damn good excuse for being up there, from both Philippe's and Parides' points of view". Hauptmann added, "Coincidence is never actionable", laughing throatily.

Señora Flores agreed, certain in the knowledge that Hauptmann was her operative and completely dependable. She wished him a good flight to Caracas and said that she'd be contacting him from Cartagena, but would stop off in Bogotá for a day or two and collect Parides to aid her in checking the Caribbean/Atlantic ports. Parides know-how around the dock areas and seamier places would be invaluable, she thought.

Philippe was organising his soldiers in Caracas, capital city of Venezuela and the glass-skyscraper capital of the world. He smiled, thinking only, that without the billions of dollars from drug-money this city would still be in total poverty. Although the city had been emasculated cash-wise to an enormous extent when five of the city's largest bankers had fled with most of the country's foreign currency reserves to safe havens in the US, Australia and Europe. What convenient hypocrisy he mused, considering that Venezuela had harboured fleeing Nazis from the second world war and given them safety within their borders, this being in return for the huge sums of capital that they had taken with them. So now it became the turn of the western nations to utilise the lack of reciprocal extradition agreements to recover criminals from each others' countries. The West, as usual, had come off best in that deal, but now Venezuela was the conduit for most of the laundered money from the drug barons. Americans and Europeans could live at sumptuous levels here at the expense of the poor and indigenous people, due to the closed economy and a rampant black-market in dollars.

His schematic map on the wall of his previous office had now been replaced by large scale maps of Colombia, Venezuela, The Guyanas and the lower part of the

Caribbean. I must find you this time my friend, he thought, there would be no room for any lack of success with Jefferson.

He rang Señora Flores in Belém and confirmed his arrival and listened to a tedious interpretation from her about Martin's possible movements. There had been nothing, not even a whisper about Martin or even any stranger who wasn't accounted for by the many holiday companies who'd booked berths aboard the ferries and river-boats. It was off-season for them and a stranger would have been noticed immediately. Even if he'd been able to blend with the other passengers, someone would have been aware of a minute difference in accent, clothing or reason for journey. There had been nothing and Flores had taken it upon herself to send her own lieutenant, Hauptmann, to Caracas to assist his old boss.

"O.K. Señora Flores, Hauptmann could be of some help in checking the ports close to the ABC Islands. You're thinking that Parides could do with your assistance in Colombia.

"Si es muy possible Señora. You could be right that he's in one or other of these countries, but don't take all your people away from The Guyanas, nor Belém. He's a sneaky one, this Martin".

Señora Flores was satisfied with her call and gave Hauptmann a call on his mobile to say that all was well and that he'd be expected by Philippe. Now for Bogotá, she thought.

Damn Bernie, thought Judy, what the hell was he playing at? She'd been in Curaçao for a week now and there had been no further communication from him. I've spent a large part of my savings on this holiday and where was he? Judy had fully intended that Bernie would be picking up the bill for her hotel costs and all the ancillary extras, so his absence was more than just nuisance value. She had hated the first few days, being alone in a foreign country, even if everyone did speak English and the hotel was as good as Bernie had said.

Now, this bronzed Adonis with perfect and sparkling white teeth and jet-black wavy hair had become enamoured by her and she was contemplating enjoying what was left of her holiday in the aura of fun and excitement that he generated. He was quite obviously wealthy and knew everything there was to know about water and all other sports. She had already been on the jet-skis for hours with him and had three practice sessions with the aqualung equipment in the hotel's pool and was getting fairly proficient in its use. He had offered to take her out to the reefs and show her the 'jewels of the ocean' as he referred to the colourful fish that abounded in these waters. He'd also occupied her bed on a number of occasions and she had enjoyed his expressive love-making and attentions. Bernie was very rapidly being replaced in her affections. His replacement was far more youthful and urgent with his love-making anyway and it now seemed that his interest in her was of a permanent nature. I must find out Juanito's full name and a little more about him, she thought, stretching languorously on the sun-bed beside the pool. I wonder who he speaks to on that mobile phone that he carries with him at all times, she considered idly. He was a bit of an enigma after all and she hadn't really been sure of how they had come to be together in this island paradise. He'd certainly paid her compliments and had been completely interested in all her chatter. She'd even told him about Bernie and been pleased to note a small streak of jealousy. Her sun-tan was coming along nicely and the stares from other single young men weren't unwelcome either. She had always attracted men and Bernie had been fortunate to keep her affections so long, she decided. Although he always returned from his foreign travels with expensive perfumes for her. Oh well, the holiday wouldn't be a dead loss anyway and her concerns over Bernie's non-appearance vanished in the heat of the sun's rays. She wriggled lasciviously at the mental pictures conjured in her mind about Juanito and his urgent passions. Would he come tonight she wondered. Tomorrow they'd be scuba-diving on the reef; that was one of the exciting prospects that she'd looked forward to. The Caribbean holiday of a lifetime, although very much different to the one that she'd envisaged!

Next morning, she was ready with a new silk kimono covering her peach-coloured bikini, her slim, lithe body tingled with excitement as Juanito stopped in the hired buggy to collect her; the tanks and gear already in the back. He drove swiftly down to the harbour and in minutes, they and all their diving gear were aboard a fast motor launch and heading out to the reef. Juanito seemed to know the skipper very well as they had shaken hands and were now in deep discussion, poring over numerous charts of the various reefs. Thoughtfully, Juanito had provided a coloured fish-identification book for her and she studied their amazing shapes and their colours in the cool shade of the saloon. This was very exciting, she thought. I could be happy with him she decided, but what about her job? There were only four more days of the holiday paid for and by this time she'd expected to be on the other islands with Bernie, the rotter! She'd make her move on Juanito that evening she decided, and to hell with Bernie once and for all! He was getting past it anyway! She giggled self-consciously, thinking, there's plenty more fish in the sea after all!

Juanito was preparing the diving equipment and soon the skipper of the launch had tied up to a floating buoy and it was time to go fish-spotting among the wonders of a coral reef. He helped Judy with her twin tanks and quickly donned his own, leaving her to adjust her mask and flippers. They descended fast and were instantly surrounded by shoals of brightly coloured, tiny fish, with larger fish in echelons of ten to twenty in number, all coming to look at the new inhabitants of their world. Juanito pointed out the fan corals and brain coral that he'd previously told her about and a trumpet fish that scudded beneath an archway. A ray glided past on its extended wings and with a start she noticed one of the ugly moray eels poking its head from a hole in the reef, a timely reminder that these coral paradises could also be dangerous. However, she had her protector and lover to guide her and show her its wonders. It was as fabulous as he'd told her it would be; sea anemones of various colours were everywhere and pretty little sea horses abounded amongst the weeds. The sea was pleasantly warm and enveloped her in the euphoria of an underwater world of colour and mystery. She lost track of time, completely dependent on Juanito who was constantly pointing at some other novelty, when her demand valve stuck! Judy didn't panic, she'd been made aware of these minor problems that happened to divers and flagged Juanito to assist her. What was he doing? He'd wrapped a trailing cord around her ankle and could see that the other end was twisted around an enormous staghorn coral. She panicked and gulped water. Her thoughts were suddenly in turmoil as she thrashed vainly to free herself from the cord. A large white light enveloped her as she realised that she was drowning. Her Adonis, Juanito, was rapidly disappearing above her. Her final thought was, that drowning was quite pleasant really.

Señora Flores received the call from Juanito soon after touchdown at Bogotá, the accident had taken place and after a search of the area for an hour the motor-launch skipper and himself had reported her missing to the authorities. The skipper had been another of her operatives, but would be plying for hire as usual for a number of weeks until all interest in the English tourist had gone. That was one less area to be concerned about, she thought and added an instruction to her underling.

"Juanito you had better stick around and see who might be interested in identifying the package, but stay in touch".

Hauptmann had taken a taxi from the airport fifteen miles outside Caracas, another half hour or so and he'd be in the city. He had already worked out that he'd entice Philippe into the city centre from his office with the opportunity to show-off his prowess at the chess-board. Caracas had many pavilions that catered for chess enthusiasts in the tiled, pedestrian shopping centre and anyone could get matches of almost international standard among the chess crazy inhabitants. Philippe had repeated, many times, his boast of meeting some of the famous Russian Grandmasters in competition there in the past. He had prided himself on his expertise at this mind-bending pursuit. He wouldn't resist the opportunity to show off his excellence to his lieutenant. The nearby metro stations however, would be where Philippe's accident would be arranged, but that would involve some necessary local help. It shouldn't be all that difficult to find. Life was cheap in Caracas along with everything else. The world's finest and most able pick-pocket gangs came from either this city or Rio and practically everything could be bought for a price, even a convenient accident.

After an hour's search, Hauptmann had located a band of youths who were prepared to assist his plan for an agreed $100 each. They would await his identification of the target beside the chess pavilions and follow them into the subway. It was a foregone conclusion thought Hauptmann as he dialled Sobatsu's offices.

"You've arrived then", Philippe remarked unnecessarily. "Yes alright, I'll meet you in Los Caobos park (the park of Mahogany trees) and get the updated picture from you first. O.K., I can show you how to play blitz chess properly. In half-an-hour then". Something jarred about Hauptmann's call, why should he wish to see his boss playing chess? He'd never displayed much interest in the game before. He made a quick phone-call to the apartment that he'd rented from the Hilton close to the complex where Sobatsu's offices were situated. Why hadn't Hauptmann come directly here he considered, relating the conversation held with him to the listener at the other end. He would ensure that there were no funny business tricks from that puzzling area.

However, Hauptmann had held nothing back and brought his boss fully up to date with the search so far and informed him that Flores had gone to Bogotá. After a couple of games of blitz chess, Philippe agreed to a coffee with a couple of brandies before accompanying Hauptmann into the Metro. It was probably faster to return to the office that way he agreed, especially with the rush hour traffic just before the siesta hours. There were some excellent restaurants in their complex also and yes, he'd buy the lunch. Philippe didn't notice the four youths who entered the underground station at the same time. The lunchtime crowds were heading home and all were in their usual hurry. At least there were only four stops, Philippe thought and aloud, "I haven't used the metro for years Hauptmann, but watch out for pick-pockets!'

The surge of bodies as the train arrived had people screaming in terror, the shriek of steel upon steel as brakes were forcibly applied, two bodies bouncing off the track and arcing out the current as the first body touched the live rail. It was all over in seconds and many of the crowd made for the escalators, none wishing to be the subject of questioning by the authorities.

In Bogotá, Señora Flores found it inexplicable that Hauptmann hadn't telephoned. Especially as she had read of Philippe's tragic accident in the local newspaper, but it mentioned that two people had been killed when the crowd had stampeded for the incoming train. It appeared highly likely that her lieutenant had been the other fatality. That's a pity, she thought, he had many abilities and was trustworthy. She dismissed further thoughts, Hauptmann had been careless, but at least the job had been done. And where the hell was Parides? His hotel said that he'd checked out two days ago after receiving a phone-call, but she couldn't even raise him on his mobile. What a nuisance! She would have to go to Cartagena without him and his knowledge of the Colombian underworld. Fortunately, Sobatsu Bogotá had been able to give her a black employee who spoke French, a necessity in that region. He did also have relatives in Barranquilla, so perhaps Parides disappearance would not be an impediment, especially as he was eager to impress and told her all of Parides and his own theories. They were very definitely plausible, she thought. There was work to do and the sooner she was in the north the better. But Mierda!, she recognised that it would be more difficult without her trusted lieutenant, although this young employee from Sobatsu Bogotá appeared to have good ideas. It was perhaps more than just convenient Parides wasn't here. She could claim that all his deductions, based on conversations with the young man, were her own.

Twenty-four hours later, the Señora and her black operative Louis were quizzing the numerous, self-employed stevedores on the wharf-side at Barranquilla. For a few dollars, they were informed about the cargo boats that had gone north to Panama and that one of them had carried a passenger. An Indian trader just as Parides had suspected, thought Flores, Parides was excellent in finding the right type of help in all quarters. If it hadn't been for the necessity for Philippe's removal and that Parides had been Jorgé's trusted lieutenant and friend, she would have awaited his return or call. As it was, she'd return to Bogotá with Louis, leaving him there and collect Juanito before taking the next convenient flight to Panama City. Louis seemed to be a loose cannon anyway as he'd wanted to take another coaster and follow in Martin's footsteps. She'd refused, reckoning that as Martin had few alternates, now he had to pass through Panama City on the Caribbean side or Colón on the Atlantic side. All the coastal traffic was being checked and any passengers out of Panama were being checked out in person. Martin's dash for freedom was fast coming to an end, she thought. It had been a long pursuit from Ushuaia though. All passenger names on all flights out of Panama City were being directly fed into Sobatsu's local office computer. They'd trace Martin's passport number before the plane took-off and the local Chief of Police was already being extremely helpful in that department.

The flight to Bogotá was without problems. She was delighted to find Juanito had arrived only minutes before her and that a flight to Panama City left in an hour's time. Flores, like most regular air travellers, hated the time wasted at airports. She hadn't even bothered to introduce Louis to Juanito as Louis was returning to the office. Juanito's bronzed good looks, dark wavy hair, perfect white teeth and his fabulous smile now commanded her complete attention. He was engrossed in bringing her up to date with his recent exploits and recognised his own potential for advancement in the work.

Juanito became aware also of the Señora's interest in his physique and mentally prepared himself for other duties that he would be called upon to carry out. At least he was assured of an increase in salary and a more permanent position with Sobatsu security. The work was most enjoyable he decided, relatively easy and undemanding and involved a lot of travel. Flores now brought him fully up to date with the fugitive Martin, and why he had to be stopped in any way possible. He learned that probably Judy's death had been unnecessary, although when he said that it was good practice, the Señora had laughed heartily and agreed. His future looked bright, but a lot depended on either Martin's capture or his permanent removal.

The Señora was saying that his daytime duties would be at the International airport where he would be in charge of the shifts of watchers and their co-

-ordination, reporting directly to herself by mobile phone at regular intervals. She would be retaining a roving brief and be checking the Canal watchers and occasionally making unannounced visits to the airport.

There was no need to visit the Sobatsu offices after their computer operators had their instructions. They would inform both her and Juanito immediately, if and when Martin's passport number showed on the passenger manifest of an airline. She decided that Panama would be a very pleasant vacation, Martin's capture was a forgone conclusion and Juanito had quickly recognised his duties. Take your time Señor Martin she thought, allowing her mind to dwell on other things.

Nine

Jack collected Myron on his way to their boathouse, one of many hundreds scattered around the Finger Lakes. Although they did most of their boating on the nearby Keuka lake, the ice was generally thicker and much safer on some of the smaller lakes in mid-winter. Myron was in deep thought, and finally spoke.

"You know Jack, there's something weird about that couple who're staying with me. They're very loving when you appear, but completely independent when they think that they're unobserved. It's as though they're playing a part".

"Many couples have tiffs on vacation that they don't want to advertise to others. You're spending too much time at your computer and then you work all hours", Jack replied, continuing, "Carolyn and I have arguments all the time, but never discuss them in public".

"It's not just that Jack. My other half, Gerald, was coming across to Penn Yan from Gorham and saw the guy in a phone booth with his wife waiting outside in their car".

"Well that's nothing to be suspicious about, he could have been phoning about anything, asking information perhaps?"

"No Jack, they have all the tourist junk, too much of it in fact. And they asked me about the best wineries to visit when they first arrived, the ones that remain open in the winter. But I met two of the proprietors, Bully's and that big one on the Interstate, when they were making deliveries to the bottle shop as I was stocking up. I asked both of them if they'd met my guests and neither had seen a stranger for weeks, but the couple left the Inn to visit both wineries the other day and when I asked them later, they said they'd both enjoyed more than enough wine for their driving. There's other little things that I can't identify, but they're not kosher. Both of them had a damned good look at Bernie's papers that morning when you were here for breakfast.

And their arrival without even a reservation, just after Jefferson's departure. Jefferson's and his secretary's names on those lists of companies, even you thought that was an interesting coincidence. His offer to finance you at your first meeting. It's all too damn convenient".

"You read too many spy novels in the winter old buddy", said Jack. "He's an exceptionally wealthy man, I'm just small fry to him. These lists would not be complete without our largest drinks' manufacturer on them. I'd say these list would be more suspicious if they hadn't included him".

"Perhaps you're right Jack, but why would Bernie send them to us, saying that he'd need our help".

"Well old man, I've sent them to the FBI and another copy to the CIA, telling them that our buddy Bernie wanted them to be sent there and to mention their agent Jim Booth. I've done that and there sure hasn't been a stampede to ask me any questions, from either Department!".

"Again, the young couple are always asking both of us independently, to go ice-boating. I never mentioned our sport to them, did you?", Myron probed. And yet another point, one of them has read my e-mail on a couple of occasions, because the voice alert was off, but there were messages from you and others still unread by me on it".

Jack pulled into the side of the road beside the boathouse where they kept their sail boat, now fitted with ice-skates.

"O.K. I don't remember telling them about our sport, but I could easily have done so, they asked dozens of questions about the Finger lakes and the area in general. That doesn't qualify them as KGB agents or whatever. Although, I do agree that there are one or two anomalies about this whole thing. What about inviting myself and Carolyn over to dinner tonight and we'll set a trap for them"

"Agreed", said Myron. "Dinner's fine, I have a large pork roast, we can all give the trap some thought, but beware of saying anything by e-mail, it will be on an operator to operator only basis. Use the 'e' for warning only, then we can arrange suitable times for the serious transmissions".

"OK, I'll discuss it with Carolyn", and with that Jack entered the boathouse. "Now this is odd Myron, there's been someone in here since the last time I came up to replace the reefing ties. The trailer has been moved, I remember thinking that I'd have to shift it myself to check all the rudder mounts. I can see them without moving it now. OK. Myron, you've made me realise there is something going on that's not on the level. I'll give Jefferson a call on his personal number he gave me before he left and ask a few pertinent questions".

"Well don't make it worse Jack", replied Myron.

"Be careful what you say to him".

"Yeah, don't worry buddy boy, I don't intend to give him the whole nine yards. I'll only ask about the ceramics deal and talk a little about our upcoming, ice boating trip with tourists from your homely small town hotel. He might just give something away", Jack replied.

Sally Martin was stunned. She'd just come off the phone from Bernard's office and had received the confirmation about Judy's tragic accident in Curaçao wherever exactly that was. Some Caribbean island near to South America his boss had said. But it was the apology that Bernard's boss said he owed to her that both annoyed and worried her and at the same time removed an enormous burden. Bernard had not been on holiday with Judy. She had been with a handsome young Brazilian during the full length of her stay.

"Office gossip was sometimes not very reliable Mrs Martin, but we would like Bernard to get in touch with us as soon as possible. If he is in touch, please let us know immediately", his boss had said.

It was very annoying and somewhat embarrassing that Bernard's office knew all about his infidelities with Judy. At least his boss was now prepared to think that Bernard was perhaps laid low by some bug or an accident, could it be something like that she wondered. She phoned Fraser at the lawyers' offices and gave him all the information and asked his opinion.

Fraser admitted to knowing nothing of importance and didn't mention having passed Bernie's letter to the authorities. There was little point in increasing her anxieties, although almost a month had passed since contact by phone had been last made by him.

"Yes Sally, I do think that there's a distinct possibility that he's been stricken by some tropical disease like malaria, or even had an accident Bernard's been very lucky for many years in that department, it was bound to happen sooner or later. I'll speak to the Chief Inspector who's been checking out those bogus police who quizzed you about Bernard. I'll be in touch if I hear of anything definite".

Sally went off the phone, her anxieties about Bernard increasing, her own annoyance about his past infidelities now forgiven. She hadn't had a postcard for over a fortnight and that was very unlike him.

Fraser telephoned Chief Inspector Thurlston.

"Yes Chief Inspector, his secretary died in Curaçao, I've already checked all the details that's known by his office. She'd gone there for a holiday and the office gossips had connected that fact with Martin's silence, but she'd been in the company of some Brazilian, Hollywood stereotype all the time. Martin was never there. It was a tragic accident whilst scuba diving as far as I can gather, but the Dutch police will give you all the details as they have full jurisdiction in Curaçao, it being one of their protectorates. No, there's been no further contact from Martin himself. He could have had an accident or have gone down with one of these tropical diseases, I do believe they're more virulent on Europeans who haven't been exposed to them". The Inspector interrupted the lawyer's soliloquy with a brief agreement over the lawyer's observation about tropical diseases and added,

"What's Mrs Martin's views on that?"

"Mrs Martin also thinks it is a distinct possibility Inspector. Certainly, I'll keep you informed of any information that I receive from his contacts at this end, what exactly do you think he's involved in? All right Inspector, I get the message, you begin to sound like a lawyer. Which of Shakespeare's plays was it in, a lot of sound signifying nothing".

Fraser rang off, a close-mouthed type that Thurlston, he thought. Mind you, speculation only aroused rumours and even greater speculation. He had more than sufficient other work to occupy himself with, Bernie would have to sort it out himself and Sally would cope, whatever the outcome.

Jefferson received the satisfactory news about Philippe and commiserated with Flores over her lieutenant's probable demise.

"That's unfortunate Señora, but I'm sure that you'll find an able replacement. It would appear that Curaçao has been an unnecessary worry, but at least Martin can't use her again to mislead you. Why don't you get your chap Juanito to join you, he sounds as though he's a good organiser and carries out his orders to the letter".

Señora Flores admitted that she'd already taken the decision to recall the young man from Curaçao, although not that it would also be pleasing to have that well muscled frame to view, if for no other reason.

"Si Señor Jefferson, esa idea es muy buen".

Jefferson chuckled and disconnected. Must keep the troops happy, he thought. At least he could go to Dubai with fewer problems to recount and Flores did appear to be hot on Martin's trail now. He certainly knew the continent of South America and its countries, he might just know Central America equally as well. Jefferson was better pleased that the third ingredient had now been added to Planet's soft-drinks.

Ardeth brought in two faxes of confirmation from the general managers in Central America. Jefferson read them briefly and said.

"No reply, but bring me the list of guests who are going to be aboard the Venus for the cruise in the Antilles will you".

The phone had been ringing as Ardeth returned to her own office, it was Mr McAllister from up-state New York. Ardeth had made up her mind, Larry was up to something and it had to do with Penn Yan and the couple who were staying at the Red Fox Inn, she listened into the full conversation. Jack was asking about how GM's director had reacted to the new ceramic catalyser and if he wished a prototype sent to him. Myron and he were going to teach a young couple how to ice-sail shortly. They were guests at Myron's hotel, taking an out-of-season vacation. Larry had promised Jack that he'd be sending a check in the mail within a few days and also have proper papers drawn up to secure the business loan. The McAllister guy was important for some reason, but what? There were no papers drawn up for the business of ceramic catalysers and certainly she'd received no instructions to make out a check for McAllister. Larry had made the excuse to cut their weekend short so as to meet an executive from GM's in the city, but who hadn't existed. She'd had to place a call to Detroit Diesels on her return, not a city hotel. And all these calls that she'd booked for Larry with Planet's chemists. No-one else had known about their competition trying to break their secret mixes. There were already some soft-drinks that were so similar that it wasn't necessary to copy their's any longer. Why the great secrecy? This trip to Dubai for a meeting with Larry's inner circle of companies, the Top Ten as they were referred to. Now one of the major Japanese companies was to be excluded and, as they had provided all the security for previous meetings everywhere, it was odd they hadn't to be informed about this one. Although all the CEO's had faxed their replies confirming their attendance, most of them were unhappy at the exclusion and said that they'd require full information on the subject to be the first item on the agenda. All of them had confirmed they'd be taking their personal communicators. Ardeth had already got Larry's one out of the vault. Seemingly, it was a short wave sender that printed the same message onto another nine machines of an identical and exact match. An integral micro-chip scrambled and unscrambled both outgoing and incoming read-outs. Similar keyboards to most laptop computers, but with larger LCD's and highly complex micro-chips. These machines ensured complete privacy to the N'th degree of secrecy. None of the machines could communicate with another until an exact code, chosen at random by one of the operators was duplicated on each of the machines receiving the message. Any machine not present couldn't access the necessary code to unscramble the messages. It was only used at Top Ten meetings.

I think it might be time to look for another job, Ardeth thought, and maybe extract her severance pay from the account that she controlled. She would calculate all that she was due to the last cent and include all the vacation time that she'd forfeited over the years, even though it might be argued by Larry that she'd accompanied him to exotic places and had many gifts and everything paid for by the company. There was a lawyer friend that she'd have a chat with, prior to taking that final step, but she was now certain that there was something that could be criminal going on. She had no intention of being an accomplice or party to it.

That couple weren't being given a month's vacation in Hawaii as a thank you for a simple surveillance job for instance. If the Internal Revenue Service checked all of Larry's, under the table gifts and handout's to people around the world; there could be hard time for all those involved. She had made certain over the years that there was nothing directly attributable to herself. She'd only carried out the boss's orders. Most of Larry's favours had been at arm's length and pretty much untraceable back to Planet Ales or to himself, but the entertainments accounts and expenses had been an ever increasing deduction from the bottom line profits. Some of the larger shareholders had queried them in the recent past and while Larry had shrugged it off with the explanation that the bottom line was always increasing faster and that the wheels of progress had to be oiled; it was bound to be investigated one day.

In Penn Yan, Carolyn was intrigued.

"What sort of trap do you have in mind Jack? I know all about the honey trap darling, but that's a girls' thing and not suitable for the CIA. I think Bernie's got you all wound up, you guys love cops and robbers or agents smuggling nuclear weapons. O.K., I haven't met the couple and only seen them from the car when you've called at Myron's, but they sure don't fit any secret agent's description that I've seen on the movies".

"That's just the point honey, they have to look ordinary for whatever reason they're here, but I'm now going along with Myron's suspicions, there are far too many coincidences". Jack added, "And another thing, someone's been tampering with the boat".

"Now that's an indictable offence Jack", laughed Carolyn, "Worthy of at least the chair I'd say".

Jack's hobbies were sacrosanct. She could no longer get her car into the large garage due to two classic cars that had been undergoing refurbishment since Jack's teen years, as far as she could gather. Those and bits of boats, past and present, and other junk that Jack was going to attend to one day. Mind you, she thought, that accusation could be levelled fairly at herself remembering her own family home. But at least she could tidy it up on a regular basis, Jack went into fits if she even cleared papers off the table to set dishes on it!

"O.K., so what's the drill? How do we go about trapping these two and about what?", she said soothingly, stroking her man's hair. "It will have to be something you send to Myron on his e-mail, if Myron thinks that they're checking it all the time".

"That's it my love", exclaimed Jack. I've always said that you were brilliant when push came to shove. Now if they work for Jefferson, as Myron suspects and I'm beginning to agree with his thinking. What would they react to in terms of a message to Myron?"

"Well let's say that it has to do with Bernie and his mysterious letter, and also those lists, but they cannot be incriminating because you'd have heard from the FBI or the CIA by now if they were". Carolyn was thinking out loud rather than speaking directly to Jack. "So we're missing something. Let's see Bernie's fax and letter again, Jack".

Jack retrieved them from his desk and spread the fax, letter and photocopies on the table. "There's nothing here to incriminate anyone", he said in frustration, pushing them over to her.

"Well he's mentioned that guy Booth being an agent", said Carolyn. "And the papers were to be sent to the FBI which you've done and also to the CIA., but heard nothing from either. What if there's someone in these organisations not passing them onto the right area? Let's work on the premise that these companies are up to something illegal and that Jim Booth stumbled upon it and that Bernie witnessed his murder by Sobatsu. How does that grab you?", Carolyn asked.

"Yeah", Jack agreed. "And Jefferson's company being one of the select Top Ten must be aware of what's going on, that's good thinking sweetheart, I'll go along with that. But how do we get the couple at the Inn to react and also, if we do get them to react, we'll have to protect ourselves from any retaliation. If things are as bad that the FBI has to be informed, then they might want to be rid of the problem, meaning us my love".

"You're certain that the boat's been tampered with?", Carolyn asked.

"Sure, it has certainly been moved honey, I couldn't be certain that there is anything wrong or modified without a full examination, but I'm now of the same opinion as Myron." Jack then continued. "There are too many coincidences about Jefferson, his visit, and these two arriving very conveniently a couple of days later. I think Jefferson's backing out of the deal too, he wasn't very forthcoming on the phone about the catalyser. Anyway the people at Corning have finally expressed an interest in it, so they'll finance it if the tests are positive. I really don't need a fat cat who will lick up most of the cream. Myron agrees that Jefferson's arrival at the Red Fox was far from being just a sexy weekend for the boss and his secretary, and the subsequent arrival of this couple is both a bit suspicious and highly convenient. His feelings are that they're definitely not kosher and must have some connection with Jefferson's visit, as it was curtailed rather abruptly and the couple appeared almost immediately after his departure. Right, Carolyn honey, how do we go about constructing this e-mail for Myron?"

Ten

Parides had his suspicions about Jefferson's intentions ever since his own boss, Philippe had mentioned the first verbal drubbing that he'd received from him. He had grown wary of both Hauptmann's blossoming friendship with Flores and her manoeuvring to lay all blame at Philippe's door when it had been she who had given him the epidiascope to deliver to the conference in São Paulo and had handed it to him personally. Parides hated the suggestion, made by Flores to others, that he was nothing more than muscle and should only be used in this capacity. At least his boss recognised his true worth and gave him due recognition for it.

Señora Flores had also claimed credit for the near miss of catching Martin at Santiago airport when he alone had organised the local team of watchers. His Indian tracker at Iquitos had telephoned to say that it could have been Martin who had crossed into Colombia with one of the bush pilots, but had only become aware of that possibility when talking to other tribes on the lower Solimões, where he'd recovered some items of Martin's that he'd obviously dumped overboard. If that was in fact Martin, then he could pass as an Indian trader. Talking to the highly intelligent young black employee at Sobatsu in Bogotá, whose parents lived in Barranquilla, made Parides think that this would now be the area to concentrate the search. Parides had made up his mind to fly to Caracas and bring his boss up to date with his thoughts, theories and suspicions. He'd reported to his boss at the Sobatsu offices and was now ensconced at Philippe's apartment. When Philippe confided his own worries about Hauptmann and his chess outing, Parides was certain that something sinister was going on.

So it was he'd received the news that Hauptmann was in Caracas and wished to meet with his boss in the Los Caobos park, and then to join him at the chess pavilions in the nearby pedestrian precinct. Parides had observed at a distance and seen the four youths, first in deep discussion together with knowing nods in Philippe's and Hauptmann's direction, then separately approach Philippe for much closer observation. It had been clear that his boss was a marked man and that whatever was going to happen, Hauptmann was a party to it. He'd seen Hauptmann order the drinks and coffee and add something to his boss's cup. He thoroughly approved of his boss's sleight of hand when reversing both the brandies and coffees. When Hauptmann and his boss, on finishing their drinks, finally entered the Metro followed by the four youths, Parides was certain of their plan.

On the escalator, he'd bumped into one of the youths and pressed on the pressure point on the left side of his neck, rendering him immediately senseless. One of his friends had stopped to aid him while the other two had followed in Hauptmann's wake. The platform was the usual seething mass of commuters and Parides had positioned himself carefully at the side of one of the pillars and close to the two youths. Hauptmann was absolutely unaware of his presence and was concentrating on Philippe a little ahead of him. When the train hurtled into the station, Parides felled one of the youths and threw the other at Hauptmann who, although right behind Philippe, appeared to be suffering a dizzy spell. Philippe had sidestepped at exactly the right moment. It had been all over in seconds and he and Philippe had made good their escape, passing the second youth still administering first-aid to his friend who was now recovering. Neither saw Philippe leave the station among the crowds, who also wished to avoid the authorities, and none had been aware of Parides, in spite of his bulk.

Later, back in the Sobatsu offices after a slow taxi ride, Philippe raised a glass to Parides, "I owe you my life amigo. You will not regret it. Now we have to make one or two decisions about our future and what we should do to ensure that there is one. But first, we'd best make sure that Flores and Jefferson believe that their plans have succeeded and that I died today in the Metro. I know the Chief of Police here very well and he'll give the names of those who died in the accident to the Press".

"Rest in peace Jorgé Philippe", said Parides who solemnly raised his glass in salute.

Philippe was studying the wall map of Colombia and the connecting Isthmus leading to Panama. He jabbed his finger at the archipelago.

"So you reckon that he crossed into Panama via these islands; he's an exceptionally clever and resourceful bird our little sand-martin, I think. I reckon that it's also time that I spoke to my boss at Central Office in Japan before we come to any decisions of where to go from here. Pour us another couple of drinks and I'll get a supply of coffee organised and book one or two calls with my secretary, this could take some time".

Philippe buzzed for his secretary and issued instructions, then cleared his desk of all material to receive the new, large scale map of Mexico and Central America that she'd immediately returned with. As the door closed behind her, Parides handed his boss his refilled glass and Philippe observed,

"She's efficient anyway, it was only this morning that I asked for this map".

The phone rang and after the usual courtesies expressed to his boss, a considered necessity by all of Japanese society, he outlined as briefly as he could, all that had happened since his last update of almost three weeks ago. As Head of Sobatsu's security, he was not expected to have anything other than have the usual weekly written reports delivered by courier. This call underlined both his own anxieties and the urgency of updating news over the handling of the ongoing situation to his boss. Nomura would want to know everything.

Parides sat patiently listening to the one-sided conversation, but understanding only a little of what his immediate boss was saying; English wasn't his strong point. An hour later, he replenished his boss's glass as Philippe finally replaced the receiver which rang again almost the instant it touched the cradle. Another minute later, it was returned to its cradle once more.

Philippe was smiling as he acknowledged the refill and said to Parides,

"Buen amigo a la salud de nosotros! It appears that a meeting has been called of the Top Ten and that Sobatsu had been excluded from the list of those invited. This was done at the expressed wish and desires of Señor Jefferson. Tokyo is not pleased and will be attending the meeting, but incognito if you like. They are very unhappy with Flores and Hauptmann and have no problem with your solution, Flores can be dispensed with in the same fashion if it is deemed to be necessary. We are to go to Panama City and co-ordinate the final capture of Martin. Your young helper had sent off your last report to Central Office before he left with Flores for Barranquilla and had included some of the points that you'd discussed with him prior to flying to Caracas. It would appear that you chose a good team player, as well as helpful and intelligent and that he is unhappy with the Señora. He overheard Flores' telephone conversation, presumably with Jefferson, claiming your's and his ideas as her own. We'll get organised and collect your young helper in Bogotá before flying to Panama City". Philippe buzzed the intercom, asking his secretary to book the first available flight next day to Bogotá for himself and Parides, adding to his lieutenant. "And we must get our timing for the final meeting with Señora Flores absolutely perfect. I wish her final realisation of my check-mate to have maximum impact and effect".

"What do you intend for her death boss?", Parides asked.

"I shall give that particular enjoyment some deeply considered thought my friend. They say that revenge and pay-back time are dishes best eaten cold. There's no rush. Remember she'll be organising all the teams for us. It will mean less work to do when we get to Panama City".

Philippe, Parides and Juanito had descended from the same flight at Bogotá, Juanito having caught a connecting one to Caracas from Curaçao and as they'd never met one another before, they were oblivious of each other's existence. Flores and Sobatsu's young employee Louis, had arrived within minutes of the other flight and Louis had seen Parides waiting in the queue for the taxi-rank accompanied by another gentleman. He hailed them and was unceremoniously bundled into the next taxi as Parides said.

"We were just coming to collect you. Where's Señora Flores?"

Philippe interrupted for brief introductions with the young man, then suggested that they repair to a convenient nearby bar where Louis could be debriefed.

"We're lucky to have just missed her, it would have been most unfortunate for us and our plans if we'd bumped into her here".

Louis told them all about Martin's passage on the coaster to the archipelago and of his conversation with the van driver. He repeated also some of the overheard conversation between Flores and Jefferson. Louis added that it was the first time and a great pleasure to have met a ghost, regaling Philippe with the Señora's enjoyment of his accident.

A grim smile played around the corners of Philippe's mouth as he listened and he agreed to Louis' suggestion of following Martin's route saying.

"You were absolutely right there my lad, you might even have caught up with him but there's no chance of that now and I need you to accompany us to Panama City where I think the end-game will be played out. Señora Flores will definitely have her game check-mated, but I think that Martin will also surface there. The next few days will be interesting in the extreme, I moved a lot of my men into Panama ten days ago and with Flores' extra watchers, even the bugs will require to show some form of identity before they can leave that country".

Philippe downed his drink, the others following suit, left the bar and hailed a taxi to take them to Sobatsu's offices.

"First", he said. "We must put a permanent tail on Flores immediately she arrives in Panama, so that we'll know exactly where she is at all times. We can't afford the advantages of my untimely death to be lost gentlemen!"

Sobatsu's Chief Executive Officer and chairman of the company, Kaitto Nomura, sat and contemplated a giant video screen on the wall of his office. It had taken him thirty years to put together the largest computer software company in the world, as well as producing two thirds of the micro-chips. He had to admit that part of his success had been due to meeting Laurence C. Jefferson and listening to his cleverly expressed plans for beating the competition in any and all the other countries, no matter what product they manufactured. Jefferson's outlined formulae definitely worked and the cherry-picking system of buying into the shares of potentially dangerous competitors had aided him to stay ahead of any competition and to buy them out when the time was ripe. Jefferson was clever and highly dangerous. He'd have to be careful if he was to sound out the other eight's views on their collective future. At least he'd be fully aware of what was to be discussed at the Dubai meeting.

Sobatsu had designed and produced the communicators after all, and his own brilliant electronics people had a safeguard built into them, just in case of an eventuality such as this, Sobatsu's exclusion from any meeting. All messages would be instantly flashed up on his big screen and a complete record would be transmitted and transcribed in the main office by a team of typists, linguists and boffins. He was taking no chances of any mistakes or missing information. He wondered if Jefferson knew that his company had installed all the UAE's telecommunications at their Etisalat building, just a few hundred yards from the Intercontinental Hotel and almost directly opposite the Sheraton. He very much doubted it and smiled wryly to himself. His company was fully prepared for this meeting. He resented Jefferson, not only for excluding his company, but mainly because of the man's desire to control the security arm of Sobatsu and to try and remove his personally appointed head man. This was a very dangerous precedent, he thought, and one that had to be fully discussed eventually with all the other eight CEO's. There were definite indications in Jefferson's character of megalomania and a wish to be more than just Chairman of the Ten. Where would it end? It was time that he knew all about Jefferson's interference with Sobatsu security and if he was manipulating any more of them for his own purposes. The security arm for the Ten had been put under Nomura's care as most of the products were theirs and none had the right to use men for individual purposes without reference to Tokyo. There was no doubt about Philippe's loyalty and especially after the attempt on his life; he could also count fully on his lieutenant, Parides. Flores would be retired in Panama. He'd given full instructions to that effect, but perhaps it was time to check on Jefferson's instructions to their New York office and their English operations. The weekly reports had shown up activity in both areas that was directly attributable to Jefferson. He would send two of his best local men, both of whom spoke flawless English, to check out exactly what was happening. He would also arrange for an emergency meeting of the Nine, but it would be Planet Ales who would be missing from it. However, that meeting would be held at a time and place yet to be determined and after this meeting in Dubai. He would await all of its information and assess the position before contacting any of the others. His large video screen now flickered into life. Aha!, he would not have long to wait, the meeting had begun.

Meanwhile, Philippe, Parides and Louis had arrived in Panama City and had taken up residence in Caesar's Park Hotel, having established that Flores and her new lieutenant, Juanito, were ensconced in the newest hotel, the Intercontinental, at 53 storeys now the tallest building in Central America. Philippe had decided to use Parides to obtain all the information on the ground about what was happening, as there had been a directive from Flores at Sobatsu Bogotá instructing Parides to follow her to Panama. Parides had telephoned the Señora from the office immediately after receipt of his orders, claiming that his disappearance from the picture had been due to illness and that he'd been aghast to learn of Philippe's accident. Flores had told him that she suspected Hauptmann was also dead. "Perhaps trying to save the boss", Parides suggested. Flores had agreed instantly and had told Parides to take the first flight out to join her. Although, she reckoned that Panama was sealed up tight, Parides knew a lot of areas that might be tested by Martin as escape routes.

It would be impossible for Martin to board any ship while it was passing through the canal; she'd posted watchers at the very few places that this could happen. The whole canal zone was fully enclosed by high wire fencing and was still controlled by the American Seventh Army. Ownership of the canal wouldn't revert to the Panamanians until the end of the century. An amazing engineering feat, she thought, and not one gallon of pumped water required; it all operated by gravity. Gatun Lake had been man created to act as the necessary reservoir, holding the 200 inches of annual rainfall in this part of the world. The runoff from the central mountains was contained in Gatun lake and channelled in both directions to facilitate shipping movements. Continuous dredging kept the channels open and a series of lock gates at both ends allowed the vessels either to climb up to the lake or descend from it. The original concept was exceptionally clever she thought, connecting the Pacific with the Atlantic and reducing the shipping movements by more than 3,000 miles in some cases. No, Martin wouldn't be able to board a ship, neither in the Canal nor at either Colón or the port at Panama City. He had to go out by air and she'd organised a direct computer link with Sobatsu's operators who would instantly inform her of developments by mobile phone. Her teams of watchers in all the sensitive areas were fully organised, it was now only a matter of waiting for him to emerge from the jungle.

With Parides en route, she would utilise him to cover the French quarter and key into the local smuggling element. Apart from drugs this was hardly a requirement, as Panama was a duty free zone for both bona fidé travellers and those in the know. She would have time to enjoy this fabulous hotel and its facilities and cuisine. Just watching Juanito in the pool was very relaxing, she considered.

Louis had been dispatched to the French quarter of the city by Philippe with strict instructions to keep a low profile, but to keep his eyes and ears open. Parides was en route to the Intercontinental Hotel and would shortly be in one of the suites on the top floor where Flores had set up her base. She wouldn't have risked such expenditure if he, Jorgé Philippe, had still been in control, thought Philippe grimly. He'd await Parides return before making any move, much depended on knowing all of the arrangements that Flores had organised for Martin's capture.

"Buenas dias Parides", Flores greeted the late Philippe's muscle and hit-man. "You are well enough now, I see".

"Si Senora, yo siento muy buen ahora", replied Parides, assuring her that he was now fully fit and well. He listened to all the detail of the arrangements made for Martin's final capture and added. "He should not evade us this time Señora". He'd taken in all the detail of the suite of rooms with its two bedrooms and the opening French windows to the balcony, which were at present, closed to enable the air-conditioning to operate properly.

Flores caught his intense look, misinterpreted his motives and said. "Yes, there's a great view of the city from here, but you'll see it another time, I want you to go down to the French quarter right away and obtain some of the local hard talent to cover the clandestine areas that Martin might be tempted to use". With a perfunctory wave of her hand she dismissed Parides, thinking only that he was after all only a muscle bound thug who could be useful in the places where his like fraternised and frequented. At least, she thought, he had accepted that his previous boss's demise had been a tragic accident. There had been no mention of it, so she could make use of him without fear. Hauptmann had been right about that.

Parides did not make for the French quarter, Louis would cover that area far better than he. Instead, Parides returned to the Caesar Park Hotel to report to his boss on all that he had learnt. Philippe was very pleased with his lieutenant's report and especially about the news of the Señora's balcony and her wish to show-off the view at a later date. He had men keeping tabs on her around the clock, also on her paramour Juanito, and he would not be startled into taking actions that hadn't been very thoroughly thought out. There would be only the one surprise and when it came, this time it would be the Señora's!

Philippe's features relaxed into a slow smile as he contemplated her fate. Vengeance, when one was completely in control of all the events and possibilities, had a very satisfying and intoxicating effect, even when viewed objectively. Soon Señora, very very soon! The mental images being conjured-up in his mind creating a deep sensation of inner peace. An almost orgasmic pleasure could be obtained from the delayed final act; self-gratification being a greater anticipatory enjoyment rather than actual.

Eleven

Jefferson sank back in his chauffeur driven limousine, en route once again to La Guardia. How many times had he flown out of here over the years, he considered idly. But this time he was concerned, all his planning over the past twenty years was coming apart and all due to some damned salesman. Or was it? If Philippe had done his job properly he wouldn't have had to clear up this mess. His organisation had been water tight for almost quarter of a century and his forward thinking and planning had made him one of the most powerful people in the world. He had the ear of Presidents, Kings and Princes, Prime Ministers and all the news moguls. He had purposely kept a low profile whenever he had been faced with the media, by putting them in touch with other famous personalities, but he'd pulled their strings. For many years now he'd watched CNN, ABC, Sky News and BBC World News and had been able to mouth the words spoken by the pre-eminent spokesmen whom he'd coached or set-up or to whom he'd had the correct scripts delivered to, prior to television interviews or Press conferences. He counted in the thousands the numerous politicians around the world who received his advice or phone-calls appertaining to global finance and those who'd enjoyed his hospitality. He'd always made very sure that his gifts to all were well understood by the recipients as to their correct provenance, but had taken care also that the reality of their true emanation would stop short of being traced back to him. The gifts, helpful information and donations to political parties were always made by others and untraceable to himself directly. Even his helpful friends in the FBI had been organised by Supreme Court Judges who'd saved their asses over stupid cock-ups in the past. The first eight companies of his inner circle, the Top Ten, had been the most difficult to recruit, but they'd seen the light when he'd formed the initial few hundred members of the Millennium Cartel.

The power of money. There was nothing it couldn't provide, do, or organise. A great friend in his early years, whose complete honesty he'd respected, had surprised him by saying to him one day, "Larry, everyone's got his price". Finding out his, had been more of a mental exercise and game to him initially, but with a mixture of sadness and excitement he'd found it and never looked back.

When on his first visit to the Persian Gulf he'd agreed to act as an ambassador for his country, the whole knowledge of the systems of control had been revealed to him, in a much smaller way of course and really not hidden either. The Arabs were only protecting their own interests from the manipulative methods of the Western industrial nations.

My God!, he considered, these Arabs had formulated a system that made them impregnable from the 'bandit oil companies' as they'd once called them. Now those same bandits operated to the Gulf Arabs' complete advantage, although the G7 nations had tried many times to re-shuffle the deck when the Arabs tried to isolate all the aces. It was little wonder the ancestors of these Arabian thieves had invented the game of chess. It was now almost impossible to outmanoeuvre them in commerce or, for that matter, in politics. They could see the advantage in the retention of such dictators and ruthless murderers as Saddam Hussein, Idi Amin, Muammar Gadaffi and suchlike madmen. They funded operations and media reports whenever the West came too close to removing one of these monsters, but paid lip-service to the G7's military strikes in retaliation for some outrage. So far, but never far enough. They were even able to claim credit from these dictators for the restraints that the western nations had shown; Islamic fundamentalism was yet another area of careful orchestration. These fatwas were very often convenient in taking up the world's attention and taking the media's eye off the ball and all at well organised times for themselves. The limo drew alongside the Lear and he was quickly aboard, all the paperwork having been organised by Ardeth. He had duplicate passports, issued by the State Department and kept in various convenient places, like this jet. There would be an almost immediate take-off, the tower had a slot booked for his flight immediately he'd entered the security perimeter - he seldom wasted the Lear on short haul flights.

Six hours to Heathrow, re-fuel, another five to the Emirates, giving him time to make a few calls, do some necessary preparation and think about the coming meeting, enjoy dinner and catch a good five or so hours' rest before arrival. He'd have to telephone his wife and probably have to listen to a long boring soliloquy about the round of socialite parties he was going to miss.

That reminded him, he must have his Caribbean yacht faxed with final confirmation that they'd be joining it for a five week cruise this next week in the Antilles. He would join it in Cancun in the Mexican Yucatan peninsula and combine the cruise with tours of the ancient Mayan ruins that his wife kept talking about. By now, Ardeth would have checked his 'favor-book' and listed all those who had done sufficient helpful things in the past year to merit a trip aboard. The lists would already be with Captain André who would be doing the necessary homework and have a discreet aide memoire for him on any salient points about his guests and a list of their first names. Many years ago he'd realised cheap flattery could be highly advantageous. Some of the guests could already be aboard and enjoying the hospitality in his absence. He used the yacht from a personal point very infrequently and then usually at the behest of his wife. There's nothing that increases support and removes doubts better about the business methods of a wealthy man than the use of their Christian names among other Establishment members. He smiled over the naïveté of people. Flights for all guests, from wherever to Cancun and onwards to convenient ports, would be included. It had been a handy book over the years but had increased in volume, year by year. The company's two yachts, The Venus in American waters and the Mercury in the Mediterranean, were almost fully engaged with guests from the favor-book. As both yachts were fully tax deductable, the returns gained fully justified their retention.

Unfortunately, the general public of many of the Western nations were now demanding an end to these open-ended agreements with the Revenue services. It was also just a matter of time before all the offshore banking was brought to book around the world. Secrecy would be disallowed by law, and the funds taxed at higher rates, although probably still giving the Island banking areas a small advantage. It would stop dead all the money laundering, he reflected, but would also stop some of his own convenient gifts and extra - curricular activities. The formation of his Top Ten would be beyond the reach of such petty controls by Governments, as they already financed a number of them. The thought made him smile again, as he accepted a Bacardi, ice and cola from a pretty hostess who asked him when he wished to eat, leaving a printed menu beside his drink along with the wine list. Flores' incoming call had him smiling to himself once again, human nature and its weaknesses were one of his specialities and the Señora was very easy to read. He was glad that she'd replaced Philippe. In truth I could never be certain of him, he thought.

The news that Flores had still not located the salesman was not what he wished to hear, although he reckoned that Panama must finally be enmeshed in the network of Flores' security people and watchers. On the plus side, it would also take Martin another few days to reach Panama City or Colón, whichever he was making for. The Darien was a difficult jungle to traverse and would take two to three weeks to cross. Flores was moving people by the hundred to cover the Canal and the airports to act as spotters, but Martin now looked like a Central or South American according to the van driver who'd ferried him from Cartagena to Barranquilla. He would not be easy to identify. He'd done amazingly well for an amateur, Jefferson thought. He could have used a salesman like Martin. For now there was this meeting ahead and, having dined lightly, although still enjoying a brandy and cigar with his coffee, he decided to catch up with a few hours rest. They'd left Heathrow a good twenty minutes ago and he would arrive in Dubai, rested, showered and ready.

The Lear drew to a halt beside other private jets and a limousine was immediately at the stairs as they were lowered. A liveried chauffeur had the car door open and collected his bags and in seconds they were en route to the V.I.P. lounge where Yussuf, the vice President of Dubai's Chamber of Commerce was waiting to greet him.

"Larry it's good to see you again, I won't detain you now, but after you're settled we must have a long talk. Would you manage to come for dinner at the villa tomorrow night, say around seven-thirty".

"Thank you Yussuf, I look forward to that", replied Larry, pleased at both the invitation and the consideration given to organising himself before attending a dinner. An invitation here was considered to have the same weight as a Royal command, the Arab households had similarities to the Chinese and would be offended by a refusal. Neither of these nationalities willingly took a rain-check. He remembered a previous occasion when he'd received a rap over the knuckles for doing just that. Well it's their country I suppose, thought Larry, and they're entitled to organise it according to their own rules, and boy did they do just that! The Emirates were the most controlled society that he'd ever come across and because of their complete hold over everything, the country ran like a well oiled watch. No-one could own land or property in their lands except the Emirati, but they imported expertise, technology and labour from around the world. Being free of all taxes and duty, the Emirates attracted every form of business and thousands of expatriate, middle and top management from all of the western nations. Around 100,000 people from these countries worked here for salaries that were tax-free and much higher than they could obtain elsewhere. Ordinary labour was supplied by Filipino, Indian, Bangladeshi and Pakistani nationals who came to make sufficient money and send it home to support their families. But all the newcomers, whether Western or Eastern had to have Visas and were here purely on sufferance. There was no crime here Larry thought, just because of this control. One mistake and you were on your way home, replacements were readily found. The streets were clear of the rubbish found in New York or London, as the fines levied on litter bugs could amount to a month's salary. The rules held rigid as the maxim, "If you're not happy, then leave", gave little option and signs or expressions of discontent were very rare. It was one of the safest cities in the world to frequent at night and it had everything made or known to man that could be bought or sold. You could meet every nationality here in the space of a week and enjoy the world's cuisine. The Emirati were building a new Hong Kong cum Singapore cum old-style Beirut here, he considered. Their gold and Persian carpet trades were the backbone of their duty free sales and they'd had the foresight to create an International airport with no landing fees levied, so as to entice the world's airlines to use it as the Middle-eastern hub airport. The world's tourist trade would be diverted through Dubai within a few years, Larry smiled wryly. Cash with control, that was the key he'd become aware of so many years ago. Oil in the Emirates was being fast depleted at the time, so they had devised a system that would maintain their lifestyle, but it had been the oil wealth that had supplied the initial impetus. The limo had pulled up in front of the Dubai Sheraton and Towers, one of the two five-star hotels in the centre. Registration was a formality, everything had been organised and he was escorted to one of the lifts and in less than a minute was in his executive suite on the eleventh floor. He had butler service on this floor and a fax machine, as well as three phones. The 28inch TV gave CNN and BBC news services along with another ten satellite channels. The music centre, video and CD players were housed immediately below the television. There were faxes on the desk awaiting his attention. Seven of the other CEO's had arrived, two staying in the Sheraton and five others, just a few hundred yards further along the road at the Intercontinental, the other five-star hotel.

Larry thought it odd how that ratio reflected the two hotels popularity from a client booking point of view, although he personally preferred the Sheraton's ambience and enormous open-plan lobby, to the more old-fashioned layout of the

Intercontinental. There was, however, some merit in the latter's greater privacy for its business clientele and guests, where the thundering herd hadn't easy access. The views across the bustling Creek were another plus. The meeting was to be held at the Intercontinental; he liked to separate his areas of business from pleasure. He placed calls to his fellow CEO's and welcomed each in turn to Dubai, letting them know that the golf-course had been reserved for their sole use tomorrow morning and also for the morning of their departure in two days time. Their meeting had been arranged for the next afternoon and the best of the conference rooms at the Intercontinental had been reserved for the purpose. He reminded all of them to take their electronic personal communicators to ensure complete secrecy from inquisitive eyes and ears.

Dubai might be one of the safest places on earth he reckoned, but there's no sense in taking unnecessary chances. Food and drinks, etc would be served during the meeting and although the waiters would be vetted by both the hotel and the Emirati, they were best kept in ignorance of the meeting's purpose.

Señora Flores considered Parides re-appearance, but discarded the nagging doubt that there was anything wrong. She was quietly satisfied that Jefferson had been delighted with her own theories and now regretted her decision to leave Louis behind in Bogotá, he had been prescient after all. The suggestion by the black upstart that he would be better following in Martin's wake had been quashed without thought. Her racial prejudice had been showing, she thought grimly. Martin could arrive in Panama City or Colón within two days after she had arrived there; she'd already warned her teams in both places. She smiled to herself, Jorgé you felt that you were clever, but I'm far cleverer, she thought, and I'm alive too! Pity that he'd been such an arrogant bastard, she reflected Although that trait had made it easier on her own conscience when Jefferson had asked her to replace him. Poor Hauptmann, she had surmised that Philippe must have taken him with him as he fell on the live rail. Ugh!, she shuddered involuntarily; it was a nasty way to go and she had liked Hauptmann. Anyway, Parides had accepted his late boss's fate as being an accident, so that removed any possible problem. It was time to ring down for the menu and wine list; Juanito would soon be joining her for dinner. She had to employ him and justify his existence, there would be an accounting for all the expenditure at the end of the day, she considered. She would put Juanito in charge of overseeing the airport watchers, they already knew what to do. All he has to do is observe, listen and report back. She could see the well muscled frame in her mind's eye. Yes Juanito just you report back, she mused, as she conjured-up his beautiful physique.

The main conference room reserved for the Top Ten was on the second floor of the Intercontinental Hotel. Five of the CEO's had already arrived and were chatting together and enjoying the view overlooking Dubai's famous Creek. It was the usual bedlam of noise, hustle, bustle and colour. Almost two thousand dhows of varying size and purpose were moored alongside the wharves immediately opposite the hotel and stretching out in both directions. Trucks, large and small, cars and all manner of transport, deposited goods on the quays for onward passage to other Gulf, Red Sea, Mediterranean, African and Indian ports. As fast as the non mechanised labour allowed, dhows were filled with all manner of goods; only one single mobile crane was in action to load the larger, heavy items. All other lading was man handled up open gangways consisting only of long, thick planks of timber.

A constant stream of smaller boats were ferrying passengers from the steps on the Dubai side, with loads of twenty to thirty people, across to the steps at the Deira side of the creek It was a fascinating spectacle and all the executives had been gathered before they were aware that Jefferson was asking them to take their seats at the smaller of two boardroom tables. The other was groaning under the weight of sweetmeats, salads, fruit and selections of nuts and of course, the UAE's famous dates; there being none finer in the world. Stacks of various sizes of plates and covered hotplates indicated a selection of savoury dishes. At each of the nine places on the smaller table were placed two bottles of mineral water, a sparkling one and a small selection of fruit juices. A can of the latest drink to be marketed by Planet Ales stood next to two, tall crystal glasses. All, as they'd arrived, had placed their files and communicators at one of the places leaving the position with the largest chair to be occupied by Jefferson who now addressed them.

"Well gentlemen, you no doubt wish to visit the gold and carpet souks in the afternoon and obtain gifts for the family or have a round of golf, so we'll get right down to it. I should prefer you to use your communicators for all business to be discussed and to voice only requests to our waiters for anything that you'd like to eat or drink. We will adjourn to the English Pub for something stronger than what is available here. But only after this meeting has finished. Unless anyone has anything more to add along these lines, I have already programmed my communicator and will pass it in a clockwise direction for you to copy my code and enter your personal number".

A murmur of general agreement followed this final remark. Two of the executives ordered coffee from the three waiters who were discreetly out of earshot and standing next to the food. Jefferson's communicator was passed around for encoding their own with the displayed operational details. The others entered their own personal number on Jefferson's and as the circuit was completed and Jefferson once more in possession of his; he pressed a key on it and all the communicators came to life.

The first query by one of the other eight was echoed by each officer in turn, emphasising their collective concern at Sobatsu's exclusion from the meeting. Jefferson however, had prepared carefully and pressed another key that transmitted all the detailed discussions that he'd had with the late head of Sobatsu's security arm. He gave an account of Philippe's unfortunate accident in Caracas and the urgent necessity for an immediate replacement. The message concluded that he'd elevated Flores to this position and expressed his own full trust in her abilities.

A lengthy transmission about Martin and the agent Booth's transcripts brought worried frowns to the countenances of most of the Executives. Jefferson enlarged on Philippe's inability to trace Martin with Philippe's request to himself that he add the third ingredient to his soft drinks in the Central American countries. Consternation and alarm was obvious and there were eight immediate No's, from the others making Larry decide that the time wasn't right to inform them that there was no going back. Question followed question, mainly fielded by Jefferson and the meeting broke up in mid -afternoon. They filtered through to the English Pub which was on the same floor, but separated by yet another high-class restaurant. Their conversation was somewhat stilted and guarded.

The bar didn't usually didn't open until six, a sop to the Islamic principles of the Emirati which were hypocritical in the extreme, but whose rules had been waived on this occasion as it was a private party. Their communicators continued to be used for business questions and answers. One by one the CEO's left to attend to other matters, but all were clearly worried by the events that had been outlined by Jefferson.

It was a rather grim Jefferson who returned to the Sheraton to rest, bathe and dress for dinner with Vice President Yussuf of the city's Chamber of Commerce. Normally, Larry would have thoroughly enjoyed the excellent cuisine his friend always provided, but this time he was more than preoccupied with thoughts about his fellow executives' disapproval of the proposed remedies for an already deteriorating situation. Yussuf's business propositions held little interest for him, even the finest of wines that accompanied the lobster thermidor, the spicy calamares and hamour fish-dishes failed to excite his palate. Finally top of the range Beluga caviar was served with crushed onions, sweetened and covered in Parmesan. This last dish was accompanied by small, shot glasses that had been frozen and set out by a man-servant's gloved hand, into each glass was poured chilled vodka. These hauté cuisine touches failed to entice him and he informed his host that he'd be returning to New York first thing next day. Larry realised that his failure to be more appreciative of his host's largesse in his honour would cost him dearly in the future, but couldn't overcome his depression at the meeting's outcome. He feigned making a poor recovery from a recent bout of angina, exacerbated by the unaccustomed, very warm and humid conditions of the Gulf. He hoped that his host would excuse him for his rudeness, but that it was unavoidable. Returning to the Sheraton, Larry telephoned his pilots, who were staying in the nearby Lords Hotel, to inform them that he'd be leaving soon after dawn and to be ready to depart. Damn it all, his planning was going down the plug, thanks to that damned Martin and bloody Philippe's early blunders. Someone would pay for this, he thought as he dialled his office, leaving instructions for Ardeth and asking her to contact him when she arrived first thing in the morning. He realised that he'd have to cancel the next cruise just in case he needed the Venus for his own hasty exit. It had been very obvious that the other eight executives at the meeting were not about to support him in his actions. He cursed Philippe again for his incompetence over the epidiascope, his inability to apprehend Martin, and for stampeding him into using the third ingredient. He recognised that if it hadn't been for that impetuous action, he could have swung the other eight to back him in his actions, Damn, Damn, Damn!. If Philippe had still been alive, he would have made him pay dearly for all the mistakes. The future looked bleak. Jefferson was now forced to review everything and consider carefully all of the possible future implications of his previously well-structured planning.

Twelve

For three days the malarial fever had me in its grip, I shivered and shook another thirty pounds of weight away while Mariella tended to me. During some of my semi-conscious moments I made her aware of the other life threatening situation I was in and she promised to keep me safe. Thankfully, she had recognised a previously good guest to the Dolphin lodge and was on my side when I explained the type of people who were searching for me. I had also taken another bout of amoebic dysentery, probably through eating with the crew on the coaster and now made worse by the malaria. I asked Mariella if she could obtain the antibiotics Ciproxin and Flagyl from Panama City for me; without them I would assuredly die from loss of bodily fluids. I was drinking gallons of untreated water which wasn't helping and even their soups were running through me.

I gave Mariella the final $300 that I had in my trousers, deciding that to tell her about my jacket would only complicate things and was relieved to see it was on a hanger beside the shuttered window. Mariella used her radio link with her relatives in the city who also operated the fleet of light aircraft that serviced the jungle outposts of Panama. She assured me that the drugs would be here the next day and for the umpteenth time changed my bedding. I resolved to give her and her people in the village a large monetary thank you before I left and if I survived.

An Islander light plane touched down next lunchtime with the antibiotics and a couple of dozen packets of Rehidrat to replenish the minerals lost due to Montezuma's revenge. It was just in time as I'd been weakening daily and had eaten hardly anything for forty-eight hours.

The antibiotics pulled me through, they and of course the nursing by Mariella and her helpers. I'd been there a week and would need at least another before I regained sufficient strength to continue on my journey. I had written two postcards, to Sally and to Fraser, explaining my debilitating illnesses and more than doubling the length of my probable convalescence. Mariella undertook to post them in Panama City. I wrote also to Juan Zambrano in Nicaragua, a guide whom I'd hired some years back and whom I'd helped to start a postcard business through the gift of $200.

He'd been a professional photographer, but had been forced to sell his cameras to feed his family during the war of attrition between the Sandanistas and Contras. I could only hope that he would help me to enter his country or to avoid questions by the Immigration authorities if I took a plane to his city. The alternative of flying out of Panama to Costa Rica was very probably the end of the road. Mariella had said that there were many strange characters at her uncle's café, that doubled as their tiny airport lounge.

The airline was operated on a shoestring and regularly lost four or five aircraft each year, but amazingly continued to operate from the centre of Panama City. Many of central America's flag carriers had unenviable reputations, I reflected. The San Salvador and Honduras airlines were known by their acronyms T.A.C.A. and S.A.H.S.A, now mercifully defunct or completely reformed as in the case of the former, had been called by their clients, Take-a Chance Airline and the latter's title, Stay-at-Home and Stay-Alive Airline. The ridicule wasn't completely deserved, but spoke volumes about their maintenance and safety records. Travel in those third world, banana republics could be more than just interesting, I thought, but they were slowly climbing the ladder. The multi-nationals had undermined the virility of their peoples, with poor wages to sustain cheap supplies to the States and Europe.

Although the western public was beginning to demand fairness in their dealings with all these countries, the multi-national companies twisted the ground rules at every opportunity.

The other side of the coin that I also recognised was, that without the work, these companies provided, many would simply starve. Panama, because of the Canal, and Costa Rica because of its tourism from the US, were the only two countries on the Isthmus with a decent standard of living.

Slowly my health returned, but there was little to do except play dominoes with Mariella's younger brother, Saoul. I watched with interest as her female helpers mixed a juice extracted from an unusual fruit to paint their black nose lines; these were considered cosmetically appealing by the tribe. I had many hours to contemplate the differences between my own culture and those of the so-called, uncivilised peoples of the world. The Kuna Indians hadn't yet succumbed to the lure of television and much of their way of life had been preserved over the centuries and still survived intact.

I planned and re-planned my escape from Panama. There was no alternative to leaving by the main airport. Private and light planes were forbidden to fly during the hours of darkness in Panama to enable the DEA to control the skies with their anti-drug enforcement systems. I would have to go through the international hub airport and risk my passport number being abstracted by Sobatsu's operatives. Again, I had to look reasonably like my photo which would mean shaving off my beard and adopting western dress once more.

Otherwise the Immigration officials would subject me to questioning and that would be it! At least flight durations would be short, two hours to San José, the Capital of Costa Rica, but I'd probably walk into the hands of my captors. They would be expecting me to make short hops so as to delay final recognition. Dare I take a chance and fly direct to the States and claim protection? No, I'd be taken out somehow. That was a risk not worth thinking about. I'd written to Juan Zambrano in Managua, Nicaragua, but I couldn't be sure that they wouldn't have him under surveillance. Although, I had made him fully aware of my own plight in my letter and of the risk to himself. I could book two or three flights and pay for all the tickets to different destinations, but could only chance that none of the flights would be fully booked as I couldn't wait around the airport. It would be last minute stuff if I were to pull it off. Timing would be critical. I spoke to Mariella and asked her to get the information I required from her uncle without raising his curiosity level.

I swam with the village children of Achitupu (Island of God) and accompanied them on forays to some of the other uninhabited islands to gather coconuts. Occasionally, I accompanied one of the fishermen when checking his traps for lobsters and crayfish and helped others hang their nets out to dry. I recovered slowly and my gut had adjusted to the raw water with the aid of the Rehidrat electrolyte powder.

Mariella's conch soup was unbelievably good and very rich and I was given seconds of everything to rebuild my strength. Her father was one of the Sahila's or chiefs. Around twenty headmen controlled the fifty or so inhabited islands in this chain of three hundred and fifty. The Kuna Indians had been given a great degree of autonomy by the Panamanian Government and made their own laws with little or no outside interference. Although missionaries had established a Christian meeting house, the tribe paid little more than lip-service to its existence and happily accepted the economic aid that the mission brought with it. The other uninhabited islands were planted with vegetables to help feed the tribe or grow coconuts for sale or barter. Hunting parties regularly went ashore to the mainland for the meat from tapirs, howler monkeys, birds, snakes, caymans (South American alligators) and iguanas (often referred to as the poor man's chicken, tasting similar and found in huge numbers throughout the isthmus).

I became expert in the handling of a dugout canoe for the crossing from the main island back to Mariella's atoll, named Uaguitupu. I had even started to learn some of the Kuna language and recognised that the atoll's name came from their words 'Ua' meaning fish, 'gui' - dolphin and 'tupu' - island. The swimming combined with the heat of the sun aided a faster recovery and after a day on the mainland with a party of hunters, I felt strong enough to continue my journey. Mariella radioed her uncle and fortunately there was a plane due next day bringing two American guests for her Lodge. It was to be a fortuitous overlap as I did not wish close encounters with Americans before I left.

At eleven next morning I took my leave of Mariella and Saoul and of the other women helpers. She tried to refuse the dollars that I pressed upon her and her father, the chief having organised a large fishing canoe to transport me to the beach. It was a far greater honour than being transported ashore by the Lodge's motor launch which followed us to pick up their new guests. I remembered to leave a signed note with the chief to give to Captain M'mboya on his next visit; he could then collect his fee from the Bank. A Twin Otter was already taxiing towards the hut that served their island as an airport as I stepped ashore on the mainland, the partial strip of bitumen and short grass being no more than a rudimentary runway. Two Kuna Indian tribesmen, myself, a net full of coconuts and seven boxes of crayfish made up the return load to the central city airport that catered for air traffic to jungle destinations. I was very, very nervous, but had still retained my appearance of being a trader, although I'd shaved off my beard to allow my face to tan. I was aware of the many watchers as we landed and taxied to a halt at the airline's collection of buildings, but Mariella's uncle greeted me with an embrace and this had the effect of removing any further curiosity in my plane's arrival. I forced myself to chat and have a coffee with the friendly owner of this fledgling airline.

All around the airfield were dozens of light aircraft, numbering over a hundred at a rough estimate. Every type of light aircraft from makers around the world was represented and in the far corner, next to the private airport stood a number of executive jets. Mariella's uncle left me with a list of the main airport's departures for that same evening with their times and destinations while he busied himself shouting orders at his pilots and organising the loads to be delivered to various jungle airstrips and villages.

On the first occasion that I'd gone down to Dolphin Lodge with Jack and Myron I remembered that we'd risen at the ungodly hour of three in the morning as we'd been told that we'd leave at first light. It had taken us all of the first two hours wait to recognise that Mariella's uncle had his own slick method of maximising his profits. This was to utilise the largest planes first if they could be filled. Two Shorts 360's and four Twin Otters were the largest in the fleet. Any remaining goods and passengers had to await the time when a profit could be made as most of the passengers arrived without any prior bookings. All loads were just allocated the next pilots to arrive whose duty appearances were suitably staggered. The three of us were slightly annoyed when we worked it out, the five hour wait meant that we consumed a fair number of beers, soft drinks and food at his restaurant. Although, it was the lost sleep that we objected to most, but Mariella's uncle apologised when he recognised that we'd tumbled to his little ploy and bought us a couple of beers to soothe our ruffled feathers. He was a character and we did recognise that his airfares were very low and that he didn't have a large margin of profit. It became a good dinner party story. I had studied the list of departures and decided that, as there were three aircraft leaving Panama within half an hour of one another at around six-thirty to seven in the evening, this would be my best time.

Watchers would be hungry, tired, or both and possibly changing shifts. A Boeing 747-Jumbo of American Airlines would leave first, then a 767 followed by a 727. The Jumbo would require a lot of passenger checking and as its destination was Miami, it would be subject to greater scrutiny. The Continental Airlines 767 was heading to San José, the capital city of Costa Rica and this would also be thoroughly checked. It was the San Salvador TACA- 727's destination of Managua that I was interested in and the fact that Sobatsu's people would regard it as my least likely choice. I hoped that this strategy of gaining sufficient time would work; the checkers would be getting fed up by that time and they'd have already spotted my name and passport number on the manifests of the other two aircraft. Would they consider that I'd buy three tickets to three different destinations I wondered. That was the $64,000 question! If only all three aircraft had available seats for purchase at the last minute. This would depend upon luck, although the tourist season having just started would help. It would take me a good hour to reach the International airport and as it had just gone four thirty in the afternoon the sun was fast dropping to the horizon. It was time to move.

I required a few western clothes to wear for passport control. Twenty precious minutes evaporated in purchasing my requirements, but I entered the main airport exactly on my scheduled time. I traced all the airline desks I required, feeling that I had a large placard proclaiming my name above my head. There were dozens of people I took for watchers, but none gave me a second glance. I realised that they were looking for a much portlier man than the new me! Having lost almost fifty to sixty pounds, I looked ten years younger, a fact that was brought home to me when an attractive blonde tried to engage me in conversation. For the first time in my life, I was rude in the face of such flattery, I hadn't time to waste, neither could I take any chances. I watched the roll-over electronic board as the time edged nearer to my self- appointed deadline of six-thirty; the three flights had been called and all were now boarding. It was now or never and screwing up my courage I approached the American Airlines desk, asking if they had a late seat and assuring the booking clerk that I'd no luggage other than a carry-on bag.

"No problem sir, but you have to hurry, they're calling the flight". I paid with the credit card I'd kept safe for such purposes.

There was no difficulty so far and no difficult questions to answer. Clutching my ticket I strode towards the international departures until I saw my clerk involved with another customer. I made for the check-in desks of Continental Airlines and went through the same procedure. Again no problems, but the perspiration was running down my face, neck and torso and I headed for the nearest rest rooms where I washed in cold water and used loads of paper towels before feeling dry and cool enough again. I had been visibly shaking and the cleaner asked me if I was alright, I said that I was recovering from a bout of malaria and hadn't fully shaken the symptoms, but thanked him kindly for his attention.

I entered one of the stalls so that I could gather my wits and gain a degree of control on my nerves. It was a very uptight Bernie Martin who finally emerged into the main booking foyer and I had gone to the wrong queue for TACA. before realising my mistake.

It was apparent that there was a flap on with some of the people I'd identified earlier as watchers. Groups of two's and three's were now apparent and mobile phones were the order of the day. A young, bronzed, film-star type was issuing orders to arriving knots of men and women, all of whom I took to be watchers. He was, fortunately for me, directing them to the American Airlines gate that had just closed. They'd tumbled to something and I was amazed to hear myself asking yet another booking clerk if there was a seat on the next flight to Managua. She confirmed that there was, but urgently repeated that,

"Si Señor, pero es necessario para tener prisa".

"Muchas gracias Señorita", pushing over my credit card and passport. I didn't require her admonition to hurry, but didn't wish to draw attention to myself by doing so. I felt like kissing her as I heard that the gate to San José had now closed and the last call to Managua was now being announced. The flight to Miami had resounded throughout the terminal, to my ears and mind, a drum-roll of victory. I was almost there, but careful, don't get cocky there's still many miles to go! However, by the groups of watchers, it was plain that they thought Martin was on his way to Miami and a few minutes later as I boarded the 727 I heard the San José flight taking off. I had to be shown to my seat, my usual ability of knowing at all times where I was, now having temporarily deserted me. The 'Take-a-Chance-Airline' had been my saviour, at least for the present. Never in the world of the condemned, I thought, had one of them enjoyed an airline meal so much, having outwitted the many; parodying a great man's words of fifty years ago. The courtesy liquors given with and after the meal were fully investigated and considerably enjoyed by me.

The next stage depended on Juan Zambrano's help. After Nicaragua it would be nigh on impossible for any organisation to track me because of the very short flights, the numerous airports that dealt with International flights and the US, now within easy reach. Panama had been a close thing. I realised that I could never expect such luck again and considered that it might be more prudent to use buses again. If only Juan has received my letter and isn't compromised, I thought, I'm almost home and dry! There was little chance of evading the Nicaraguan authorities. If they had been nobbled by Sobatsu's people, then without Juan's help I intended to plead for political asylum and consular aid. I hoped that he'd received my letter and would be at the airport to help me. I'd done all that I could by myself.

A shivering bout reminded me that I hadn't fully recovered from the malaria and that the tension of the previous three hours had taken an enormous toll of my physical strength. Beneficial, health-giving sleep finally overcame my feverish thoughts and I slept the sleep of the just.

Thirteen

Ardeth had made up her mind. She had spoken with her lawyer who had said that while technically she might not be justified in the removal of salary and supplements due to date, possession was nine tenths of the law, but advised her to leave full details of the money she was removing prior to leaving her job. She should also leave a letter of explanation together with her letter of resignation and a complete account of any cash discrepancy from the funds that she'd had in her charge. These, with the written reasons, would await her boss's return.

The lawyer added that it would be sensible to place the money into a deposit account with himself until he had established her legal entitlement. She had already taken the decision to phone Jack McAllister and warn him of Jefferson's operatives who were presently staying at the Red Fox Inn. And she had faxed both managers of Planet's Central American canneries, amending Jefferson's instructions to distribute the soft drinks in their territories and instead, make a limited batch with the third ingredient addition and to hold it for testing at venues convenient for Jefferson. Ardeth hoped that these measures would exonerate her and leave her free of complicity in anything illegal. It was with these points in mind that she was now in the process of clearing her desk and carrying out her lawyer's instructions.

Faxes from both Panama and Mexico confirmed that Jefferson's programme had been altered in time. There's something funny about that formula, she thought, as the fax machine spat out a message from Sobatsu Tokyo, confirming that they too wished the third ingredient to be put on hold. I'm glad I organised these changes, she thought as she re-read it before photocopying all the relevant faxes for her lawyer. She typed a reply to Tokyo confirming that the third ingredient had been used on a test batch only and that it was being held for inspection and would not be in general distribution. She added that she had taken this decision herself, Jefferson being unavailable and that she was terminating her own employment with Planet Ales Incorporated at the end of that present day.

"Now for that call to McAllister!", she said aloud to an empty office.

In Hampshire at Police Headquarters Portsmouth, Thurlston pondered over his phone call and the long conversation with his opposite number in The Hague.

The authorities in Curaçao were far from happy that Martin's mistress had met her death accidentally. They had recovered her mutilated body from one of the reefs offshore. Although the body had been badly eaten by sharks and other fish, their forensic medical team had found distinct signs that the young lady had been tied to the coral before drowning. The Dutch police were holding the skipper of the motor launch under suspicion of complicity and were trying to find the young Brazilian.

Thurlston dialled the M.I.6 number and spoke to one of the senior officers, receiving information that they too were now interested in the case and had transcripts of other calls made by Martin from various parts of South America. These had been passed to them by G.C.H.Q. who monitored phone calls that they plucked from the ether on a worldwide basis. The Central Intelligence Agency of the US had been informed and were also showing great interest in all relevant information and wished to be fully updated on developments. He placed a call to that agency and quickly got through to the agent in charge, a Jim Turner, whereupon he rapidly brought him up to date with all that he knew. As he replaced his own receiver he was aware that although the agent had been pleased to get further information, most of it was already known to the CIA and that they were pretty much on top of whatever Martin was up to. This chap Martin has got himself involved in something that's decidedly dodgy, thought Thurlston.

Meanwhile in Panama city, Señora Flores was en route to Sobatsu's offices to check the information on Martin's flight to Miami. Or was it yet another red herring, she wondered. They'd tracked another booking in Martin's name for a flight to Costa Rica, but had been delayed in the relay of this new information because of Juanito's officious and interfering orders to the team of watchers at the city's airport. Juanito had drawn all the watcher's off the wider hunt in a vain attempt to stop the Miami flight that had, by all accounts, taken-off before they could do anything about it. At least there was sufficient time to have her people organised for reception committees at both arrival points, she thought, but Jefferson would be furious and would no doubt be looking for blood. It wasn't going to be her blood, she decided, and ordered Juanito to return to the Intercontinental Hotel to await her arrival while she sorted out the mess.

"Mierda! Esta es un problema major", she voiced aloud. She had now decided that Juanito would have to be sacrificed if she was to escape Jefferson's wrath. Ah well, she sighed wistfully, he had really only been good for one thing, perhaps even the best ever, but the memory would have to suffice.

Nomura meantime had had his electronics boffins re-programme a message to the other eight's personal communicators with an urgent request for an emergency meeting of the nine, but this time minus Planet's CEO. The message left the other CEO's in no doubt that he was fully aware of the meeting in Dubai and of their discussions, but that he acknowledged all of their concerns and worries over his own exclusion and also that of Sobatsu's security arm. All of the CEO's would have the message before they left Dubai. His hope that all were in a like mind over Jefferson's paranoia and their own vulnerability had been fully justified by the faxes of confirmation to the immediate meeting. The venue in Cancun Mexico was certainly off the beaten track for the majority of them, but all would attend it in three days from now. He called Philippe in Panama City and in a carefully worded message gave him the authority to remove his annoying two thorns from the scene, prior to reporting to him again from the offices of Sobatsu where secure communications would be assured.

Nomura had chosen Cancun for the emergency meeting for a number of reasons. He could protect all from prying eyes and ears, as so many of his security people at Sobatsu were on the doorstep so to speak. Again Philippe was available for a full debriefing and new orders, after the nine had taken final decisions about how to deal with the problem. Jefferson would be cruising in the Caribbean, the working port for his yacht being Cancun. All guests, extra supplies, mail and banking facilities were now being channelled through this Mexican Riviera resort. He considered what was best for the test batches of soft drinks that had been made and canned, finally deciding to call Jefferson's secretary and have them delivered for Jefferson's attention at Cancun. They could then be dumped at sea as he was certain that the other eight would insist on the scrapping of the plan. Glancing at the clock, he realised that he'd just catch Jefferson's secretary before she terminated her employment.

Philippe received his boss's call and immediately recalled Parides and Louis to have a council of war in his room at the Caesar Park hotel. His next two calls were to the people who were shadowing Juanito and Flores, instructing those who were tracking Flores to contact him immediately she left the Sobatsu offices then headed back to her hotel. Now Señora, he contemplated. It's almost check-out time - permanently!

He poured himself a Margarita from a jugful on the coffee table and sat down to await his men. Nomura's not happy with Jefferson anyway, he considered, that much was evident and he'd learn the full details later when he called him back from the secure phone at the Sobatsu offices.

Flores sat fuming, as she listened to the final details of Martin's exceptionally clever second booking to San José in Costa Rica. It should have been obvious to her people at the airport. She'd already warned them about his cunning and his regular use of false trails. Damn Juanito, she'd better get it over with, she thought. She had better report to Jefferson, he would be on his way back from Dubai and the meeting there and she wondered also what the others had said about Philippe's permanent removal. There was just a slight chance that her people could get to the San José airport in time to grab Martin before he cleared Customs, but she doubted it. She wondered too what Nomura would think about it when he learned that his head of security has been retired for good and that Jefferson had appointed her to replace him? The Japanese had funny loyalties and sometimes didn't take kindly to being outmanoeuvred or outvoted, she reflected. Losing Martin yet again wouldn't enamour her to anyone, even if she could blame it on Juanito. She'd been in full charge this time, there would be no ducking of that responsibility and passing the buck would cut no ice with either Jefferson or with Nomura. Perhaps she could blame Parides somehow. Where the hell was he anyway? He kept dropping out of sight! This whole thing was a complete mess, she thought. We should have caught this 'hijo de perra' Martin. Damn and double damn Juanito! She dialled Jefferson's personal number and heard the call being forwarded to the Lear from New York. The wonders of technology, she thought, immediately coming to attention as a sharp "Yes!", announced that her boss had answered. Jefferson was livid beyond belief, she'd never heard him like that and his almost demonic screams of abuse made her quiver with fear. He was changing the Lear's flight plan and diverting to Panama.

Jefferson called his office in New York and left a message on the answer phone for Ardeth to deal with his faxed instructions when she arrived. He then instructed the stewardess to send Ardeth a fax with his intention to divert to Panama City for a business meeting and then go to Cancun to join the Venus. Would Ardeth also make arrangements to abort Mrs Jefferson's plans for the Antilles and make excuses to all the invited guests, giving crew illness as the excuse for the cancellation.

He buzzed for the hostess, ordered another Bacardi and cola, then pressed the intercom to the cockpit and snapped.

"You can cancel our refuelling stop in London and make a forty-eight hour stopover in Zurich instead. Then you can file flight plans thereafter for both Panama and Cancun, I haven't yet decided which I wish to visit first". Damn Martin and also Philippe and now, Flores' incompetence.

It was time to arrange his new life elsewhere and the necessary instructions had to be given to his Swiss bankers; he'd prepared for all eventualities.

Jack McAllister emerged from the bathroom, his face covered in lather, a small cut oozing blood as he'd nicked himself with the razor just as he had started to shave. The harsh ring of the phone had been a jolt to his nerves at the critical point of a clean stroke. He had been considering the impact of the e-mail that he and Carolyn had finally worked out, although he had to admit that the brilliance had been all Carolyn's. Devious that's what they were, he'd been thinking about her sex just as the phone had rung.

"Mr McAllister, this is Ardeth, Mr Jefferson's secretary phoning from New York. There is something I feel you should know".

Jack listened, his eyes narrowing. Well that's confirmed that, he thought, thanking Ardeth for her information and call. He telephoned Carolyn at her home. She'd been about to leave and come over to his house. Bringing her up to speed on the substance of Ardeth's call, had Carolyn saying that there was little point to their well planned e-mail.

"Send another Jack, asking Myron if he could give you a hand for ten minutes to move a new refrigerator or something you've just bought".

It was imperative that Myron knew of Ardeth's phone message immediately, but out of earshot of the couple. Jack punched in the keys to alert Myron's e-mail, requesting him to call as he needed help to move the fridge and had just replaced the phone and re-lathered when it rang again. A man's voice, identifying himself as Jim Turner an agent for the CIA., asked if he could call on him personally with regard to the papers that Jack had sent.

"Anytime you like", Jack answered. "And the sooner the better, it would appear that my friends and I are in need of your help ourselves. Whatever's going on now seemingly involves us". Jack proceeded to outline the Red Fox Inn's mysterious couple, their own suspicions about their presence and the rough outline of Ardeth's call. He answered the agent's questions quickly and accurately, agreeing to continue as normal and attend dinner at the Inn.

The agent and his partner were close by and would be with Jack in less than thirty minutes; delaying dinner would have been helpful, but he countermanded Jack's request for Myron to come round.

"That won't be necessary Mr McAllister", said the agent. "The couple will be arrested tonight before they even finish their dinner and possibly before they start".

Jim Turner turned to his partner Chuck Hanson saying,

"Drop me off at McAllister's, then head for the Red Fox and stake out the couple's car. You'd better call the office to have someone pick-up this Ardeth babe at Planet's offices; she sounds as though she could be a mine of information".

Ardeth read Jefferson's fax about the cancelled cruise, deciding that she'd better carry out these final instructions as the guests would shortly be making arrangements to join the Venus in Cancun. Mrs Jefferson was most upset having her holiday cancelled, but the guests were more understanding about crew illness and quarantine requirements.

Ardeth was carefully gathering all the papers that her lawyer had said were so necessary when the phone rang once more, "This is definitely my last action for Planet", she thought, and breathlessly replied.

"Yes Mr Nomura, I shall see to it before I leave. Thank you sir", as Nomura had congratulated her for her actions, indicating that her now ex-boss was mentally unbalanced.

The two faxes that Nomura had asked her to send were speedily typed and sent and as she put on her coat, the acknowledgements were coming through. She took the copies with her and left by the private entrance door, locking it behind her just as two men flashed their CIA identifications and asked her to accompany them.

Jack was relieved to see Jim Turner's ID, the agent rapidly asked questions as fast as Jack answered.

"Yes", said Jack, "Jefferson definitely sold me a bill of goods and because I was strapped for cash; I didn't notice the warning signals, it was Myron who became suspicious first".

Carolyn's car was turning into the drive and she entered as Jim Turner said,

"O.K. Jack, Hi there Carolyn, you guys go to dinner as though nothing is wrong. Maybe you should check your e-mail before I go, in case your buddy's replied".

It was Myron; e-mailing Jack on an operator to operator basis, there being no one else in the Inn. What's the problem buddy? Is the trap set?

Jack rapidly typed the reply, No problem, changed circs.- no need for a trap will reveal all in due course! Clue you in later. - Jack.

Promises, promises, that's all I ever get from you buddy boy, get your asses over here - the roast's ready!, Myron's reply had both Carolyn and Jack laughing to the agent's total bafflement.

"Private joke", said Jack and escorted Carolyn out to her car. "We'll take yours honey".

Five minutes later they were at the rear door of the Inn. Carolyn was given the job of chatting to the couple and dispensing glasses of wine while Jack helped Myron to carry through foodstuffs from the kitchen. Snatched opportunities with convenient clatters of various pans and dishes allowed Jack to say that the couple would be departing shortly, courtesy of the CIA.

Myron said,

"I hope someone's going to pay the bill, they've had nothing but the best since they arrived. Dinner's going to be a chatty time, I don't think". Myron was relieved of this particular strain with a rap on the fly-screen. Jim Turner entered the kitchen and asked if the couple were in the lounge. Jim indicated to Jack and Myron that they go into dinner and organise the seating areas, his partner would be ringing the front door bell in exactly two minutes. Turner was taking no chances and with Hanson's arrival at the front, he entered from the kitchen and identified themselves. There were no histrionics or attempts at escape, although the male suspect was found to be armed.

"If you hear anything further about your friend Bernie, Mr McAllister, you have my mobile number. Let us know instantly. Your own personal problems about this matter are over, but I think your friend's are just starting".

Handcuffed by light chains to ankle-cuffs, the pair were led to the car by Hanson leaving Turner to wish the three friends, "Bon Appetit". Myron's culinary efforts were fully appreciated, to a background discussion and immense speculation about Bernie and his whereabouts.

"At least said Jack, he's now got official backup".

"That's if they can find him", replied Myron.

"And there's no indication of where to start looking for him", Carolyn chipped in.

"Uh Huh!, these guys know what they're doing and never reveal what they know until the information is history", Jack replied between mouthfuls of roast pork and tiny roast potatoes. "You've excelled yourself tonight Myron, I'll bet you're glad that it wasn't wasted feeding those two Black widow spiders".

The pudding was followed by a selection of cheeses and coffee with choice of liqueurs. Carolyn added. "It's most unfair that my roasts don't have the flavour of Myron's, what's your secret?"

"Tender loving care", replied Myron.

"Right Myron old buddy, we'll give you a hand to clear the dishes before we head for home, why didn't you ask Turner who was going to pay your bill?"

"Damn-it", Myron grumbled. "With all the excitement, I plumb forgot".

As Jack and Carolyn entered the house, the telephone was ringing. Jack answered and spoke slowly and precisely with many, "No comprendo, and "ahora", or "en Ingles por favor", interspersed. After five minutes, he put the phone back on its cradle, Carolyn had been prepared with notepad and pen and looked at him expectantly.

"O.K., I know that was something about Bernie. Give! What's happening? Do you know where he is?"

"Si Senorita", Jack laughed, whirling her around.

"How d'ya like a vacation in Cancun? I've got some time due and Bernie will be there in a week. That was a friend of Bernie's in Nicaragua, saying that he left there yesterday and to let me know as long as it was safe to do so. Or words to that effect, my Spanish is rusty, much like that guy's English".

"Do you think it's wise Jack, it could be dangerous", said Carolyn. "And then again the CIA might not let us go".

"I don't intend to ask them and I know that if we needed Bernie's help, he'd be there for us. Cancun's a big place, but I'll bet that Bernie will try for that top hotel he bragged about. You know the one that he'd said deserved six stars, but where he got a discount just through asking. If we spot him we'll let him know that we're around, but let him contact us. We're highly unlikely to bump into Jefferson, whatever he's been up to; that man hires all his specialists and we don't exactly travel in the same circles".

"Shouldn't we phone Sally and let her know that Bernie's O.K.?", Carolyn asked. "She must be worried sick about all this".

"Yeah, although I'm pretty certain that Bernie's kept her pretty much in the dark so as not to worry her, but you're right. She deserves to know that he's safe and well. We can put her mind at rest and let her know that we're going to meet him in Cancun, but when you speak don't mention the CIA or any possible problems. We don't know what it's all about yet anyway and it'll only complicate things. In fact sweetheart, if it's necessary, cool the situation down", Jack added. "Bernie would appreciate it. I don't know if we can do anything to help down there, but it will give Bernie a tremendous lift to recognise that he's not alone. And he'll have a contact if he wants", he added.

Fourteen

As the aircraft emptied of people, I sat until the final passengers were about to leave before joining the crowds of people who had lined up in front of the Immigration officials.

Nicaragua was far more particular about passports and took an inordinate length of time to examine them. I felt certain that Sobatsu would have some form of contact with the Nicaraguan officials and reckoned that I would have to rely on officialdom's consideration and honesty. As the country was just recovering from a civil war which had occurred soon after the ousting of another bloody dictator, Somoza, I didn't place a great deal of faith in their fragile fledgling bureaucracy. My confidence was fast ebbing as there was no sign of my friend and I had resigned myself to my fate when a hand grabbed my upper arm from behind.

I turned in alarm to see Juan's grinning face and embracing me he almost shouted,

"¿Como esta mi buen amigo, tu es bien?"

"Muy bien amigo.¿Y tu?", I replied.

As on the first time that I'd met him upon visiting his country four years previously, he led me around the passport control and customs, giving a friendly hello and cheery wave to one or two of them as we went. "Regulations are for ordinary people", he said, and embraced me again.

In the battered old Volkswagen, tourist minibus we drove at breakneck speed out of the airport, his chatter amplified by many hand explanations that had me on the edge of my seat. Amazingly we avoided all other traffic and the numerous pedestrians who were sublimely unaware of my friend's devil-may-care attitude. In less than twenty minutes I'd answered a hundred questions about my problem and been regaled at length about the success of his business. I was very pleased to hear about the in's and out's of his postcard business which he ran alongside his job as a guide to his country. He delivered his company's postcards to the tourist hotels when he delivered or collected the tourists, so reducing his overheads.

His regular driver and friend, Bismar, would join us tomorrow as he was also involved in the business that had grown immensely during the past few years. I asked him how he'd found out which plane I'd be on and received the simple answer that his uncle was one of the senior immigration officials that he'd waved to at the airport and that there were only two flights from Panama every week. Juan had been called on his mobile phone (an essential aid for both his business and that of the agency) and told of my name being on the passenger manifest before my plane had been half-an-hour into its flight. As he'd been taking the tourist bus home every day, collecting and delivering Bismar to and from work, he had just driven directly to the airport when he heard of my name on the passenger list. I asked him if he'd had any contacts with the Sobatsu people and was relieved to find that there had been none. Sobatsu had offices in the city; Juan had checked on them after my letter, but was certain as he could be that they were supremely unaware of his existence. That was comforting at any rate, I thought. It was also good to relax in the company of a friend who was both on my side and willing to help.

Because of my insistence Juan agreed very reluctantly that we would not return to his apartment and have me stay with his family. It was too much of a risk for him and them. I would sleep in the minibus which would afford me reasonable comfort, because of its side door and large space immediately behind the front seats for luggage accommodation. We would eat at some roadside café. After our meal, having first obtained a couple of blankets, Juan drove to a locked compound where he parked near the rear, away from any prying eyes, saying that he'd return at dawn.

It was a long night. A single mosquito had gained entry and annoyed me on a regular basis until I finally nailed it and fell asleep. I woke with the door opening, relieved to see Juan's grinning face as he said that my bed hadn't been as comfortable as the one that I'd first enjoyed on my first trip to his country. I agreed wholeheartedly, remembering the comfort of Caesar's Palace, a five -star hotel at prices which Westerners found to be ridiculously low. We drove through the suburbs to collect Bismar. They used the bus for their own use with their boss's agreement as there was little tourist work.

During the journey Juan brought me up to date on his country. Manual labour was still paid little more than 50 Cordobas or around $7 per week, Bismar and his own average remuneration from the travel agency amounted to little more than $35 on a good week.

The postcards added another $10 to $15 during the tourist season with the occasional good week of double to triple that. Tourist tips added $5 as an average, depending on the clients' generosity.

We were taking a long detour to collect Bismar who now lived near to their new Cathedral. It came into view, its pink, red and green walls startling in their modernity, a gift from the International community to Nicaragua after the devastating Christmas earthquake of 1972. This magnificent place of worship with its palm-lined avenue and massive wrought iron gates had been a replacement for the original that was destroyed in the quake. The whole of the city centre had been wiped out and was being reconstructed away from the fault lines. There were still many gaunt, skeletal - framed buildings still occupied as housing for the poverty stricken country. A gigantic figure of a Sandanista waving an AK47 echoed the bloody birth of this nation into a young democracy. Somoza I thought, had wrought terrible havoc on his people whom he'd treated as little more than animals. Juan had shown me on my earlier visit, the dungeons where Somoza had incarcerated his enemies. They were underneath a Romanesque amphitheatre where lions and panthers had once torn the prisoners to pieces for his own personal pleasure.

As Bismar joined us, he shook hands vigorously with me and I felt humbled by the warmth expressed by both these men who had so little and whose nation had undergone such trauma. We called at the travel agency where their boss was delighted with the $100 for a supposed fast tour of Lake Nicaragua, the second largest freshwater lake in the world after Lake Baikal in Russia. There were no other tourists to service and Juan photocopied all the papers I carried, so as to retain a set in case of any misfortune happening to me. The road structure had vastly improved and the general infrastructure was geared for tourism. Nicaragua was making the most of its finest asset. It is a truly beautiful country of stunning perspectives with very friendly people. I reflected, that the ability to recover from such horrors, devastation and degradation was a great tribute to the indomitable spirit of humanity with the will to rebuild still retained. Bismar read the photocopies during the journey and related their contents to Juan, both were aghast at their implications.

We stopped for breakfast and a council of war and I explained to them that the sooner that I was across the border into Honduras the better. I'd been on my journey almost three months, Heaven alone knew what my boss and my family were thinking and I had these final papers to deliver to the FBI. Juan suggested that he telephone Sally and put her mind at rest, but I was not happy with this suggestion purely because Sobatsu operatives might trace the call and that would compromise the safety of his family and mine. I finally agreed to his call to my lawyers and gave him their number, agreeing also to his telephoning my American friend, Jack McAllister. If he were convinced that it was completely safe, then to inform Jack of my whereabouts and say that I expected to reach Cancun within six days or so.

It took the rest of the day to cover the appalling roads after Lake Managua which were dominated by the volcanoes of Masaya, smoking and still active in the distance, and also that of Mombachu. We finally reached the border crossing town of Ocotal and my friends refused the $200 that I entreated them to accept. I surreptitiously slipped them into Juan's coat pocket when we embraced again, before passing through immigration control, as I recognised that the costs of his telephone calls would eat into his fragile capital.

"Buena suerte mi amigo", said Juan and Bismar added.

"Vaya con Dios!"

It was with a heavy heart that I walked to the waiting bus bound for Tegucigalpa, the Capital city of Honduras. I could see the pair of them waving their goodbyes as the bus pulled away and I offered a fervent silent prayer for the safety and future of my two worthy friends. It never ceased to amaze me, the friendliness, compassion and true strength of character exhibited by the Central and South American peoples who had endured so much pain and poverty. These Latin peoples, with certain exceptions, were truly the salt of the earth, I thought. An awful sense of loneliness now overtook me as I tried to make up for the previous night's lost sleep.

The overnight coach had pulled into Tegucigalpa before I came awake once more, my loneliness increasing as I remembered my friends' salutations of "Good luck" and "Go with God". I daren't risk staying in the city for long and quickly found that another coach was leaving for the two day trip to San Pedro Sula in the north of the country in a few hours. Sufficient time for a wash, bolt down some food and obtain a ticket for that journey.

The roads in Honduras were, if anything, somewhat worse than those of Nicaragua, reflecting yet another poverty stricken country. I watched a flock of vultures rising in unison at the approach of our bus, the driver not slackening speed. Another guide had informed me when I'd travelled in the opposite direction many years previously that they were the scavengers that cleaned up the road kills and kept the country free of disease.

The bus stopped at Lake Yojoa where all the passengers descended, many of them to enjoy the freshwater bass that made the lake famous and which had dozens of restaurants alongside. After my meal I walked along the lakeside, there being two hours to kill before the next stage.

I disturbed a Quetzal, one of this area's most beautiful birds that resembled the lyre bird of Australia, if somewhat more colourful and, I recollected idly, the name given by the neighbouring Guatemalans to their currency. Finally I returned to the coach before it filled up with other travellers and to preserve a window seat to view the scenery. I had decided to rest for a day in San Pedro Sula, Honduras' second city, and would fly from there to Belize, a flight of little more than an hour and a half.

I spent my time with memories of another happier visit to this beautiful country when my guide, a young man of twenty-four who was training to be a lawyer, had supplemented his meagre income through escorting tourists. We'd driven down to Copan, the Athens of the lost Mayan civilisation, situated on the border with Guatemala. Honduras lost out to a large extent, their larger neighbour organising tourist visits from the other side of the border.

It had been a trip of visual magnificence with wonders equalling anything in Europe. The Mayan King, old 'Eighteen Rabbits' had been his titular name, had created an ancient city which compared well with the treasures of Greece. I smiled at the invading thought of the 'maybe later' kids who frequented the access to this site. Their begging methods from wealthy tourists would end with the plaintive cry of 'maybe later' when tourists weren't forthcoming with their money. As most generally agreed to this final request, to rid themselves of the little nuisances, they were amazed to be confronted upon exiting from the site, the urchins reminding them it was now, later!! I had also been highly amused by my guide's fast retort to my own observation about a cocoa tree outside the old museum in the town. I'd never seen cocoa beans growing before and volunteered that "it had been the currency of the times". His snappy reply of,

"Who said that money doesn't grow on trees", had me chuckling. The extreme poverty of his people had been emphasised on that particular journey by the sight of hordes of six to twelve year olds packing quicklime into plastic bags from a working lime kiln. He had told me that the locals used it to cook their food of maize cobs which they wrapped in leaves and that UNICEF had provided the kids with gloves and face masks to prevent their early death from lung cancer, as few lived into their twenties. The kids had sold the protective clothing and returned to their previous system, oblivious and uncaring about their own bleak future.

As the bus approached the outskirts of San Pedro Sula so the dead dog count rose, providing the vultures with many extra meals. It was a relief to relax in a room at the Gran Sula Hotel, although its displayed five-star rating belied the reality. Two restaurants and a swimming pool entitled it to the claim and it was also clean and relatively comfortable. The requirement of pouring Ron (their Rum), around the bed-legs was a necessity to prevent the occupant sharing a night's rest with hundreds of ants. It was a minor inconvenience and after a shower, I descended to reception and found that there was a flight to Belize City at lunchtime the following day. I spent the time wandering around the city, avoiding the many hundreds of cables connected to as many generators that gave power and light to traders' stalls and other businesses in the neighbouring streets. Honduras had suffered badly from 'El Nino' or global warming, no rain having fallen for years to replenish their reservoirs for their hydro electric facility. As I wandered through the streets I realised that I'd never seen so many pretty girls anywhere else in the world, but also that I'd never seen so many knickers and bra shops either.

There were sufficient of these to give all of the Honduran ladies a daily change of underwear for a year each! The mind boggled.

Returning to the main square, I had my shoes expertly cleaned by one of the dozens of 'limpiabotas' and listened to a lecture being given to a huge encircling crowd of people of all ages. It was on family planning, the birth rate and illegitimacy rate of the country being of worrying dimension. The speaker cleverly and astutely penetrated my disguise to recognise 'el gringo' among their number and made some pointed and unwarranted remarks, so I hastily retired for dinner and a bottle of wine before an early night. I had gone over my intended route to Cancun, both in my mind and on paper, and was now confident that I could now get to safety without encountering any of the opposition. My confidence was increasing with the extra 'Rons' after dinner and I'd also enjoyed a half bottle of Chilean wine. I counted my expenditure in Honduras for the three days, it hardly came to $150 dollars including bus fares, a night in a hostel and dinner bed and breakfast at the European equivalent of an excellent three star hotel. My cash dollars had lasted well, I thought, and I would treat myself to one of the best hotels in Cancun on my arrival there, although my credit card was nearing its expiry date. With that final thought, I fell asleep.

Next morning after breakfast and having paid my bill the night before, I went shopping for some clothes and a suitable suitcase. I would leave my check-out until later. Finding a small enough suitcase was a problem as the Hondurans appeared to wish to travel with almost literally, the kitchen sink. Their cases were generally enormous. It must be all those knickers, I thought wickedly! The average suitcase was one and a half times the size of the largest available in the rest of the world. Having found what I wanted, I collected my purchases together, returned to my hotel and asked them to order a taxi to take me to the airport. While awaiting its arrival I was highly amused to spot a sign at the rear of the hotel lobby advertising Blitz Rental Cars. It was, I thought, a typical example of Honduran humour, as the sign was in the colours and style of the famous Hertz. A fast trip through banana plantations to the city airport had me joining a small queue at the check-in.

The aircraft was far from full, but I'd been assigned a seat next to a young couple from New Zealand. Murf (Claire's pet-name for her long-term partner Stephen Murphy) and Claire were enjoyable company. They were part of that happy band of antipodean travellers who had between them covered every part of the world and continued to do so on a regular basis. Both in their early thirties, they were full of vim and vigour and echoed my own sentiments about the Latin Americans and their beautiful countries. Murf's heavy frame contrasted with Claire's svelte figure, but the couple complimented one another in their love of life and go-getting attitudes. As we passed over the port of Cortes and turned north we could see the machillas or industrial factory units that surrounded the town. Murf and Claire had been staying near there for a few days and explained that these factories were practically slave labour for the local population. Multinational companies paid miserable rates for production of their own branded goods which sold for enormous profits in the States and Europe; I agreed with their caring attitude, but said that it was almost impossible to alter the system. Without the work, many of the population would starve and the multi-national fruit companies had a monopoly over the country's fruit growing production. Murf advised against stopping off in Belize City, as many of the black inhabitants were on drugs and very dangerous. As they were heading for a week on an offshore island paradise and I had already been informed that my air connection to Cancun wasn't due until two and a half days time, I decided to join them.

After Juan and Bismar's friendship I now craved human contact and some form of European company, Murf and Claire's friendly disposition, chatter and world awareness was just the tonic I needed. Most of the next forty-eight hours was spent in their pleasant company, and as I kept my own counsel on the problems facing me for that length of time, I escaped into the unreality of San Pedro.

San Pedro is as close to a desert island as its 2,500 population would allow. This number increased fivefold during the height of the tourist season. The sandy beaches, its flora and fauna, the low cost, friendly people and the famous coral reef were among the many reasons for its popularity. The world famous Blue Hole was a diver's must and attracted the finest aqualung and scuba divers from around the globe. This, the second largest and completely unspoilt coral reef in the world was a temptation that even I couldn't resist. Murf, Claire and I found one of the worthies of the island, a Captain Ramon Badillo, who with skill and absolute knowledge of the reef, proceeded to show us the magnificent underwater world of corals, seaweeds and fish. The old Captain's leathery skin was burnt to an almost dark mahogany, his open smile revealing many missing teeth, but his extensive knowledge of his home-waters and life beneath the waves was encyclopaedic. We saw sea horses by the dozen, colourful parrot-fish and sergeant-majors whose strutting form of passage and their stripes evoked immediate recognition of their name. It was truly a paradise of monumental dimension. The pelicans fishing just outside the block of our self-catering apartments dive-bombed the fish in a continuous display of aerial agility, the screaming frigate birds making many of the gulls abandon their own hard-won booty. The mimosa grass that curled up at the slightest touch was fascinating. The natives who delivered freshly squeezed orange juice, coconut milk, banana drink and guava juice for just pennies in cost were an added, low-priced addition. Three or four good restaurants gave stunning meals of shellfish and other cuisine. The blue Morpheus butterflies flitted around the edges of the jungle area where bird life proliferated. It was truly an island paradise. Even the two nasties, a biting sandfly and an ant with huge pincer jaws, that the Indians used for stitching wounds, were reasonably easy to avoid and I vowed to return to this Eden wilderness before tourism destroyed it completely. Murf and Claire's knowledge of the mainland had me wishing I had more time, but reality returned and my leave-taking of these two friends over a couple of dozen Beliken beers in the Purple Parrot, a neighbouring bar with live music, was a sad affair in many ways. I did not wish to entangle my new friends in my problems and had to be on my way. I spent an hour of my final evening before retiring, walking along the beach, disturbing hundreds of crabs that scuttled for cover in the mangroves. These bushy trees with their long roots stabilised the silt from the flash floods in this part of the world and I found the tropical downpour, suddenly upon me, highly refreshing. It was like standing under a waterfall and cleared my head of the effects of the Beliken beers and I found that I'd walked down to the working fishermen's wharf. Two of the names of their boats, 'Salt an' Pepp' and 'Bottom-scratcher', raised my spirits once more helped me to face the two flights in the morning in a much happier frame of mind. The two days of friendship shared and the fun experienced with those two from down under had cleared the dark thoughts and refreshed my soul. A fast leave-taking of my friends, before they were up and about, had me heading for the airstrip and an hour later I was awaiting the arrival of my Air Jamaica flight to Cancun. The turbo-prop aircraft had Rolls Royce Dart engines which increased my faith in its ability, but I was shaken slightly by the fact that there was only one other passenger, a swarthy young Panamanian who was heading for the bright lights; our two pilots and the two air hostesses outnumbering the clients. With a degree of misgiving for choosing this route I thought that I couldn't exactly disappear in the crowd when we landed. However, it would be a totally unexpected direction for any watchers to concentrate upon, but I felt a little naked and vulnerable as we touched down in brilliant sunshine at Cancun airport.

Fifteen

The Venus slipped her moorings at Fort Lauderdale, making passage to Cancun in Mexico as per Jefferson's instructions. At 180 feet in length and fitted with twin 650 H.P. turbo -charged G.M. engines and fuel tankage of 6,000 gallons of diesel she could cruise the world, although she was generally confined to the Caribbean and her home waters. Fresh water tankage of 2,000 gallons and a further sewage tank of 2,200 gallons for pumping ashore for effluent disposal, were placed fore and aft of the fuel tankage to aid her stability and trim. Her sister ship, the Mercury had the same layout and equipment and cruised the Mediterranean, the Red Sea and the Gulf. She was eighteen months younger than the Venus, both having been built at the top Italian shipyard Benetti's in Viareggio. Radar, satellite navigators, three echo sounders, S.S.B., V.H.F. and ship to ship radio communications together with an auto-pilot were standard. A security vault was built into the superstructure and a large walk-in duty-free store and cellar were centrally placed below, forward next to the engine room which was kitted out with a 1,000 piece toolkit, various engineering equipment and impressive spares lockers. Each yacht had been completed at the bargain basement price of $25 Million, but were fitted with helicopter decks, carried twin 18 foot Rivas as tenders and a Mini-moke beach buggy. Jet skis, a four-wheel motor-bike, and a small sail boat were also carried along with all the usual scuba gear, skis, fishing equipment, etc. The main deck saloon had bar facilities that catered easily for 100 guests, the galley could cope with dinner parties of 50. A crew of sixteen serviced the needs of the vessel and its passengers. Twenty, twin and double cabins with en suite facilities were for guests. The crew were accommodated in three forward cabins. A luxury suite for the owner and a small double cabin for the Captain next to the wheelhouse completed the accommodation. Air conditioned throughout and with every known modern convenience fitted or at hand, the Mercury and the Venus merited their titles of 'floating gin palaces'. They were floating, five-star hotels, the last word in luxury that could go anywhere in the world. At their top cruising speeds of 16 knots, they were far from the fastest of their type as they had been built for maximum comfort and stability with reliable equipment that could be serviced anywhere and spares obtainable worldwide.

Captain André Schiffé was an Austrian by birth, his Yacht Master Ocean ticket having secured the position he now occupied. He was an experienced and highly competent man who looked the part. He and his crew wore whites whenever there were guests aboard, which was during seven months of the year. The Captain and his first-officer also wore braided caps and epaulettes; it impressed both guests and harbour masters alike and added to the ambience. The crew wore white shirts and white trousers or shorts, depending on the prevailing weather conditions, their shirts emblazoned with the yacht's name, embroidered in blue and gold. Cabins were equipped with soft, luxury towelling gowns and soft, Muslim-style slippers which were monogrammed with the yacht's initials. As in all luxury hotels, the guests were expected to retain them for their own future use. The Waldorf, Savoy, Danielle, Raffles, Mandarin or Ritz would be hard pressed to deliver greater luxury.

Captain André found the lifestyle much to his liking, as did most of the crew, generally all of them appearing for all of the trips and few replacements were necessary. They were well paid, but the 'pourboires', thank-you's or tips from the passengers could double or even triple their salaries. Work was hard and long days were expected by himself and the crew when they were at sea or had guests aboard. Eighteen hour days were the norm, but the working trips flew past and there were many other extra compensations.

As the Captain, André was expected to join the guests at all meals and make himself available for small talk with the ladies or enter discussions about the ship with the men. Occasionally with the top VIP's, he'd have to escort a guest on a tour of his vessel, but thankfully he could mostly delegate this chore to the first officer or the senior steward. So it was that the Captain read the list of passengers who would board at Cancun to cruise in the Antilles, the pecking order that Jefferson placed them in, with the specials in dark print for extra attention. The boss might be a difficult man, André thought, but at least he was exact with his stated requirements and it made life aboard that much easier. All of the crew would be informed of the guests names, their foibles, needs and wishes. By the time they'd arrived in Cancun in another ten days, each crew member would know them personally as the boss's secretary provided photographs of all the guests as standard procedure. All the lady guests would be presented with a memento of their trip, a tiny yacht carved in lapis lazuli set in silver on a solid silver anchor. The male guests could have their choice of cigars, quality malts or the top bourbons. The gifts for the men were specially labelled in the company's colours with the yacht's name on attached small silver plaques. Nothing was left to chance, the final detail on the instructions giving a list of those who had especial preferences for certain wines, cigars, spirits, teas and coffees. These last specialities would come down from New York by FedEx, or on occasion, by the Lear. The Venus carried a wide ranging wine cellar, fully gimbaled, so that the wines were not disturbed by rough weather. Her storerooms were the envy of all visiting Captains, even those of the classic Ocean liners.

It was a most satisfying position to hold, Captain André considered, it was only a very few of the guests that he'd personally wished to cast adrift or maroon on a convenient desert island over the years. Most of them had been very gracious, heedful of his orders and careful with the yacht's equipment. Very occasionally there would be an arrogant loudmouth who demanded that the world crawled on its hands and knees around him and who could endanger his ship through stupid requests as well as make life unpleasant for all. Unfortunately his boss fell into this category; it was always a relief to see a manifest without his name on it. This voyage was not to be one of the easiest, Jefferson's and his wife's names headed the list, although Mrs Jefferson was a far more pleasant person than her husband and often defused potentially difficult situations. At least there would be some control on his bombast, André thought wryly.

The crew were hard at work repainting the upper sundeck and all the davits, rubbing down the teak handrails for the umpteenth coat of varnish. He'd lost count of how many coats his crew had applied, the depth of varnish now shone like glass. The engineer was stripping all the shower units and pumps for the lavatories, it was funny how all landlubbers felt that facilities afloat should be the same as those at home. Toilets gave the greatest problems as guests ignored requests not to use them as disposal units for trash, etc. All those who hadn't sailed before were quickly identified by blocked loos and flooded shower compartments, usually once but often twice before they came to terms with it. The pressure sets for water circulation around the yacht had just been returned from a full service, so at least there would be no trouble with that particular area, he thought. The two chefs declared themselves satisfied with the stores carried and their expertise was ably supplemented by other members of the crew behind the scenes when it was necessary. Two massive deep-freeze rooms and a large chill room were situated at the after end of the engine room. These together with the stores at the forward end, ensured that noise from the engine room wouldn't disturb the guests.

The two stewards could be temperamental, chosen more for their looks and charm to the lady guests than for work output, although they did serve the guests perfectly. It was with their other duties where they didn't pull their weight fully. He sighed; it was a price that had to be paid. If the ladies were happy on the cruise, then the men were usually delighted as they were assured of pleasant partners for many months to come. The helicopter was in use most days, obtaining newspapers, mail, fresh fruit and flowers or taking guests on sight seeing tours of the uninhabited islands in the area. The pilot, who wore light blues to signify his specialist position, doubled his duties by laying off all the new courses for the yacht and priming the satellite navigation with the information prior to the Captain's final check. None of the crew was allowed to be idle at any time, although regular breaks were given to all except when entering or leaving port. The stewards, when on duty in the saloon serving either food or drinks, wore neck-high, fitted white jackets and white gloves.

Video tapes of the latest films and CD's of a wide variety of music were available from a well stocked library in the saloon. All cabins were equipped with TV's, VCR's and CD players, the large screen in the deck saloon being used for the CNN or ABC News broadcasts almost exclusively. An M.16 automatic rifle, two .38 revolvers and four shotguns were located in a security gun-cupboard in the Captain's cabin. The shotguns were used for skeet or clay pigeon shooting from the fore or after-deck and the rifle and pistols in case of pirates. Thankfully, this problem was not common in either the Mediterranean or the Caribbean, but could be encountered in the South seas.

The Captain laid out the new Log that detailed all of the yacht's daily functions, courses, distances, servicing, weather both expected and encountered and all other active duties undertaken by himself and crew during the cruise. He'd learnt this trick from a Scots Captain when working in the Western Mediterranean. The Scots Captain had found that it was avidly read by all the passengers that he'd had aboard. It greatly reduced the problems and more especially, the aggravation caused by unthinking landlubbers who would go out on deck at night during night voyages without informing the bridge first. Many did not realise the dangers of a sudden gust of wind, a freak wave or even night blindness causing a passenger to stumble over the deck furniture and fall overboard. Lower handrails on luxury yachts, mainly for aesthetic reasons, hadn't the inherent safety of the chest-high ones found on ocean liners and ferries. Again by itemising fuel, food, harbour fees and services with costs; he'd found that the final accounts rendered at the end of a charter were much easier to understand by whoever was paymaster. It had proven to be so and also ensured that guests were aware of just how hard the crew worked, so alleviating the uncaring actions of the few. André had cause to bless that canny Scotsman on many an occasion, and none could argue with what was entered in the Log. It was a permanent record and stupid mistakes or thoughtlessness, while often entered in a diplomatic fashion, were seldom duplicated by the same passenger. Pretty much like an end of term report card, he thought, smiling to himself.

Captain André sighed with quiet contentment, everything was in order and in perfect condition. The Fax machine was spewing out another message as he entered the wheelhouse/Bridge of the yacht, but he left it for later as he checked the course and radar. A few words with his helmsman, one of the senior crewmen who was entrusted with Bridge duties, confirming that all was well. Dependable people made the job that much easier. Venus would be tying up shortly as they were now in the approach channel for Cancun where the final stores and extras would be taken aboard. The guests would be arriving in another ten days and he felt confident that everything would be perfect for their arrival. The crew would be given a few days shore leave prior to the guests arrival.

The bleep of the fax reminded him of the awaiting message and he picked it up en route to his cabin; it was his habit to read all of his instructions in private before relaying the content, if necessary, to crew members. Captain André couldn't believe his eyes, the cruise had been cancelled; he had to read the fax twice before coming to grips with it. Never, in his seven years of service aboard the Venus, had there been such a last minute cancellation. What did it signify? Was the yacht about to be sold? There had been no mention of another being built, and the fax had included orders to have new charts and pilot books aboard for a trip to Rio de Janeiro. Why there? A possible buyer? Or another movie in the making? Both the Venus and the Mercury had played starring roles on celluloid in the past; although their true identities had been masked. Charters and these valued extras helped to pay the bills of many of the large yachts. But there had been no indication of this and Jefferson wouldn't cancel a cruise just for money. It was inexplicable. He would follow the orders and be ready for sea when Jefferson arrived, but he'd no doubt the crew wouldn't like being put on a short leash when in port with no guests, having also their lost shore leave. He'd have to make sure that they were fully occupied by inventing other work to be completed before Jefferson's appearance, but which would keep them within an hour or so's mustering time. Apart from the first night ashore, the bars would have to be off limits as they were when cruising. If Jefferson was only by himself, a full complement would not be required, but the delay with Port authorities, the form-filling and leaving missing crew members' passports with Immigration could take-up considerable time. The crew would be unhappy without their tax-free cash from the cruising guests; André knew that many of them lived to the maximum and depended upon the generous tips. He would have to give careful thought to his strategy and rang the galley for a pot of coffee as they would be docking in another two hours.

Ah well, he thought, without Jefferson there would have been precious few problems, but without Jefferson there would have been no job. I suppose this is one of the times where I justify my salary and the extras, he reflected. A knock on his cabin door, preceded the steward's entry with a steaming pot of coffee, china cup and saucer with a matching sugar bowl, their blue and gold motifs reflecting upon the silver tray.

A good hour later, Captain André had made his plans and flipped the switch of the Tannoy, connecting all parts of the yacht.

"This is your Captain, I've just received a fax from Mr Jefferson, cancelling the cruise around the Antilles, our scheduled guests will not be arriving and instead we will have Mr Jefferson only. He wishes to sail to Rio within an hour of his embarkation and will be arriving sometime during the next forty-eight hours. Accordingly, I have decided that we will not require a full complement and will extend paid leave for half-a-dozen of you, but those who volunteer to go ashore or return home will hold themselves available to return within thirty-six hours notice. Flights will be paid by the company both ways and will be conditional on compliance with this requirement. As we have never had the time during the past year to tidy our dry goods storage and bring its inventory up to date, as well as clear any outdated stocks, the store will be cleared into our onshore storage and the storeroom cleaned and disinfected while we are in Cancun. There will be no shore leave on this occasion apart from a four hour initial break on first docking. Any crew member who fails to return after this break will have his contract terminated immediately and have a one-way flight back to the States. That is all. Thank you for your attention".

The First Officer was at the cabin door as he opened it, his facial expression denoting his annoyance.

"O.K. First, there's nothing I can do about it. Read the new orders, then organise us with the necessary charts and pilot books. We'll also need tide tables for the eastern coast of South America".

In reply to his First officer's queries Andre replied.

"I know nothing more than what the fax states, I don't even know what it means, but we have our orders. Let me know who wishes to go home on paid leave, we'll still require one of the chefs and a steward and of course the Chief engineer. Our chopper pilot and yourself will stay aboard for the trip, I'll review the others when you give me the list of those who wish to go ashore. Reinforce my warning about tardiness in returning aboard tonight, there will be no second chances given or excuses accepted. Understood?"

"Yes Captain", the First replied, recognising that to argue with Captain Schiffé would be pointless.

"Organise the men to start on the storeroom first thing in the morning. And you'd better order the transport tonight for first thing tomorrow", André added.

Half-an hour later they were tied up alongside one of the working wharves of Cancun's merchant port facilities. They shared part of a large warehouse facility with their parent company's distribution arm and could draw on its transport when required. The shore connectors for electricity, telephone and fresh water supply were quickly run ashore and within ten minutes they had a quiet ship as the generators were shut down. The four hour shore-leave break would begin at the top of the hour. André retired to the chartroom to check his manifests and requirements for morning, having already ordered bunkering for delivery mid-morning next day. Whatever Jefferson had in mind for the Venus, she would be ready. Speculation as to what Jefferson had in mind was a useless exercise. They'd know soon enough. He knew without overhearing the muttered, but muted comments that his crew were far from happy with their new orders.

All of the crew had returned well within his deadline, which made selection for shore-leave an easier task. Six of them would fly out the next morning. A flatbed truck was already being loaded with the storeroom's dry-goods. The usual good-natured banter from the crew was missing on this occasion. It took five trips to empty everything, but the storeroom had been thoroughly cleaned and disinfected before mid-day. All afternoon would be necessary to have the stocks replenished and any old stock changed, but there had been no further contact from Jefferson, so André relaxed a little. There would be no delay to sailing within an hour of Jefferson's arrival. It was unlikely that he would arrive that night and in a further four hour's they would have the work completed. Fuel tanks had been topped-up, water, oil, charts and pilot books were aboard and the engineer could be allocated two crew members to help him with last minute painting and tidying of the engine-room. Jefferson demanded that the vessel looked like new on every voyage. There would be no reason for any complaints in that department, André considered, now that the storeroom had been given a thorough cleaning job.

The four deckhands who'd been assigned to the heavy work of removal of all the goods to the warehouse and their return had been grumbling amongst themselves. The loss of their tips was a severe blow to all of them, their future drinking and gambling money was now much impaired. Guesses as to what was afoot gave nothing but possibilities, none of them was comforting. The leader of the shore detail said.

"O.K. mates, we're out of luck this trip. It's time to make our own", and pointed to a stack of Planet soft-drinks on a shrink-wrapped pallet which had a large label proclaiming its special delivery for Mr Jefferson's personal attention.

"We've skimmed in the past guys and this sure looks like the last trip of the Venus to me, these shiny bastards don't give a shit for the grafters. We'll collar this lot instead of what the Cap'n ordered, he'll never know the difference. There's a cool thousand dollars worth on those planks of timber. It'll divide nicely. With the last couple of cruises, we have already cleared another two thousand each through buying Planet's soft drinks in Cancun rather than having them loaded at Fort Lauderdale, so this will help compensate us this time for the loss of our beer money. It has beaten me why our boss always insisted in taking his products with him rather than buying them at less than a third of the price down in Cancun, but that's these clever dicks for you, can't see where true profits can be made!"

The others laughed at their leader's remarks, all of them shared equally in the scams that he'd devised over the years. The bosun had established a dummy company many years previously for the supply of goods to the Venus and all of the deckies had kept a weather eye open for the opportunity to make an extra dollar or two. As they handled all of the stores, it was a simple matter to change purchase orders and direct payments to their dummy company.

"Will the check be issued in time for shore leave in Rio, bosun?", asked one of the deckies. "No problem, it will take three weeks to get there, maybe a month and the mail will be collected as we go".

Another one of them remarked,

"How about the tag, it's designated - for Señor Jefferson's personal attention".

"Get rid of it, it's not important, we'll bill the local distributor for this load. Get the numbers off some of those crates destined for the offshore islands, so that we can be paid immediately. No hold on. Better put the tag on one of the other pallets, just in case there is someone delegated to trace it. It wouldn't do to have the company's inventory upset. We might not be paid for a couple of months and I hear that these Brazilian dames can be real friendly".

Captain André was both puzzled yet relieved at his crewmen's changed attitude when they delivered the last load to the storeroom and presented all the dockets for his signature,thereby sanctioning payment for the goods.

"Well Bosun, the crew seem to have accepted the loss of their extras and taken it like men".

"Yes Cap'n. They've decided that they like the sound of Rio if they get some shore-leave there".

"Good, then take these dockets to the First and have him despatch them ashore for payment", handing the sheaf of papers to the Bosun. "Tell the men that they've done a good job".

"Yes Cap'n". There was broad grin on the Bosun's face as he left the chartroom. Crew moods, André pondered, I'll never figure them out! Ah well, he considered, it was always best to have a happy crew, but he doubted that there would be sufficient shore leave in Rio to satisfy their needs.

Sixteen

"Fraser, this is Sally speaking, where the hell is Bernard?"

"I'm sorry Sally I'm not at liberty to give you that information", replied Fraser.

"Damn it Fraser, I'm your client too, and if I don't get your co-operation this instant I'll see to it your firm never gets any of our business ever again, and I'll spread the word. I've had a postcard from Bernard that was posted in Panama and I know that he's been very ill, but also that he's involved with something much more dangerous than just malaria. If you don't give me some information I'll crucify you and your damned business!", Sally almost shrieked down the phone. "So you had better tell me something believable! I'm sick to death of this, he'll be alright patter and your other palliatives that you trot out for widows and orphans! Am I making myself clear Fraser?"

"Perfectly Sally and I do apologise, I've only tried to protect you from unnecessary worry. I had a phone call this morning from one of his friends in Managua Nicaragua, a Juan Zambrano who's brought me up to date with Bernard's movements, but don't go off half-cocked, I'm going to suggest that you phone Chief Inspector Thurlston and ask him all about it. I've already telephoned him with Zambrano's information and the Chief Inspector is the best person to advise you of any further action. I'll give you his number, you should get him in just now".

Sally rang off and dialled Thurlston's number. Her temper was up and no-one was going to stand in her way! The duty officer who answered her call was told that if Thurlston didn't immediately answer that she would be around to the station and would await his arrival. She considered while waiting on the line, that Bernard had been a good, even a great provider for the family and herself and a very good father. The children definitely loved him, she reflected. Perhaps I haven't shown enough interest in his work, but then I had more than sufficient cooking, housework and clothes to wash for the family, it hadn't been easy, especially in the early years. With two children, the scraping to make ends meet and a large mortgage, much of the early stresses had concerned money. They had come a long way. Her reverie was interrupted by a smooth, controlled and soothing voice as the Chief Inspector introduced himself, he'd just heard from the lawyer of her Boadicean outburst on his other line.

"Mrs Martin, I think that it's now time for us to have a long chat, when would it be convenient for me to call upon you? After lunch around two? That will be perfect for me. Until then Mrs Martin, goodbye".

Thurlston looked at the clock. Eleven. Not yet office hours in New York, but I'll book a call to that chap, what's his name, Turner? Aha! that's it, he thought. Might as well make it all the CIA's problem. After all, they're nearest and I still don't know all the angles.

Sally opened the door to the policeman precisely at two.

"Good afternoon Chief Inspector, won't you come through to the sitting-room", as she led the way. Thurlston studied Mrs Martin closely and agreed mentally with the lawyer's assessment of her character. This was a powerful woman with definite strength of character and a very attractive one. At five foot nine inches in height, her dark frizzy hair had just been re-hennaed, adding to her aura. The high cheekbones and her green eyes, high-lighted by subtle shading of eye shadow, were even more impacting than the obvious intelligence she displayed. A well distributed but trim figure enhanced the smartly tailored tan trousers and peach-coloured cashmere sweater that she was wearing. Thurlston decided that the whole truth was best or this formidable lady would be looking for someone's blood and he was too near retirement to sustain any blasts from his Chief Super.

"We know that your husband is heading for Cancun Mrs Martin and should be there within the next few days. We've been informed by one of his friends in Central America that he's now fully recovered from his tropical illness and that he's carrying written material that others would like to have returned. He has witnessed the murder of an American agent in Tierra del Fuego and somehow obtained these writings that all the security agencies in the West would now like to study. Our security agencies believe that he is being pursued by the killers of the murdered agent and so aim to recover the missing documents and they too are converging on Cancun. As I speak special agents of the Central Intelligence Agency of the US are en route, to ensure your husband's safety. They have strict instructions to protect him from these killers. We shall be advised immediately they have him in their protective custody and they would much appreciate a recent photograph of him for identification purposes. If you could oblige me with one Mrs Martin and if you have no other questions I can assist with, I'll return to my office and fax the photo immediately. From what we've learned, you have an able and courageous husband who puts duty and country before his own safety Mrs Martin".

"Thank you Inspector. Yes I have a recent photograph, taken just a week before he left on this business trip. I have it waiting for you as I anticipated your request". Sally handed over the photograph saying as she did so "and I'm flying out to Cancun on the next available flight, so don't bother to advise me against it, you'll be wasting your breath. I don't know what I can do, but I intend to be there if my husband has any difficulties".

A very strong woman, thought Thurlston, as he was shown to the door.

"Good afternoon Mrs Martin. Your husband is a very fortunate man to have such a wife. I hope that everything goes well for you both".

Sally closed the door and lent heavily against it. The final truth and enormity of it all was now turning her legs temporarily to jelly. My goodness Bernard, what on earth have you got yourself into my impetuous darling? Hold on my love, I'm coming to support you if nothing else.

Sally's mind settled and calm resolve took over. The phone was ringing. Jack and Carolyn's call reinforced her decision to fly to Cancun. Bernard was definitely in need of all the help that he could get and she was going to be on hand to do whatever was necessary. Where the hell was Cancun anyway and how do I get there?, she wondered. I should have asked Carolyn. Oh well, at least I know the name of Bernard's favourite hotel. The Fiesta Americana, if I remember rightly. It's odd, but I never thought to ask where the city was. My fault there I think. Now for that matter, where was her passport and was it still valid? She would need money too, although Bernard had insisted that she had her own credit card. Bernard's solo foreign travels would be curtailed after this, she determined. They were very well off with major investments and Bernard could afford to take early retirement and enjoy more of life. There was much to do and organise, the travel agent would be her first call.

Jorgé Philippe had issued his instructions to Parides and Louis who had acquired the assistance of other two local men just in case extra manpower was required. They were now about to leave for the Intercontinental to pay a final visit on Señora Flores and her bodyguard/gigolo. Philippe allowed his mind to dwell on the envisaged actions that were about to follow. The accident that you intended for me Señora, is now about to happen to yourself. That final thought left him smiling in an anticipatory, calculated fashion.

As Philippe sat back in the rental car, driven by Parides with Louis beside him, he said to his men.

"The hired men can stick around the elevators on the penthouse floor, there's already two Sobatsu people covering the lobby. I want both of you with me in the suite to take care of the Señora's accident. We shouldn't be interrupted, but if it's necessary to shoot both of them, then we get out fast. I want you Parides to give glamour boy his first and last flying lesson, but allow sufficient time for Flores to take it all in. Then she can follow. We'll leave the cars a little away from the hotel and get out quickly after the Señora has made her own graceful exit. The area will be swarming with police within twenty minutes after glamour boy's flight, so we will only have five minutes or so to get completely clear, allowing just sufficient time for the first lesson to be fully understood by Flores".

The Lear had hardly come to a halt at Panama city's private airport when a limousine came alongside. Jefferson entered quickly and was whisked over to the Immigration Office. A perfunctory examination of his passport was made and the requisite stamp applied, the authorities having been made fully aware of his flying visit en route to Cancun. He would not be staying in the country this trip. He'd already telephoned the Señora and was only in Panama to get the full details about Martin from Flores in person. If he, Jefferson, had to flee into exile in Brasil, then he would make certain he didn't leave any loose mouths as convenient witnesses for the authorities. She had, after all, been worse than useless as Philippe's replacement.

The two cars had been parked within two minutes fast walking from the Intercontinental. Philippe made certain that they wouldn't be hemmed in by other traffic and that both vehicles were ready for an immediate getaway. The five of them entered the hotel lobby to be met briefly by the other two Sobatsu operatives who then stationed themselves at strategic points, leaving the group to enter one of the elevators on their way to the penthouse suites.

Señora Flores was in a state of distraught anger as she berated Juanito for his incompetence. She had just received Jefferson's call that he was about to land at the city centre airport and that he'd be with her within the hour.

"Mierda Juanito, what the hell did you think you were doing? Martin was in the bag, you should have left my people to do their job. It's down to you that they missed him, but I'll pay the price - make no mistake!"

"I'll explain that it was my fault to Señor Jefferson, Señora", mumbled Juanito nervously. Anyway, no-one saw Martin, so he must have been disguised and again no-one could have expected him to book three different airlines, let alone all three leaving within half an hour of each other", he added lamely. "Martin must have researched the flights very carefully and must have had help to gain such accurate information. It was almost split-second timing", he continued, trying to justify his precipitate actions.

"Get that Juanito", the Señora said as the buzzer sounded at the suite's entrance door. It can't be Jefferson already, she thought, with a rapid look at her reflection in her mirror while searching frantically for her make-up. Her world was falling apart, the comfortable salary and perquisites were about to vanish. Her perceived early retirement from Sobatsu security now seemed imminent. There were no excuses for any of it.

"Buenos tardes Señora", Philippe said as he, Parides and Louis entered the room. Parides had Juanito in an arm and neck-lock while Louis blocked off any chance of escape. Señora Flores' face reflected a whole gamut of emotions, disbelief changing to astonishment, then panic and sheer terror as the final knowledge of who was addressing her fully sank in. Her jaw dropped and she croaked,

"Señor Philippe, I read about your accident. You're dead". Her final words were hardly above a whisper and the lipstick dropped from her nerveless fingers, smudging the application. A crooked smile of tortured realisation now adorned her pasty features as she sank back into one of the armchairs.

"The reports of my demise were greatly exaggerated Señora, with a little help from my friends as you can see", Philippe replied, now greatly enjoying her extreme terror.

"Then who died?" she croaked.

"Your lieutenant and assassin Hauptmann, Señora and one of his hired hoods from Caracas", replied Philippe, opening the French windows to the balcony.

"You have been a thorn in my flesh ever since I employed you Señora and given me nothing but problems. It is now time for me to collect on your debt. I have learnt from Parides that it was you who ordered him to deliver the epidiascope to São Paulo and it was you who should have had it checked, yet it was me who was blamed for that incompetence, which was then ably amplified by you".

Flores sat ashen-faced, her panic-stricken eyes darting here and there, any pleas for clemency would be a waste of breath. Juanito had sagged in Parides vice-like grip, there was no help forthcoming from that source.

"What do you intend Jorgé?" she asked, recognising the close proximity of death. Jefferson will be here shortly, I'll explain to him that it was all my fault. He'll re-instate you as head of security".

"No Señora, it is much too late for that and Jefferson is not known for admitting his mistakes. He prefers to remove them, as I also intend to do. It is a magnificent view from here, as you observed earlier to Parides. I think it's time that both of you had a much closer inspection of it". He stood adroitly aside as Parides propelled a screaming Juanito over the edge. A full three seconds of screaming was cut short and Philippe looked over the balcony observing,

"Such a mess on the sidewalk and he was such a pretty young man. You will cause me no further annoyance Señora Flores". Flores' rush for the door was easily prevented by Louis and her snarl of defiance was silenced by Parides who grabbed her from behind and frog - marched her to the balcony. Spitting with hatred, she was forced to look at the dread spectacle five hundred feet beneath, with many tiny figures rushing hither and thither. White faces were looking upwards and muted shouts reached their ears as Philippe finally said in a calm and controlled voice.

"A fitting end wouldn't you say Señora, a lover's tryst with sweet death", nodding to Parides who pitched her over the edge.

"Let's go!" said Philippe, not bothering to look, and headed for the door.

Collecting his men, they used the fire exit to the floor below and took one of the elevators to the second floor before using the fire exit again to the lobby on the ground floor. The Sobatsu operatives beckoned the group to a side exit and they made good their escape, unobserved by the hotel staff, who were in a state of great consternation. Philippe's little group regained their cars and made a clean getaway, heading for the offices of Sobatsu. Philippe had a report to make and receive fresh orders.

Jefferson's limousine drew up at the gathering knot of people in front of the Hotel Intercontinental. Señora Flores' body hit the sidewalk beside the car just as he exited. Abruptly, he re-entered the limo saying only, "The airport driver, and quickly!"

Philippe poured large rums and colas for the six men and himself,

"Al salud de nosotros compadres, eso trabajo haciendo muy bien!"; saluting his team on a job well done, continuing, "Louis you can return to Bogotá. Parides, my friend, I require you here. My operatives will pay you two others in the outer office as I shall only require their expertise from now on. Thank you for your assistance", thus dismissing the local talent. He looked at the clock. Eleven p.m. It wasn't too late to phone Nomura.

"Nomura speaking". He'd been expecting Philippe's call for over an hour and was anxious to be apprised of what had happened, but first castigated Philippe for encouraging Jefferson to use the ultimate sanction without reference to himself.

"All the members of the Top Ten were against such an action and they insist that you face disciplinary action. There is a meeting of the nine where everything will be reviewed, without Jefferson. It is scheduled for tomorrow morning at the Fiesta Americana Condessa in the hotel tourist zone where we are staying. Report to me there!"

Philippe apologised profusely about advocating the use of Jefferson's ultimate sanction, saying only that Jefferson's requirement of Martin's immediate removal and demise had stampeded his own thinking.

"And where do your people think Martin is at present?" Nomura asked, after hearing that the Señora and her paramour had been liquidated and would no longer be a nuisance. Their incompetence in Panama had been unpardonable.

"As his Passport number came up on a flight from Honduras to Belize, we have worked out that he used overland buses from Managua and flew into Belize City from San Pedro Sula yesterday", replied Philippe. "We reckon that he's heading for Cancun and may even be there already. He's been exceptionally clever and eluded all our people, none of whom have even seen him apart from brief glimpses in Santiago and Iquitos. Martin's definitely not like his photographs and must be receiving outside help to get this far, but what he's calling himself and what he looks like we have no way of knowing. It's been like pursuing a ghost, Panama was quite literally, our last opportunity of catching him. His method of booking and paying for three different, but consecutive flights out of Panama, all of them leaving within a half hour of one another, was brilliant and never even remotely anticipated. I am now organising men to move into Cancun, but now that he's in Mexico I have little faith that we can stop him delivering the papers to the Americans".

"Thank you Philippe, that's my own reading of the situation I'll now prepare an alternative strategy that divorces the other nine members of the Top Ten from Jefferson's actions. Advise Sobatsu security to be in attendance at our first meeting in the morning".

"Yes sir! I'll see to it immediately", answered Philippe. Nomura disconnected.

"Gentlemen we have a problem", began Nomura to the assembled executives. "Laurence Jefferson referred to it briefly in Dubai, but did not give you the whole truth. Our meetings in São Paulo were not only fully taped by the FBI agent who was terminated in Ushuaia, but these tapes were fully transcribed and copies now exist in the US and the UK. These documents were picked up by a British salesman who has undertaken the personal task of delivering them to the authorities. He has already sent copies of all the companies who were present at the meetings with names, etc. We remain unsure if the details of the following meetings have been sent, but we can assume this to be imminent as he has so far, cleverly outwitted our security net and may even be here in this city. I do not hold out much hope that my security people will apprehend him and it is now urgent that we take steps to protect ourselves in some other fashion. This emergency meeting will have to make some hard and exceptionally difficult decisions. Decisions that have to be taken quickly if we are all to avoid the penalty of long prison sentences. It is due to Jefferson's crazed desire for total power and his megalomania that we are now in this position and I now propose that we throw him to the wolves and pre-empt any judicial moves against ourselves. We can do this by first agreeing a strategy that is followed by all of us and then, by informing our separate Governments of the situation immediately. Jefferson's plans of population reduction would be dynamite if generally known and far exceeded the top ten's programme that we agreed. If we assist the authorities by nullifying and emasculating his overall plan, our respective governments won't wish to pursue us for breaking the anti-trust laws and creating monopolies. Such news if made public, will wreck the global economy and all nations will suffer; it would be in the interest of all Governments to have our help in defusing any potential backlash. As we're all in this together, I propose that each of us speaks in turn and voices his independent opinion; then a plan can be formed and a vote taken on how to proceed. If we stand together, then we can come through this mess relatively unscathed. Although I foresee strict and controlling International legislation being passed by our governments to limit the powers of our companies. It is something that we'll have to learn to live with. Gentlemen - your thoughts?" So saying, Nomura sat down.

The CEO of the French company asked. "What are the exact chances of terminating this salesman Martin and recovering the transcripts?"

"Slim to zero with time running out fast", replied Nomura.

The English CEO asked. "Has Jefferson's third ingredient been introduced to his company's soft drinks and, if so, where are they being distributed?"

"I'm afraid that I was too late to stop a test batch being made, but it is restricted to that batch only and it will not go into general distribution. In fact the contaminated batch has been delivered here to Cancun, where it can be disposed of at sea. I'm expecting my head of security to arrive here early tomorrow and he will see to it that it goes aboard Jefferson's yacht for safe disposal".

The German CEO spoke. "Someone's going to have to pay for the FBI agent's death; that agency won't accept either fudges or explanations. They'll demand vengeance or some form of trial for those responsible".

"That problem is also in hand and as three of those responsible are already dead, there are only two others who were directly involved", answered Nomura. "The authorities will take care of that area with my help".

"What about the Millennium Club, the inner circle and our top ten?", asked one of the Americans.

"Obviously they will have to be disbanded, for the present anyway, but we'll stay in touch, it's in our interests to do so. We must stick together". Nomura made these final points to murmurs of agreement from all members and he proposed a vote on what had been discussed. It was carried unanimously that they proceed along the lines discussed and to put his proposals into effect simultaneously in approximately seventy-two hours from now. The other American CEO asked if that were to be on a GMT. basis or whether they made allowances for the different time zones around the world.

"It will be up to each member to decide what's best for him", Nomura replied. "The seventy -two hours will give you the necessary leeway, as there's an office-hours' time discrepancy of sixteen hours between us".

The Swiss CEO made the point that it would be better to freeze the Millennium club's membership account and place it into a direct investment bond that wouldn't mature for five years. A murmur of general agreement greeted this proposed action. To a final query from the Korean CEO as to Jefferson's whereabouts, Nomura said,

"He's in Panama right now, but is due to fly here tomorrow and join his yacht which is presently docked at the commercial port".

Jefferson's consternation increased when he arrived at the city airport to find that the Lear was in a hangar for the servicing of an oil leak and would not be flying before mid-day next day. He telephoned the Intercontinental and booked himself into one of the suites. There was little alternative, he decided. It was better to take the yacht to Rio than the Lear. Flight plans had to be filed a good twelve hours in advance, allowing the authorities time to move against him and there were many alternative areas to be dropped off by the yacht in the Caribbean before they reached Rio. It was ironic that he was now forced to use the methods of subterfuge that the salesman had used so successfully against Sobatsu security. Planes were much easier to track than ships. He pondered his options, instructing his driver to use the side entrance to the hotel to avoid any curious onlookers. I wonder how much time I've got before the authorities start to look for me, he thought. I'll telephone Ardeth in the morning and find out the latest position he decided. God what a mess!

Philippe was carrying out his instructions and had booked himself and Parides on the next available flight to Cancun. Thankfully, there was a regular air service between the two cities and they would be there soon after dawn the following day. He was far from happy at his boss's comments and only cheered himself up at the remembered vision of Flores, just before she followed her pretty boy with his flying lessons. Vengeance is definitely a dish best eaten cold, he considered. It had been very satisfying to witness the terror of Flores when she too had witnessed the exact method of her own final departure. It had also been very convenient to have pretty boy there for use as a practical demonstration.

Seventeen

In the headquarters of Central Intelligence at Langley in Virginia, an agency meeting was underway. Nick Vyon (pronounced vine), area controller of the CIA for the Latin American countries, sat at the head of the conference table. Four of his field agents occupied other chairs. An air of anticipation as well as urgency hung electrically in the room as they awaited their boss's instructions. Nick was leafing through sheaves of paper and making notes with an occasional "Harrumph", as though about to speak, then subsiding once more and referring to his notes. Finally, as though just airing his thoughts aloud and to no-one in particular, he said.

"It looks kinda likely that this guy needs our protection, "cause sure as hell, there's something funny going on. The Fed's man, Booth, has now been claimed as theirs. They think that someone in their department has been tampering with their mail, their lines of communication and all the informative sources that should have shed light on this guy Martin long ago. They're in the process of cleaning house and are now happy to work with us, as they don't know at what level they've been penetrated. We have been given copies of their file on The Millennium Club which their guy Booth was investigating. Now Jim, bring us up to speed".

Jim Turner, the agent in charge of what had now been designated as the Millennium/Martin case interjected

"We've gotten an update from that civil cop of the Brits, Chief Inspector Thurlston, and there's been much more information gleaned from both McAllister and the Planet secretary, Ardeth. I can now give you all the relevant points and information; the scenario is briefly not very helpful, as far as the missing pages we know exist, but we are aware that they could be explosive and could compromise the security of the States. However, the lists of all the companies that are involved in this thing is frightening. The economic and political power they wield between them practically keeps old mother earth spinning on her axis. We have to tread warily when and if it comes to dealing with them on an individual basis. Collectively, just the US Branches of these thousand companies probably pay the salaries of all the administration. The following is what we know so far and is open for comment. This guy Martin witnessed the murder of the Fed's agent, but somehow grabbed the vital information that the agent wanted the bureau to get. The company or companies involved in the murder and whatever else they're up to, have been moving heaven and earth to track him down, but we've still no hard evidence on anything so we have to be extra careful. The hit-men were mighty unlucky to be observed by this guy Martin as he's way above the average in the necessary smarts and there's few people around with a better knowledge of the Latin American countries. We have part of Booth's information including the lists of the companies who may be involved. Martin has sent these; we need the rest of it. From Thurlston's last message, the Brit cop that I've been liaising with, it would appear that Martin's wife is now heading to Cancun in the Yucatan peninsula of Mexico. Martin is, at this moment, also headed for Cancun, Thurlston having elicited that information from her husband's lawyer. As far as we can ascertain Sobatsu's hit-men are in the area to take Martin out, then cover their tracks once they've recovered the missing papers. It's all going to happen down there and we've nobody in position". He continued,

"If you say go boss we're on our way; the DEA have a special flight going from Dulles airport to Cancun via Oaxaca that leaves in another hour and we can join it. The couple whom we picked up from Penn Yan were special operatives of the Japanese electronics company Sobatsu, who also run the security for the Millenium club and have been singing like canaries. Unfortunately, apart from being told to organise an accident for the two sailing buddies at Penn Yan and then take a hike to Hawaii, they can't be of much assistance as to why. It appears that this guy Jefferson, who is head of Planet Ales, has been pulling all the strings for some time. Our friends in the DEA have tracked his private jet on its way to Panama City and it should be arriving there shortly. This guy is heavy time for all of us if we make any moves that are not fully justified. According to the DEA he's exceptionally well connected and that they walk on eggs around him and his possessions. They have also informed us of their suspicions about Jefferson's yacht, the Venus. It could be involved in drug running, but in spite of two previous searches and extra surveillance, they can't make anything stick. They suspect some of the crew might be in business for themselves. The DEA's now scared shitless to check on Jefferson, except at a distance. However, we do know that his yacht is in the immediate vicinity and carries a chopper, a Bell Ranger, and a variety of arms. The Seventh Army Intelligence Unit has been on the horn to advise us of odd goings on at the International airport which, unfortunately, is outside the canal zone's military jurisdiction, so they can't investigate further. Something's happening boss, but we're still guessing and pretty much in the dark. Martin seems to hold the key and if we don't get to him first, we may never know the answers".

Nick Vyon rocked back and forth on his chair, silence prevailing, expectancy mixed with excitement now visible on all the others' faces. The adrenalin surge of impending action was having its effect.

"Harrumph ! Then guys go get him", said Nick. "But just remember that it's not our country and not tread on local toes. It's too late to get official permission and have the operation sanctioned by the Mex Government, so dance lightly and don't blow it. I'll get in touch with my opposite number in Mexico, but he's unlikely to be of much assistance at this short notice. He'll probably inform the local carabinieri, but after your last little jaunt to their country, you can't expect them to fall over backwards to help you".

Vyon was referring to a hot-pursuit through Cuidad Juarez, in the north of the country when a Colombian drug gang escaped southwards from the States to Mexico; three carabineros had been killed in the resultant shoot-out.

"If you're caught doing anything you shouldn't, you're on your own, Capiche?"

"Yeah boss", a general murmur of recognition was voiced as the four agents headed for the door.

Nick shouted after them, "I'll call the DEA and let them know you're on your way and for God's sake, no Goddamned international incidents!'

Belize City had been a drag for Ramon Gutierez and his partner. The airport was worse, he reckoned. They had been posted there for the past six weeks by Sobatsu, just in case some guy passed this way. Already a thousand or so operatives and God knows how many more computer experts and extra local help had failed to find him, he pondered. As far as he was aware, no-one even knew what he looked like. What a bloody waste of time! His partner had gone into the city for some action with the birds and he didn't mean the feathered variety, at least the beer, birds and food were cheap, he reflected. Help! Apart from a couple of plane loads of tourists inbound to the country, then continuing south to another destination every day and three other flights to the north weekly, there was little to remove the boredom. If it wasn't for the steady flow of tourists to and from the offshore island of San Pedro, he could have just turned up for the main flights.

Gutierez had examined every shop in the small airport's lobby, in fact he'd examined minutely everything that was for sale. This country is strictly for the birds he thought, smiling to himself at his own unconscious humour. It was home to an enormous variety of them. That's what made it so popular with the tourists, that and their damned coral reef - it seemed to be a popular place, and by all accounts, more fun than Belize City. Too many around here were crack-heads and rife with Aids and other sexual nasties, he reflected. With little work available, crime was rampant in the city. The sooner he was back to his home in Panama the better. Thoughts of his beloved novia crowded his mind, his girl-friend was very beautiful.

Hang-on, the British Airways check-in girl was making wild hand signals to him, have to investigate. He ambled across.

"I thought that you were in some sort of hurry to get hold of your friend Martin", she said. But you don't seem to recognise each other; that's him going to board the Air Jamaican flight. It leaves in ten minutes!"

"Book me on it Cariña, there's a bonus in this for me and another fifty dollar bill for you as I promised".

Mierda!, he thought smugly as he belted himself in, the engines were now being warmed up. All those computer operatives checking tickets against passport numbers when a good old fashioned bribe will always do the trick. Ramon had been slightly hesitant when he'd first boarded, there were only the two of them; this hombre, Martin, and himself. The two and a half hour trip passed at a snail's pace for Gutierez, although fortified by a couple of rums. His quarry could consume the liquor though. Especially when it's free, he thought. A few words were exchanged over the crowded state of the aircraft and he agreed with Martin that he was personally in search of more vibrant entertainment in Cancun. Belize was for the birds, he'd said, echoing many of the tourists he'd overheard during the long boring hours at the airport. Yes, he'd heard that the offshore reef and islands were worth visiting, but that wasn't his scene. He didn't swim and preferred all his fish on a plate. Conversation, thankfully, dried up.

Bernard realised that his companion on Air Jamaica was no travel expert, yet he knew all the buttons to push when asked questions. His radar bristled and he quickly retrieved his case from the carousel and grabbed a taxi as soon as he'd cleared customs and immigration. It didn't appear that the other passenger was following and he relaxed as he directed his driver to the hotel.

"El Fiesta Americana, por favor. Ah! Lo siento, yo olvido, es en el zona turistico, el Condessa por favor".

"Si Señor, immediatamente!"

He should have remembered about these damn franchised hotels, there was more than one of them with the same name. He'd forgotten and had to apologise to his driver for the wrong first choice. Damn-it! He'd already spent a couple of times as an exceptionally dis-satisfied customer with that annoying system. There was some American city, where was it?, Miami? Where there were no less than five Holiday Inns! And their supposed four star rating was as bad as two with one of them, and another actually meriting six. It all depended on the management. Bloody hell!, it was an irritation that these multi-nationals created in the pursuit of money. When a specific area was coining it, they expanded the franchise and to hell with the quality or customer satisfaction. The consumer was just a form of cannon fodder after all, he thought. Cash was king and bugger those who complain! Tough! was the comment that he'd heard more and more often when using these franchised businesses. It was a gamble more often than not and could be a substantial rip-off in many cases. The taxi dropped him at the foot of the escalators, taking guests up to the lobby and reception area of this luxury hotel, his case had already been grabbed by a porter and was half-way up the escalator before he'd paid his driver. He was looking forward to the sheer unadulterated luxury of a weekend in the sumptuous surroundings of this hotel. There had been no watchers at either Belize City nor Cancun airports; he'd lost his pursuers. He could relax for a couple of days, then prepare for the final surge towards his goal. He had fully earned this break, he decided. He intended booking their fabulous top restaurant for dinner that evening. The one where he couldn't quite justify the expenditure the previous time he'd been here. Signing in had required his passport details, but he had chanced that risk, reckoning that Mexico was a large country and even computer checking would take a few days for Sobatsu. He was surprised at his sang-froid, but happily accepted his room key-card and followed the porter to the elevators. The room had pile carpets, an area outside the bath, bidet and shower suite had two wash basins, a his-'n'-her's, he surmised. The fridge-bar was huge and crammed with a wide range of goodies. He'd seen less well-stocked corner shops in the UK, he thought. The room even had a door-bell! Wow! The balcony had three loungers and a table with two chairs, overlooking part of the golf-course and across the hotel strip and over the inner sea where yachts, both sail and motor abounded. Jet-ski boats and pedalo's were closer in to the sandy beach; further out catamarans and water-skiers vied for manoeuvring space with luxury motor yachts. Pouring a couple of the miniatures of Scotch into one of the crystal tumblers, he came to a decision. Hang the expense, just relax and switched on the box to check the satellite programmes. Picking up the phone, he booked the Restauranté Rosato. Ye gods, Sally would have a fit if he told her about the night's expense without her. He resolved to say nothing about it. Bernard ran a bath for himself and caught up with world news, O.J. Simpson was in deep shit, Clinton was heading for the next presidency, the Tories were in definite trouble with their mid-term elections, poor old Ronald Reagan had Alzheimer's. It was the same old thing, mainly bad luck stories made the headlines. He hadn't missed all that much anyway.

Luxuriating in the bath, he considered how he would travel from there. Taking all the possible routes and methods under review. He could fly to Oaxaca in the Chiapas, then take coaches right up through to the north of the country and cross into Texas. If he headed to San Antonio, the rest was a "walk-in-the-park", as Jack would have put it. The warmth of the bath combined with the headiness of the whisky and his mind floated off into memories of happier times spent in Mexico.

This country had a history worthy of greater investigation. Their Aztec pyramids outside Mexico city were of equal impact as those of the Egyptian Pharaohs, he considered. He wondered if there was some linkage, the similarities were, after all, just too many to be pure coincidence. The Mayan civilisation too had been influenced by the Aztecs and the Yucatan had more than 1,400 archeological sites within the peninsula. Monté Alban, just outside Oaxaca had impressed him when he'd visited it a few years ago. The Mayan studies of astronomy and medicine in particular, where they'd even had all their diagnostics recorded on stone tablets. They defied belief.. Humanity hadn't advanced much in many ways, he thought. Although, the Zapotec Indian peoples had been truly great in their time. Probably their greatest citizen had been Benito Juarez who had been a Zapotec Indian, Bernie considered. The great man's immortal words were carved on a hillside outside Oaxaca —"El respeto al derecho ajeno es la paz!" — Such wisdom from a central American Indian whose education had been rudimentary. 'Respect for the rights of others is the way to peace!'

And yet, the early Zapotecs of Mayan society had missed the full mechanical significance of the wheel. As it had been an integral part of the Mayan religion and its use restricted to either their ear-rings, their national ball game or for their calendars. The religious aspects of it overrode any other possible use. A form of bigoted, religious insularity, he reckoned. It was time to get organised for dinner, Bernie decided. The bath water was cold now and his dram was finished. He splashed himself off under the shower and a hard towelling made him feel ten times the man once more. Bernard was now looking forward to the magnificent meal as he caught the elevator to the lobby below. This hotel even had palms growing inside, a waterfall, a large integral shopping precinct, three bars and four restaurants. There were four outdoor pools that he knew of, one of them with a fitted bar actually in the pool with underwater seating and he had read in the hotel brochure that there was another one inside, next to the exercise facilities.

The Restauranté Rosato was all that was expected, their 'sopa cebolla' or onion soup was as good as any to be experienced in Paris. The steamed, then grilled poussin which had an unusual sweet tomato gravy had been liberally covered in Parmesan before grilling. This was served with new potatoes and selected vegetables, lightly cooked to perfection, further complimented by a white (blush) Zinfandel. It was heaven. The hierarchy amongst the waiters here was very noticeable, he thought. One couldn't get either butter or water from any other than the boy who dispensed these items. Apart from a table of nine businessmen, there was only a foursome and three other couples in the restaurant.

Bernard remembered his first trip into Mexico and another visit to a good restaurant in Maztalan, when he thought he would starve before being finally served. He had sustained a severe crick in his neck from constantly requiring to turn towards the swing doors to the kitchens. He had learnt the hard way, that if you wish to eat in Mexico, then face the kitchen doors and get the waiters' attention on immediate entry to the dining area or they would be doing something for someone else. In the Rosato, the waiters outnumbered the clientele and an expression about the excellence of the meal evinced a free coffee and mints and a visit from the chef to whom he gave his congratulations. It was a satisfied and pleasantly tired Bernard Martin who wound his way to the elevators, one of the young bell-boys in hotel livery, scuttling in advance to call the elevator that arrived as he reached it. The tip was instantly accepted and into the lad's pocket. Wishing him a "Buen tarde", Bernie felt a comfortable tiredness and in less than five more minutes was in bed and fast asleep.

Ramon Gutierez had done his job well, Philippe congratulated him for not spooking Martin and obtaining the taxi-cab's registration number. Immediately they'd arrived at the airport, Parides was despatched to track down the hotel where Martin had been deposited. The day being Sunday, Martin would probably be thinking that he'd eluded his pursuers permanently and would take it easy for a day or two. He'd elicited a full and detailed description of Martin from Gutierez.

Martin was now athletically fit. No wonder the watchers hadn't seen him, he was nothing like his old photographs. Chameleon-like he'd even changed his skin. You're a clever and able adversary my friend, but I've got you now, Philippe reflected.

Just in case Martin decided to leave before Parides located him, Philippe instructed Gutierez to remain on watch at the airport until he'd organised others to be fully apprised of Martin's new description. Then Ramon could have a roving brief in the city, with luck he could spot him quickly. He could now report to Nomura with much better news this time. Directing the cab driver to take him to the Fiesta Americana Condessa, Jorgé realised that the sooner he reported this news to Nomura, the better it would be for himself.

Nomura led Philippe to the balcony, having ordered a pot of coffee from room service. He listened to his security head's report. Martin's description exploded upon his memory.

"He's here man, in this very hotel, I saw him at dinner last night", Nomura gasped. Philippe was halfway to his feet when Nomura placed a restraining hand on his arm.

"Sit down Philippe. Organise the coffee will you", as a waiter entered with a loaded tray, "Just give me a moment to consider what would be best. But first you have to see that the contaminated batch of Planet Ales is placed aboard Jefferson's yacht, the Venus, it's lying down at the commercial port". Nomura had already taken the decision that his head of security and his lieutenant Parides would both have to be sacrificed to appease the wrath of the FBI. He'd made an anonymous call to that same organisation first thing that morning. There had been no alternative to giving up the two men as the murderers of Booth and where they could now be found. However, this was an unexpected bonus; Martin here! It was incredible. As Philippe poured out the coffee, he said.

"I'll need Martin alive to answer questions first and to recover the copies of the meetings, so don't let Parides loose on him, not until I say so, O.K.?"

"Yes sir. Shall we bring him here?", Philippe queried.

"No, for God's sake no! Keep him out of sight in the old city, but you have yet to pick him up. I think that I saw him walking in that direction about two hours ago. You'd better get organised now, and don't contact me here again. Let me know of any developments by phone only. Although I'm returning to Tokyo on an afternoon flight, so I'll be unavailable for directions from four until late tomorrow. There's to be no killing until you have the green light from me! Understood?"

"Yes sir", Philippe replied, standing up and preparing to leave. "I have your mobile telephone number if we catch him before your flight departs. I'll enjoy meeting Martin face to face once more", he added.

Sally had cleared Immigration and collected her luggage, joining the queue for taxis to the city. She had changed some cash into pesos when collecting her tickets at the travel agency and was fully prepared when the time came to pay her driver. She'd even remembered to get the driver to write down the fare before leaving the airport. Prices must have gone up she thought, when seeing the fare of twenty-six pesos. She was sure that Bernard said that the fare he'd paid just two years ago was half that. However, the Fiesta Americana, while very elegant, wasn't nearly as grand as she had been expecting after Bernard's lauding of it, and they wouldn't divulge any information about other guests. What a nuisance, but it was probably more secure that way. She was about to follow the porter to her room when she was hailed from the lounge.

"Sally, Hi there honey", Jack and Carolyn came over to embrace her.

"No, we just arrived last night", they replied together to Sally's immediate query.

"Have you seen Bernard yet or had any contact?"

Carolyn said, "Come on Sal, we'll get you settled in first, I'll come up with you, you just have another coffee Jack, we've some girl talk to cover first".

"O.K. sweetheart" Jack replied, "I still reckon that this is the wrong hotel, so I'll check with reception first, this one is too reasonably priced even though it is a five star hotel".

"It's not what I expected either Jack", echoed Sally, "I'm really glad to see both of you, I'd forgotten that I was flying to a foreign country and I don't speak any Spanish. Give Carolyn and me a few minutes to help me get organised and we'll be right down, I don't want to waste any time. Bernard's in danger, so the sooner we find him the better, he must be under a dreadful strain".

Bernard had risen at first light, showered and enjoyed a light breakfast. It was Sunday so he reckoned on having a lazy time watching the ubiquitous Sunday fiesta and parade that all Mexican towns and cities held. If you organised yourself early enough and obtained a seat at one of the café cum restaurants that lined the main street, you could have a pleasant couple of hours' free entertainment watching the colourful parade pass by. He had risen early enough to enjoy a pleasant stroll along the promenade of the hotel belt into the old city proper. The sunshine and sparkling modernity of this hotel zone had boosted his joie de vivre, he felt good.

Jim Turner and his team had arrived in Cancun. They would take three separate taxis so as to place an agent at each of the Fiesta Americana hotels.

It could have been worse, Turner decided, saying to Hanson and the others as they split up. "Stay put in the lobby until you've either made contact or I come to relieve you". Even with Martin's photograph that each of them carried, it would be like looking for a needle in a haystack unless he could persuade the local Police chief to give them some help. These five star hotels didn't take kindly to questions about their guests and he'd need the authority of the local cops to have them check their registers.

"Al distrito de la Policia amigo, por favor", he instructed the driver of his cab.

Chuck, his partner, and the other two agents, Joe and Hank, he reflected, were probably three of the best field agents that he could have on this job.

"No Goddamn international incidents". The boss's final words were resounding in his head. He'd have to make certain there weren't any!

Eighteen

Transcripts of the Tapes.
Address to the Millennium Club.

"Ladies and Gentlemen, thank you for your support and one hundred per cent turnout to this conference. For those in the audience who do not know me, my name is Laurence Caldicott Jefferson and I'm the Chief Executive and Managing Director of Planet Ales, Incorporated. We are indebted to Sobatsu Electronics and their bankers who have provided the facility of this conference hall in São Paulo. I'm assured their dining hall can seat and feed our full complement at one sitting. All the food and refreshments are provided free gratis by Sobatsu whose security arm of the company has the remit to ensure that no part of our meeting or its content leaks out to the world's press and media. The checking of your invitations against the exact names was, I assure you, as much for your personal protection, as it is for ours in general. There will be time for a limited number of questions after I have outlined the purpose and reason behind this conference and a number of colleagues and myself will be available to head discussion groups in the afternoon. They will all be wearing the same yellow-bordered name tag as I, myself, am wearing. The rest of you have light or dark blue-bordered name tags.

Now, to cut immediately to the purpose of this meeting; it is to make each and every one of your companies, the largest, best and strongest of its kind throughout the world. Indeed you will have no other competitors in your field and be completely safe from any predatory takeovers or buyouts from others.

As ours is the United States' largest single company with our products on sale in at present 200 countries and territories; I have developed systems that make my company not only impregnable from attack by any and all competition, but from any attack by the wheeler dealers of the city. I shall explain how to make use of these systems and reveal how to turn them to your advantage. The thousand companies represented here today control over one third of the world's wealth and between us we will be able to dictate the terms of all trade anywhere in the very near future.

As most of you are aware, the Millennium Club has been in existence since its formation in 1975 when there were fewer than a dozen companies taking part in the programme that I'm going to outline, once again, for the benefit of the more recent members. Today, with the registration of another 197 companies, I'm glad to report that the original number envisaged for our club has now been reached and that no further members will be admitted to it".

(Strong and loud applause)

"A lot of the information that you will hear today will be old news as many of the business communities have latched onto some of our ideas and the methods are disseminated by their accountants and tax-advisors. Needless to say, we have the largest company of that breed amongst our numbers today".

(Cheers and light applause)

"The saying that success breeds success definitely holds true in business and all of you here are aware of the value of Brand names, strong identifying colours, clever Logos and regular advertising to imprint upon the minds of your buyers. On a worldwide basis for many of us here, we are now in the realm of subliminal advertising without the actual requirement of invoking its use. We all know the power of television with its ability to channel the thinking of the masses. Let me tell you some of the facts that I've elicited from a specially conducted poll for my company. A poll that revealed, not only how the public saw our Planet brand, but why they purchased it. Identity was obviously number one with the impacting colour and name and the worldwide advertising driving the message home. I understand from friends that you can no longer go into the jungles of Indonesia, nor of the Amazon without the extreme likelihood of encountering our products. Some of the remotest tribes in the most outlandish parts have been found not only with colour television working on generators or twenty -four volt systems, but also drinking our products. The importance of branding, colours, logo and advertising have therefore been established beyond all doubt, and most here would agree".

(Murmur of approval and agreement).

"Most here know that 85% of the public get their knowledge and information about life and the world from either the soaps they watch on television, the tabloid newspapers or the latest blockbuster films. It is relatively simple arithmetic to work out your return, if you have a strong enough brand name and to convert that percentage into sales made, now increasingly available through these advertising promotions, to X- numbers of people. Hence the ever accelerating equation of advertising costs with an ever-widening audience for certain sporting events. These facts have also not been lost upon the world's largest advertising agency, now also within our ranks".

(Laughter and light applause)

"All these afore-mentioned points are already known by most of you and some of what follows may also be known. But it is these latter points, combined with the former that will make you invincible, unstoppable, and totally protected from predatory buyouts. These facts will ensure that you stay in the driving seat. This conference is to give the newcomers to our club a knowledge of the methods that have already been proven by the majority of you. The dark blue name-tags signify the old lags (Laughter), the light-blues are the new boys. In the afternoon session, it will be up to the new boys and, of course girls, to elicit further information from their elders and betters". (More laughter)

"All our companies have proven that collectively, we can aid one another through utilising one another's products where we can, at minimal cost to the club's members, and so strengthen our worldwide control of our markets. Again, through the sensible use of combined promotions, we can avoid the anti-trust laws but obtain the maximum benefit of advertising. Numbering one thousand of the world's largest and best companies and through changing the promotional venues for our products will make any accusation of collusion between us, almost impossible to prove. Any improved discounting by any one of our competitors should be reported immediately to the member company concerned, so that appropriate action can be taken.

Almost all of you here know the advantages of scale and of concentrating on the core business that is essential to your growth and profits. We're all aware that diversity in business can be divisive and corrosive, especially when one sector of a conglomerate hits bad trading conditions, such as peaceful conditions for the arms -makers". (Ripple of amusement)

"The Millennium club's members have been chosen very carefully and none of your core businesses are liable or subject to the vagaries of fashion or short term projections. Avoid such businesses, buy them only if you are going to asset strip and then dispose of all the pieces except those which relate to, and enhance, your own core business. Remember that maintenance of your club is essential. Utilisation of one another's products where possible gives strength in depth to its members. Although faulty goods, poor products or bad service will not be accepted. Helping club members through information about price-cutting by competitors or marketing changes will enable you to stay ahead of all competition. Our members cover the world, as do our factories and offices, so unless someone starts a soft-drinks company on Mars or another planet, we're safe!".

(Loud laughter)

"It is a necessary part of your membership to pass on information to each other and aid other members to beat any local competition. There is one danger that we have all to be aware of and avoid having levelled against us. It is of creating a monopoly situation where governments will take powers to reduce your size. A special pamphlet has been written on how to avoid this problem and can be obtained here. Our club has recently engaged a team of psychologists to profile the buying market, break it into economic advantage and disadvantage so as to increase the sales potential. It is only through increased awareness of consumerism that we can improve profits and push our salaries and perquisites into the mega-bucks region. An information sheet will elaborate on all these points and many others and this will be given to all our new members. Updates are sent regularly to all of you. We will now adjourn to form discussion groups. Those who wish to listen to a specific lecture from any of the invited lecturers who are, at present, awaiting their students in our hospitality room can do so. Or if preferred, just enjoy a coffee and chat with your fellow members".

(Heavy applause, following which a large notice was erected on the podium with details of various subjects and the lecturer's name next to the conference room being used.)

Note: This enabled the members of the Century club to make their way to their own conference without arousing comment from others.

Transcript of the taped meeting of the Century Club

Jefferson brought the meeting to order and gained the attention of the audience.

"Ladies and gentlemen, today we are favoured with an address by one of our own inner circle of the Century Club. He is well known to all of you and needs little introduction, except to say that under his company's tutelage and guidance, our profits have soared and taxes have been contained. He will outline how best to do it which probably includes hiring his company, (Laughter) and set you up with systems that are impregnable from Government inquisitiveness and the demands of bureaucracy and the Revenue services. Simon, the floor is all yours". (Applause)

"Ladies and gentlemen, I believe that few of you are not clients of our company already and this talk is preaching to the converted". (Loud laughter) "However there are one or two recalcitrants among your number and I shall address them with some of the major tenets that we advise our clients to follow, so that they will be free to run their company profitably, enjoy the fruits of their labours", (Loud Hear Hear's), "and at the same time not have to worry about predators or being sold out by the city financiers.

"Three of these major league players, I see in our midst". (More laughter) "Ladies and Gentlemen, it is insufficient just to aim at producing rising annual profits year on year. You will just become bait food for the larger fish in the pool who, in time, will swallow you up. What I want is to make you into is one of the whales of the world's oceans, so that you can go where you will without fear. You can harvest what you need, but will be too big to be harvested in turn, and will be protected by Government legislation. We recommend that our clients use simple business methods. Some of these I will now outline once again.

Set-up your factories in the black-spot, unemployment areas of the world. You will receive massive tax advantages and even tax holidays for a number of years as an enticement from the incumbent Government who will probably give you a major, non-returnable subsidy as well.

You have then created a shared vested interest that properly used becomes a licence to print money. The unions will be easier to deal with, as they won't wish to lose the jobs of their members to another part of the world. The employees will become your supporters, as long as their standards of living are on a gradual incline upwards, but they'll realise that their work could evaporate and so they will be more pliable. Employee share ownership will strengthen their loyalty. Governments will toe your line as they cannot afford to alienate their voters and it is as easy to work with one political hue as another, because all will recognise the reality of the situation.

In effect, it is we industrialists, who now control the wealth creating aspects of all nations; and it's their Governments have to pay heed to our requirements and wishes. Having lobbyists on your payroll in the Parliaments of the world may no longer be a necessity, but it does make things easier. Many politicians look for this extra remuneration and will support your company's future during votes that can affect profits and secure advantageous contracts if you subsidise them in turn, especially holiday jaunts and expensive gifts. Remember to oil the wheels of progress". (Loud applause)

"I have asked for the epidiascope to be brought into the small chamber, so that I may illustrate the linkages of our suggested, command structures. Any queries over these layouts may be taken up with me personally, afterwards. Another requirement we suggest that you follow immediately, is to strengthen your share value and buy at every sensible opportunity, some of your own shares and so increase their value. You will then be less likely to become fish-food for the sharks". (Muted applause)

"Always be aware of who your share-holders are and who can trade off large slabs of shares that can make you vulnerable. Likewise be prepared to purchase your competitors' shares whenever there is a downturn in business and their cashflow is weak. Keep sufficient reserves for this purpose, if you can always guarantee your major shareholders of a reasonable annual return. They can, in turn, plan their own strategies. Always be aware of your strengths, one of them being the vested interests of your shareholders. Use these correctly and you will retain their loyalty for life. I see five of the largest pension fund holders and another half dozen of our largest insurers amongst our number, keep them with that smile on their faces". (Laughter)

"After all, the money you make goes into their pockets, those of the company lawyers or of our own at the end of the day". (More laughter)

"Our firm has had a number of pamphlets printed with the latest information on all the topics that are to be discussed today. These contain points that are restricted to our inner circle of the Century Club and will be subject to 'D' notices being issued - in other words not to be passed on.

I suggest that we now adjourn to create smaller discussion groups where new ideas can be floated for onward dissemination to this inner circle of one hundred companies".

Transcript of the taped meeting of the Top Ten

"Gentlemen", once more Jefferson addressed the meeting. "We have now put in position our lines of defence in case of interference by Governments and their departments who may wish to hamper us in the attainment of our aims. Our thousand companies are a force that's greater than either the Government of the United States or even the European Federation and certainly the loose confederation of Asian nations. We can now dictate terms to almost all countries around the globe and expect to have them accepted. The Millennium cartel will ensure, by the lobbying of their politicians, that the decisions taken by us will not be opposed nor become the subject of corrective legislation. Due to all of the information given to the outer circle of the Millennium cartel and the known inner circle of privy councillors that is subscribed to by the Inner 100 companies; the Century club has now strength in depth!.

Finally, our secret Top Ten, who know all the rules and understand and agree with this knowledge that has been carefully researched over many years; we ten, now control, not only our own destiny, but also that of our planet. We all recognise that our planet is under strain from over-population, pollution and the depletion of its resources. There will be two speakers who will address us on these subjects today. They will outline some pertinent facts. They belong to an elitist group of ten thousand scientists who collate all the relevant information from around the world and present it in a fashion that can be understood by national Governments. These two professors will address you first. Then I shall continue with my own solutions to some of the problems outlined.

The two professors are only aware that they are addressing a small group of influential people who are interested in the environment and wish to improve the lot of humanity. They are well paid for their time and trouble, but are held incommunicado in the hospitality room until their lectures have been delivered. You may question them freely over coffee after their addresses, but for the purposes of retaining your anonymity, I propose that all of us remove our name-tags until they leave".

"My name is Prof. Chuck Simon and my job is the collation of factual and detailed information from around our globe. My colleague, Dick Arnold runs our mainframe computer, feeds collected information into it, and makes the judgements about the likely outcome of the various agricultural, industrial mechanical and social changes that occur in the world. Its accuracy can be evaluated from the following simple fact. To establish figures for death from smoking cigarettes, various factors have to be calculated. These give us approximately the number of deaths expected in each country dependent on a variety of vital input detail that influences the actual number. Such evaluations are only 88% accurate. Dick's box of tricks can evaluate a projected outcome to within 99.9% accuracy, so its theorising can be taken as facts. I shall outline some of the facts that I have collated first and then Dick will give the probable outcome of a continuation of the various policies. All of you here are aware that we cannot go on breeding and live with the systems that are in place today. The world's population has doubled twice this century and is set to double again within fifteen years, then again in twenty years after that. These projected figures are obtained by taking all present policies into account. The climate is rapidly altering due to the expelled greenhouse gases of the combustion engine and other pollutants.

The following are known facts.

1. Prior to 1950, there were only 82 countries in the world with another 56 dependencies, colonies or territories. Today there are 201 countries and another ten territories making movements towards division and wishing independence. There are still the original 56 other colonies or dependent territories although not entirely the same ones.

2. In 1950 there were 2.8 billion people in the world, today that figure is 5.7 billion and increasing at 90 million extra people annually, allowing for births minus deaths. The projected population figure for 2020 is 8 billion.

3. In 1950, there were only 5 nations that didn't have the required 0.125 acre of necessary agricultural land that's required to fed each person of its population. Today that figure has increased to 15 nations. The projected figure for 2020 is that 27 countries will be unable to feed their citizens and will be forced to import food. One of these countries will be China.

4. The fact that every food-producing country in the world is suffering from reducing crop-yields due to a diversity of factors has to be addressed. Climate change, soil erosion, storm damage, water scarcity and polluted land.   The increasing loss of land to buildings, roads and general infrastructure all contribute to an ever shrinking pool of the available food-growing land. Global warming influence is also accelerating a movement of the prime growing areas in a northerly direction creating shorter growing seasons and making an added reduction in the world productive capacity.

5. Thirteen of the world's fifteen major fisheries are in decline. Fishing conflicts and international fish quotas are now, a source of greater and greater difficulty.   The shortfall in fish protein has been partially replaced by a massive increase in fish-farming which, in turn, is creating other imbalances. Disease in farmed fish-stocks due to escapees has wiped out many of the natural, healthy, indigenous stocks. The use of chemicals to control these diseases has caused untold damage to many of the local environments and could be causing even greater problems that we're unaware of at present.

6. The ninety million increase of population annually has to be fed or die from famine or disease. It required the equivalent of 300 kilograms to feed each individual in the world in 1995, on either a direct or indirect

basis. This takes account of the wasteful, food-producing methods of grain-fed, meat producing animals and also of the millions who die annually from starvation or of the severely undernourished dying from disease at a young age.

7. To grow the extra food required for another 90 million annual increase, requires an additional 27 billion, cubic metres of water for the production of the necessary, extra grain. Dick Arnold will show you that the projected population in 2020 will need a further 780 billion cubic metres of water. To put this into a simple perspective, it is more than nine times the present flow of the River Nile. I have brought graphs and charts to illustrate the various problems that I've outlined, but will now hand over to Dick as he has many more graphics to demonstrate by use of the epidiascope. Dick Arnold, gentlemen".

(Light applause)

"Gentlemen, the state of the world is far from good as my projections will show. My graphs illustrate the different problems that, when they are taken to their limit, destruction of the human race becomes possible. You will be able to see that this apocalyptic scenario is to all intents and purposes just around the corner, and is certain to occur within the next century unless drastic modification to our systems of living and lifestyle is put into operation very soon. The world population cannot continue to increase at the rate it has been doing. In fact we are probably at a point where reduction of population could be argued for the future health of our planet and the humans who inhabit it.

One of the facts that Chuck left me to illustrate is our inadequate water resources. There are 214 major rivers that are shared by at least two or more nations. Various treaties have been made and written agreements drawn up on the usage or amounts extracted for all the required purposes. These agreements are far from watertight, to use an apt expression, and many countries are finding ways to opt out of inequitable treaties or simply ignore them and take more of a vanishing resource. Those down river are at the mercy of those who are first in receipt of the water.

High Dams are being created to conserve this resource and utilise its power for hydro-electricity, but at terrible cost to the environment. In 1950 there were only 5,000 of them around the world, today there are more than 38,000. Local climates have altered because of them, water tables for hundreds of miles downstream have altered drastically and irrigation systems that have functioned for decades are no longer operable. Some of the largest aquifers in the world, many of them thousands of years old, are now drying up. Water usage and its consumption, will become an ever increasing reason for conflict between nations. The majority of these High Dams have been built with technology that did not take into account possible future climate changes. Greatly increased rainfall in some areas could have disastrous consequences; unforseen at the time of design and construction.

I have programmed the computer to take into account severe legislation on water usage and to project the food growth through use of artificial fertilisers and by maximising water usage through extensive use of hydroponics.

Such methods will give us a few more years of breathing space, but where do we go from there? Desalination plants for seawater, not only are fearfully expensive, but are wasteful in energy terms and release extra pollutants through the use of power generated to drive them. Collection of the meltwater from icebergs has also been studied, but this too would be a sticking plaster remedy.

I have taken many of the specific leaflets on various subjects to this meeting as requested by your Mr Jefferson and shall leave the slides of graphs and charts for your further examination. I had extra copies made for this purpose. Chuck and myself agreed to address you briefly on our findings about the state of the world. Mr Jefferson made us aware that we would be talking to highly influential industrialists from around the globe and we hope that we've given you food for thought. The future is in your hands gentlemen. Thank you". (Loud Applause)

"Well gentlemen", said Jefferson, "We'll take a coffee break and you can ask our speakers any relevant questions".

Jefferson returns, having escorted the two professors back to the hospitality room where they would then be escorted from the building by Sobatsu's security people. This was ascertained by me (Booth) later and accounted for a blank section of tape that contained only background noise and other conversation that was indecipherable.

"Gentlemen", Jefferson continued. "We have among us one of the largest chemical companies in the world whose speciality has been modifying the genetic structure of plants, so as to obtain the maximum return. It is incidental that such production methods, not only increase the supply of food, but also increase the dependency of those who grow it. A captive market for all time, a veritable milch cow. It gives control of populations and nations, that none can break free from, but which with judicious use, could aid our top ten companies to re-shape the world to our own advantage.

This brings me to something that my own company's chemists have been working upon for many years. You're aware that my company, in common with most of yours, has been subject to industrial espionage over the years. However, in our case, it has been the formulae for our soft drinks that have been the target and they have been researched by chemists around the world who've tried with varying success to duplicate exactly our ingredients. Since the mid -sixties, our chemists have been trying to thwart these thieves by making different compounds that are in themselves so complex they defy all attempts at chemical analysis. These chemists have among their number, an exceptional man who for ability and comprehension regarding difficult problems has no peer. He used to work for the Nazi war machine during the last war, but escaped to Argentina where he was working for a soft drinks firm that my company finally bought out. His analysis of our original product was unbelievably accurate at the time when he came to my attention and I brought him to the States where he is now my senior chemist. We have discussed many of the problems of the world together, as outlined by our two professors. He has been working on various solutions that could resolve the major problem of overpopulation in an ingenious manner and in an undetectable way. For many years, he has been isolating the various ingredient amino-acids and linkages with other lethal compounds, for example curare and digitalis. He has invented an untraceable drug that will work, but only if all three ingredients are included. Each is colourless, odourless, tasteless and harmless by itself, but most importantly, completely untraceable and totally unidentifiable. Chemical analysis of this deadly compound which induces sleep and eventual heart stoppage within a few hours, results only in the revelation of three, each harmless in itself, chemical ingredients. These three additives can be administered separately without any effect on the individual, but are retained within the human body and will link chemically with the other two when they are eventually ingested. It is only after that third ingredient has been introduced that the first two ingredients combine with it to produce the desired effect, namely loss of consciousness, followed by death within twelve to eighteen hours. When they are combined with my company's soft drinks, this results in complete un-traceability. Result, a safe way to control sectors of the world's overpopulation.

Together we control the world's wealth and have secured our own personal future and the position of our companies. We now have the means at our disposal to control populations or remove the undesirable portions. My chemists are now experimenting with various foods to see if it can be included with similar un-traceability, even with the most stringent analysis.

Gentlemen, your thoughts".

(Silence for a full minute with muted murmurs that are indistinguishable)

Finally, a voice (later identified as the CEO of Sobatsu), Kaitto Nomura;

"Mr Jefferson, as you say we are all aware of the world's problems and the fact that it is overpopulated, but you cannot have serious intentions to remove sections of humanity in the way you suggest. Who is going to arbitrate on which nationalities are to be removed? You? — Our top ten companies? Your Government or mine? I agreed to form the security arm for the Millennium Club as we have the expertise in the electronics that are necessary for such a task. However, I did not agree to signing up to mass murder and I think that you will find all our fellow executives here present would insist on the most stringent controls being placed upon such an apocalyptic solution". (Murmurs of agreement)

"Mr Nomura, under my tutelage and guidance the Millennium club has prospered and succeeded beyond all your dreams. This has been due to my foresight and vision. We now effectively control the world's financial systems, and in many cases, the political aspects of its operation. Our Millennium cartel, of which the controls lie only in the hands of the top ten assembled here, can manipulate Governments together with their masses, exactly as we wish and completely to our advantage. My chemists have given us the final power that will only be used in case of dire emergency, such as plague or war. It is little different to the world's armies training with the latest technological weaponry or in a more domestic situation, through having fire brigades that sit around doing little, and whose cost effectiveness against losses can be debatable. They are there, in case of that major conflagration which could happen. Being prepared is exactly what I'm in the process of organising".

Nomura replied to Jefferson's explanation, insisting that the top ten be fully informed about the chemicals use. - - - - - - - - the tape ran out!

Nineteen

Jim Turner found that the Mexican Police Commissioner was in possession of far more information than he'd expected. His own boss Nick Vyon had obviously been moving heaven and earth to help them since they'd left Washington.

"We have been keeping an eye on Señor Martin since he arrived and also have located the Chief Executive of Sobatsu who is staying at the same hotel. I have just been informed by our Immigration officials of the recent arrival of a number of Sobatsu employees who do not appear to have come to our city for their vacaciones, eh Señor Turner! Is that not how you would say it?"

"Si Comisionado, esta es exactamente las palabras que yo hace uso de por un descripcion", replied Jim Turner who received the soubriquet from the police officer in turn, "Bueno, habla Espagnol muy bien Señor".

If one addressed the authorities of foreign countries in their own language, it was always more acceptable, Jim reflected, and resulted in greater help too. They should be able to tidy up this situation very quickly.

"However Señor", the commissioner was saying, "With these people I have only issued orders to my own men to observe, no more. We shall allow your team to be at the cutting edge, O.K.? I am already short of manpower if you get my meaning".

"Perfectamente Comisionado. If I can call on you later and obtain an update on all of the interested parties' movements I shall be most obliged".

"And when you return to Washington thank your boss, Señor Vyon, for his most generous gift", said the Commissioner, rising and shaking hands with Turner.

Nothing much changes down here, Jim thought. I wonder how much the boss sent as a gift?

He hailed a taxi and entered quickly, directing the driver to the Fiesta Americana Condessa. Pulling out his mobile phone he instructed Chuck Hanson to rent a car, collect Joe the other agent and return to the Condessa as soon as possible. If the carabinieri were keeping tabs on all the vital players it would make their task that much easier. He checked his watch. It was only 0930. The Mexican police department worked very odd hours in comparison to ourselves, he reflected. They insisted in keeping their three hour siesta at the height of the day, too hot to work or chase thieves and criminals, he decided. Perhaps it was also too hot for the criminals.

Bernie had reached the old city outskirts and walked along the main thoroughfare looking for a suitable vantage point from which to view the parade. Already there were sufficient numbers of onlookers gathering and many café tables were occupied. He grabbed the last vacant table in a café cum restaurant which had a wide angle view at a convenient corner and ordering a cola he settled down to write two of the hotel's postcards. One was to Sally and the other to his boss explaining the delay in contacting them had been due to malaria and the long convalescence required. He would be home shortly, Bernie wrote, but first he had to fly up to Washington and not to expect an early appearance. He had completed this task when the patron of the restaurant asked him if he minded sharing his table; the parade was about to begin and the crowds were increasing.

There was no problem with that, Bernie smiled, recognising a good businessman who was maximising his profits. Two exceptionally well dressed Arab gentlemen nodded to him politely and took the other chairs. Their Armani suits spoke volumes about their wealth and the better-looking one of the two men wore Italian, hand-made, blue crocodile shoes with a shine that vied for attention with the sun. Bernard couldn't help but notice.

The parade was most enjoyable and Bernard left the café, having first been asked to organise a meal for the two Arab gentlemen, neither of whom spoke any Spanish.

He wandered back towards the hotel strip, not taking a direct route and found himself on the main street leading to one of the other Fiesta Americana Hotels. Heading towards it, he decided to make use of its rest room facilities before catching a cab back to his own hotel, when once again his heart leapt. A bulky figure was emerging from a taxi-cab further down the street and was entering the hotel. Although the glimpse had been momentary and at the distance of a good five hundred yards, Bernard would have recognised that shape anywhere, it was Parides! Hell! Sobatsu knew he was here and staying at a Fiesta Americana hotel, how did that happen? He hadn't mentioned it to Juan and Bismar, only that he was going to Cancun, they couldn't have traced the hotel registration or they wouldn't be checking them all out. Was it all hotels or just the Fiestas? He crossed to the shadow side of the street and approached the hotel cautiously. Entering that hotel was now out of the question.

Damn it, he'd become too confident and made a mistake somewhere. He cursed himself for his stupid pride. He'd been so confident about his own ability to out-think them. His heart raced again and a rush of blood to his head almost made him black out. Sally, Jack and Carolyn were coming out of the hotel!

Bernard pinched himself. He wasn't dreaming. They were real alright and Jack was now hailing a cab. He was unable to think and couldn't concentrate, so slunk into a doorway as the cab passed. He daren't risk the arrival of Parides at an inopportune moment. Hell, this was unbelievable! Choosing a small, nearby bar where he could see the front steps of the hotel, he ordered a beer while keeping a keen lookout for the bulky frame of Parides. Good old Jack, a definite stand-up guy, in the parlance of his country. But Bernard worried about Sally's and Carolyn's presence; they didn't, even remotely, understand the dangers.

Things would have to be worked out very carefully, at least he now knew that they were in the city and he could phone them later. He would arrange a meeting with them tomorrow. He daren't return to the Condessa, it would shortly be swarming with Sobatsu's people if not already. Thankfully, all his cash and the relevant transcripts were on his person, it would only be his clothes and suitcase that he would lose. And all his toiletries, yet again! Ah well, another razor to get. This was becoming an irritating habit!

Chuck Hanson was about to leave the Hotel Fiesta Americana in the city when he noticed Jack McAllister, his girlfriend Carolyn, and another woman leaving the elevator and heading for the exit. They were deep in conversation and paid no attention to his scrutiny, Chuck reckoned that he'd better inform Jim immediately. The other stunning broad must be Martin's wife, he reasoned.

Jim Turner was unenthusiastic about the news. "Shit Chuck!", he exclaimed. "My chat with the local Commissioner has established where all the other main players in this game are, if we can keep McAllister's lot out of it we should now be able to scoop the pool very quickly and get back stateside. Stay put until I send Hank round to you, then you can identify these three to him, but don't reveal yourselves to them, it's best that we keep our powder dry for the moment. I've just updated Joe at the Condessa, so I'll give him this extra news and send him for a rental car; he can then join up with you two for an update in recognition also, leaving you to take the car over here, O.K.?"

"Yeah Jim, got your drift. Will do!", replied Hanson. As he disconnected the call he noticed a large, bulky gentleman leaving the lobby and entering a taxi-cab. Built like the proverbial brick outhouse, he considered idly. Wouldn't like to meet that in the dark.

Jack, Carolyn and Sally chatted in their cab, Jack had established there were other two Fiesta Americana hotels, but that the best one lay in the new tourist zone. They were now on their way to check out the Condessa.

"This is more like the description of Cancun that Bernard gave me", said Sally.

"Yeah me too Sal", Jack answered as the taxi drove through the sumptuous tourist hotel zone.

"It's a bit like Vegas" Carolyn observed. "Only greener".

"And with a lot more water honey", Jack laughed. Although there is a slight similarity. Ah!, this looks more like one of Bernie's hangouts", said Jack, as they swung into the approach to the hotel. "Sorry Sal, it's just a form of speech that we guys use when bragging, there's nothing more to it than that".

Jack had caught sight of Sally's look of disapproval and decided he'd better not drop his buddy into it. "O.K. girls, let's go see this Taj Mahal", he said lightly, holding the cab door open for both and expertly proffering a twenty peso note to the driver. "I might be able to buy you two a coffee here without having to see my banker first", he added and all stepped onto the ascending escalator.

As they arrived at the lobby, Sally observed "Goodness me, it's definitely all that Bernard said it was, Jack. Perhaps we should stay in the city one and take shifts of sitting around here. This place's prices will be astronomical".

"Yeah Sally you're right", agreed Carolyn. But I'm sure as hell going to get Jack to transfer here for at least a couple of nights and Bernie owes you that little bit of luxury too Sal girl".

"O.K., and Bernard will be much easier to spot if we're around this place. At least he has to use the escalator to gain entry to the hotel. One of us can cover it easily", exclaimed Sally.

Jim Turner had seen the trio enter the lobby and made himself less conspicuous, but made his other field agent aware of them for future recognition. This was going to complicate matters. He pondered over the complexities that their presence could bring. Why the hell had McAllister and his girlfriend decided to come down here. Was it to accompany Martin's wife. Had she asked them to help? He could have done without their assistance. Bloody amateurs interfering were always a nightmare for the security services, but there was nothing he could do about this situation. He sighed deeply, just as his mobile alerted him to a call. The number was that of his boss and on answering, "Yeah boss", he was given the information about an anonymous call that FBI headquarters had received. A gorilla by the name of Parides and a smoothie but lethal bastard called Philippe had been the two guys who were responsible for Booth's murder in Ushuaia. The others involved were already dead due to internal squabbles amongst the hit team.

"Our buddies in the Hoover building are calling in a favor Jim, they don't want those two guys to go home, nor to face a court of justice if you get the drift. Can you live with their request Jim?", Nick asked.

"Yeah boss, that shouldn't be a problem, but we have not only Martin's wife on the scene, but also McAllister and his girlfriend. I hope to hell they don't get in the way. They're staying at one of the other Fiesta Americana hotels in the city, I'll give you the number. Perhaps you might give them a call and persuade them to leave it to the professionals?"

"Yeah, O.K. Jim, I'll see what I can do but they're free citizens and can do as they please". I'll try to scare them away". And with that Nick Vyon signed off as soon as Jim relayed the phone number.

Philippe had decided to rent a car, but have one of his operatives drive. As all of them carried mobile phones, his team of thirty soldiers could be distributed throughout the city and yet he'd have some of them on instant recall if and when required. When Martin returns to the hotel he's mine, he thought. There were only two routes out of the hotel zone and all points were covered. The rental car had been delivered to the hotel. Five taxi-cabs had also been hired and with two of his men in each. They were now systematically scouring the city for Martin. What was he up to?, Philippe pondered. You can't be going sight-seeing my little sand-martin? Or do you feel safe and secure and think that you've eluded us? Or are you running again, but where? He had all the possible routes out of the city sewn-up. Martin couldn't escape this time.

He left three of his men to watch for Martin at the Condessa and had himself driven to the commercial docks to see that the soft-drinks were put aboard the Venus. He arrived just in time to overhear the bosun of the Venus outlining his money making scheme to the crew. That's very appropriate, thought Philippe. I won't interfere, and quietly slipped away. He ordered the driver to pick up Parides from the city Fiesta Americana.

Philippe related the incident to Parides who chuckled at the thought of Jefferson being hoist by his own petard, "That's justice boss!", he exclaimed and Philippe agreed.

Bernard had seen Parides being picked up by a cab, but decided to await the return of Sally, Jack and Caroline. Definitely Cancun was crawling with Sobatsu people, he'd seen three cabs cruising down this street already during the couple of hours he'd been watching. Each had contained two men obviously checking both sides of the street.

It was almost dark when Jack, Sally and Carolyn finally descended from a cab and entered the hotel again. Giving them a full twenty minutes before dialling the hotel from a pay-phone in the bar, Bernard asked for Señor McAllister. Thankfully Jack answered, and rapidly he brought him up to date with both his own situation and the fact that Sobatsu security personnel were everywhere.

He had to talk to Sally but would do so later and was pleased that she and Carolyn were in Sal's room, giving him time to fill in all the details to Jack.

He daren't risk returning to the Condessa and no, it would be silly to risk joining them in their hotel, although Jack had informed him that they were moving to the Condessa, the day after tomorrow. "You see Bernie, we do listen and have been putting some of your tricks to good use. We got a good discount on their normal rates at the Condessa and all of us would like a night or two of luxury there".

"O.K. Jack", Bernard had said, "That's not a problem. You reckon that you saw one of the CIA agents at the Condessa but can't be certain, but would bet your life on the fact they're here, that's great. The news was very comforting, as he was sick to death of running and had thought Sobatsu's people had lost him permanently when he had arrived there. He had slipped up somewhere. His brain was getting tired. However, he wanted his buddy to phone the CIA's HQ. in Washington and let them know that he would head for Merida the next day and then fly to Oaxaca where he would stay in the Hotel de Los Angeles until they collected him. He would use the name of Señor Pilay and pay cash so he couldn't be tracked.

"O.K. Bernie but what are you going to do in the meantime?", asked Jack.

Bernard replied that he would find a cheap bed for the night then catch one of the tourist buses for Chichen Itza first thing in the morning. He would get a connecting bus from there to Merida. He would give Jack a couple of hours to inform Sally and Carolyn about everything that had been discussed before phoning Jack's room again later that night. With a "See you chum", Bernard disconnected before Jack could persuade him to do anything else. He felt a lot safer when he had only myself to think about. The saying that, 'he travels fastest who travels alone', had got it spot on, he thought. It was time to find a cheap hotel and eat before phoning again. At least it was now dark and it would be easier to dodge any of Sobatsu's men.

There were dozens of bed and breakfast areas and many cheap hotels around the Convention Centre and a row of telephone kiosks within it. It was a perfect situation and Bernard soon secured a room for the night, but he'd use the phone from one of the kiosks for safety. He found a restaurant nearby and ate a light meal. His stomach acid had been playing up again, ever since he had recognised Sally and his two friends. Bernard couldn't decide whether he was pleased to have them here or not and after enjoying a coffee and cigar; he slipped into the Convention centre to call Jack once more.

Sally answered, "Hello darling, how are you? We've been discussing all that you told Jack and there's been some bigwig from Washington on the phone to him soon after your first call. Having listened to everything both you and he said about the dangers out there, we're going to leave the final problem to the professionals as they seemingly have everything tied up. Please be careful dear, but there's one thing that we're going to do and that's join you on your jaunt to Chichen Itza. It will be safe there and we can at least be company for you for most of the day. Here's Jack wanting a word, bye see you tomorrow".

"Hi buddy, how's it going? Found some jungle lodgings for the night, eh?" Jack at least sounded in good spirits, Bernard thought, as Jack continued. "Had the main man of the CIA on the horn, re: the bad guys. They would like us to stay clear. I gather there might be some real action. Guess we might just be in the way old buddy and that you're probably safer on your own, so we'll confine ourselves to the daytrip to this Chicken Pizza place, then let you continue to Oaxaca by yourself. Hell!, the names they give these places. How do you pronounce that Mex city again?"

"Wah -hah -kah", Bernard had enunciated slowly. It was relatively simple to pronounce and Bernard couldn't resist the final repartee. "And it's 'Chichen Itza", not 'chicken pizza' you uneducated sod!" Jack's humour had cheered him up immensely as Jack then recounted the conversation with Nick Vyon and that he knew at least two of the agents who were in the vicinity.

"Vyon approved of your thinking buddy, but thinks that it will all be over by tomorrow night. Seemingly the main man, a guy Jefferson who is behind everything, arrived in the city yesterday and has now left for a destination unknown. Myron and I tangled with him and a couple of his hoods in Penn Yan, but more of that later. Some of the other main players have now abandoned the sinking ship and are helping the security services. They've only to mop up here in Cancun, so hang in there! We'll see you tomorrow at the Convention Centre and we have already organised the tour tickets from the hotel for all of us".

"That's great Jack, and thanks old friend for coming to help me. We'll have a ball for a day or two when this is over. Love to Carolyn". Bernard was feeling tremendous relief just knowing there was now support out there. He would have a quick word with Sally before he hung up.

"Sleep well darling", he said to Sally. He let her know that he had appreciated her support immensely and continued, "I have some fence-mending to do when I get back to the U.K., I reckon".

"We both have darling", Sally had replied. "I've realised just how lonely your job can be at times and I've decided that we're going to share more of our lives together, not separately as the past twenty years have been. Sweet dreams my dearest, see you tomorrow".

It was a slightly misty-eyed Bernie who put the receiver back on its cradle and headed for his hotel.

Ramon Gutierez recognised great opportunities with Sobatsu security and had been satisfied with the bonus dollars given to him by his boss; he was doing his utmost to repeat his lucky break by heading to the seedier part of the city in search of Martin. He had decided to hang around the main Convention Centre from early next morning, as he decided that was the only escape route left uncovered. With so many tourist buses leaving for places like Cozumel, Tulum, and Chichen Itza amongst many other ancient ruined sites, where better to hide he reasoned. Ramon was no fool but unfortunately could not also forsee the future.

Twenty

I'd been awake early, showered and scraped off my bristles with a safety razor that I'd bought the night before, teeth cleaning was confined to using my finger vigorously around my gums. My agitation at my wife's, friends and Sobatsu's appearance causing me to make mistakes and forget essentials like toothbrush and paste. Today would either be the end of my problems or the end of me, but Jack's news about the CIA's agents being in the city had been more than uplifting. It was a beautiful, warm and sunny day. It would be hot out at the Mayan ruins, I decided, and stuffed my Panama hat in my pocket for later. With my sunglasses, my hat would offer me some small degree of anonymity, but checking myself in the mirror I looked more like one of Philippe's hoods than a respectable British sales executive.

I laughed inwardly, Sally, Caroline and Jack were going to get a shock when I boarded the bus. I'd told Jack that I'd observe from a distance and get on the tour bus at the last moment. He'd recognised the caution attached to this piece of thinking and had remarked, "I see why you have survived this long Bernie".

There were fifteen coaches at the Convention Centre when I finally spotted Sal, Jack and Carolyn arriving, hundreds of other tourists were sitting on the steps or milling around. As the destinations hadn't been allocated to each coach, none displayed the sights so that the tourists couldn't board. I decided that this was a more sophisticated form of Mariella's uncle's methods of maximising profits with his aircraft. All tickets would be sold first, then the number of coaches to each tourist sight would be allocated.

I couldn't detect any of Sobatsu's people, but I kept a low profile even to the point of keeping well clear of my wife and friends. I noticed the guy with whom I'd shared the flight from Belize City by Air Jamaica to Cancun, but he was engrossed in his newspaper and killing time like most people. Odd thing that, he hadn't come across to me as the type to take an interest in his heritage. Ah well, I thought, one can never be sure of anything. The coaches were now displaying their destinations and a surge of humanity descended upon them, almost overpowering the drivers as they sought to check the tourists' tickets as they boarded. I saw Jack, Sally and Carolyn entering one of the double decker buses and Jack giving my ticket to the driver as we'd agreed, I would board almost at the last minute. It increased my margin of safety although I was pretty certain there were no Sobatsu people around. I slipped aboard the coach at the final moment, accepting my half-ticket from the driver on identifying myself.

I was soon on the upper deck hugging and kissing my wife and shaking hands with my friends. The degree of curiosity aroused by this reunion soon dissipated and our fellow passengers were soon engrossed in the guide's commentary about the journey. Sally, Jack and Carolyn couldn't believe my appearance, Sal was ecstatic. "You are the handsome man I first married Bernard and with that tan you could get a job in Hollywood".

"Must admit buddy that you're casting a smaller shadow", Jack added, patting my mid-riff. Reckon you could sell your slimming system on its results".

"You look absolutely gorgeous Bernie, if Jack and Sal weren't here — well!", Carolyn had laughed as we had embraced.

The guide aboard our bus was announcing that the tree we were now about to stop at temporarily was one of the chewing-gum trees; a chicklet.

It was the reason that had been behind the discovery of the Mayan ruins, the gum hunters had stumbled across them in their search for the gum trees and brought them to the attention of the archeologists. Otherwise the Mayan civilisation might have lain undiscovered for many more hundreds of years. Satellite technology had then been employed to find the hundreds of other sites in the peninsula. It's an ill wind, I reflected, that blows no good to anyone, although in my opinion it was long past time that the governments of the world should apply a tax on the product to clear the mess from city streets.

I echoed these thoughts aloud to Jack who agreed, parodying yet another phrase, "Make the bucks stop in the right sticking place and not on our shoes, eh! Bernie".

On the single deck coach behind which hadn't been quite full, sat Ramon who having paid cash to the driver had saved half the usual fare. He was now calling Philippe.

Philippe had been enjoying his breakfast. Parides was in the lobby keeping an eye on the escalators; this hombre Martin was becoming a problem again. Where the hell was he? He was still somewhere in the city, he'd bet his life on that, but where? He hadn't returned to the Condessa where they had now established his room number and checked out his clothes and suitcase. There had been nothing of interest. He must have been alerted to Sobatsu's presence, but where had he gone? His soldiers were now checking every hotel and bed in the old city. Martin certainly wasn't in the hotel zone. This damn salesman is going to be the death of me, he thought. He just disappeared into the woodwork or definitely into the fabric of a place.

His mobile bleeped and Philippe listened to his operative, a slow smile of contentment spreading across his face. Leaving a five hundred peso note and forgoing any change, Philippe was on his feet and out into the lobby. Telling

Parides to get the driver organised, then to rent another car and follow him to Chichen Itza, he quickly apprised Parides on Martin's movements. Philippe called two of the nearest Sobatsu security men and told them to meet Parides at the car rental booth immediately and was soon entering the other as it drew up at the escalators. Six of them should be more than sufficient to deal with Martin he decided; how helpful that he'd chosen his place of execution conveniently away from civilisation and out in the jungle. The instructions from Nomura were now obsolete, Philippe considered. He'd present his boss with a fait accompli. His driver, having had his instructions, was now following in the wake of the tour buses.

"Just take your time. There's no hurry. We don't want to get there ahead of them. Keep the coaches in sight, but stay well back".

Having given his driver full instructions, Philippe confirmed that Parides would follow shortly with other two men and settled back for a siesta. The next three hours would be pretty boring, he decided.

Jim Turner's mobile was also bleeping. A friendly Mexican Police Commissioner was alerting him to the fact that Martin and his party, all three of them, and Philippe, Parides and three of the Sobatsu soldiers were also en route to Chichen Itza.

Jim said to Chuck, "Get the others, it's going down".

Five minutes later, the four agents were on the road to the Mayan ruins. Chuck was saying, "Both of the targets will be there Jim, I've already given Joe and Hank their descriptions and they're anxious to assist the FBI with their needs. It's pretty damn convenient that we can get it together out in the jungle and away from people".

"Forget that Chuck, there will be far more people than just the two bus loads that we're following, buses come from another half dozen cities and towns for this important Mayan ruin. There could be five or six hundred people there; maybe even more".

"At least there's only five of them", Hank added, "We are not heavily outnumbered if it comes to a fire-fight".

"The most important thing is the safety of Martin and his group, but I don't want any of you to get trigger-happy, O.K.!"

"Yeah Jim", the others replied together, voicing recognition to his seniority and position.

"When we get there, you Chuck will stick to Martin like glue unless they split up, then it might be better if you keep the women safe. Joe will keep the group in sight at all times, ready to assist and take over Chuck's duties if the group does split. Hank and I will go looking for the gorilla and his sidekick and dispose of them as quickly and quietly as we possibly can. Martin has the papers on him and has to be protected at all costs, so no mistakes. If anyone fucks this up he's out of the service. Got it?", and repeating more loudly, "Have you got that?"

"Yeah Jim" the others chorused.

They realised now how important it was, none had heard Jim swear before. The tension must be getting to him,Chuck decided.

Aboard the double-decker, Sally was listening to the tour guide. This was a fascinating tour, she considered. The guide had just related that, although a unique four nostril-led Nauyaaca, the most poisonous snake in the world inhabited the jungles of the peninsula, the site was continually patrolled by park rangers who removed all the dangerous nasties. However, it was strongly advised that tourists kept to their groups, stick to the paths and remain within hearing of their guides if they wished further information.

The guide had extolled the virtues of the Mayan Calendar, stating that it was the most accurate in the world because the Mayans had designed a system of time-keeping and date calculation based on four methods acting concurrently. Their early astronomical buildings gave precision to both the hours of daylight and darkness. There was a unique souvenir available to the tour groups whereby anyone wishing to have their birth date recorded on hand-made paper in the hieroglyphic language of the Mayans. Visitors could obtain them, if ordered at the hotel, but prior to visiting the site. The souvenir could then be collected before the return journey. There would be four hours available for visitors to wander around on their own. The first hour of the tour would be with guides, speaking five different languages, so that all visitors could get an appropriate understanding in their own language. After that they were free to go where they wished and view everything on a personal basis.

Bernard was pleased to see that Sally was thoroughly enjoying herself and plainly excited at the imminent prospect of viewing the Mayan ruins, although he suffered more than just a twinge of guilt at her news about Judy's death. Her murder had not been anticipated and it underlined the callous brutality of Sobatsu and Philippe's hoods. Judy had not deserved to die at their hands and in such a way. Bernard hoped that it had been quick.

The coaches pulled into a large parking area in front of the Mayaland Hotel to disgorge their passengers prior to parking in an area well away from the site. All private cars were similarly directed to this parking area which meant that their occupants had a good quarter hour's walk before reaching the hotel. Sally, Bernard, Jack and Carolyn placed orders for their mementoes of the calendar before joining the queue for a buffet lunch. Folkloric and comic dancers entertained the tourists as they consumed their meal, but soon the friends had joined the English speaking guide for a tour of the site.

"It's magnificent", Sally breathed as the main pyramid came into view, "I had thought that only the Egyptians and Aztecs built such things. This one is if anything "la crème de la crème". The guide was now describing it.

"The pyramid was built to give the Indians their calendar and so has 91 main steps on each of its four sides, the other step into their religious temple that sits atop of it, makes up the 365 day year with the leap-year accommodated by the altar-step". She continued that visitors were free to climb it, but pointed out that it was far more difficult to descend, due to the depth of each row of steps and the vertical nature of them.

"It is best to descend backwards", she cautioned. A solid gold Jaguar had been found in a central chamber, reached by a labyrinthine tunnel, but those who feared enclosed spaces were not advised to investigate it. The gold Jaguar had long since been looted. The Mayan ball-court was another wonder. The carvings of the players on its walls depicted the sacrifice of the winning team's captain who then became a God according to their religion. "Definitely better to be in charge of the losing side", Jack observed.

The temple of the Eagle Warriors was another mind impacting building, as were the rows of stone columns beside it.

I whispered to Jack and Carolyn. "A bit like Karnak, the Pharaonic temple on the Nile in Egypt, only with much smaller and thinner columns".

A fascinating description of the Eagle Warriors who had worn a feather body sleeve that was then heavily lacquered with thick varnish, then followed. Cortes' conquistadors had difficulty conquering the Indians as the body sleeve had deflected even bullets.

"An early form of body armour", Jack surmised. Our group had now drifted down to the raison d'être of the site, the deep well that gave this place its eponymous name. 'Chichen Itza', our guide was saying, "means in the Mayan language - In the mouth of Itzae's well. This sinkhole was their source of water for the whole community and the lifeblood of their survival. The whole site", she continued, "is built upon nine massive structured platforms that keep the buildings from sinking out of sight in the swampy jungle, these platforms are eighteen miles square each. If you climb to the top of the pyramid you can see how enormous the site is, extending to the horizon".

Sally and Carolyn were determined to climb the pyramid, Jack and I were less enthusiastic, but said that we'd catch up with them after we'd examined the raised sacrificial altars where thousands of slaves had been beheaded or sacrificed. The girls departed as I lit a cigar and leant over the edge of the well, its deep green translucent colour was fascinating. "Look-out Bernie!" - Jack's yell of warning came just in time and I dropped to the ground clutching at masses of outgrowing tree roots.

Parides bulky figure almost stunned me as he crashed over the top of me and over the edge of the well. An enormous splash signalled his entry to the pool where he disappeared!

"That's one of the Sobatsu hit-men, Jack!. Let's get the hell out of here! There's bound to be others around". Both of us made haste back to the main site where there were no other tourists to be seen. However, Carolyn and Sally were visible at the top of the pyramid with a few other tourists either halfway up or coming down again.

Jack shouted to me, "That's one of the CIA agents beside them Bernie. At least they'll be safe. What do you think we should do?"

"Stay with the crowds Jack. Look there's our guide and some of the others at the far end of the pillars".

"I'm with you buddy", Jack shouted as I raced to catch up with our group. There was a degree of safety in numbers, I calculated. I felt my left shoulder-pad slipping as I ran; I was about to lose my last wad of dollars. I clutched at my shoulder as I'd already lost my hat and sun-specs. We were half-way through the columns when I ran full into a man. He'd stepped out intentionally and floored me. I was gasping for breath, now being partially winded from the impact. Shading my eyes from the bright sun, I looked up at another figure bending in my direction.

"Buenos tardes, Señor Martin, we meet for the last time". I briefly saw the muzzle flash as the sun went out.

Jim Turner had cursed when directed to the main car and coach park, but the metal barriers were down and staying there. They had been built to stop tanks obviously. Letting the other agents out, he directed Joe to park the car quickly, then join them in the site or wherever. He could see the big gorilla and the Sobatsu foursome a good five hundred yards ahead.

"We'd better get a move on guys. There's our targets".

Philippe had directed Parides to speed on ahead of the group and scout out where Martin had gone and to make contact with Ramon who was with the main tourist group. His mobile was bleeping and Philippe stopped briefly to receive the news from Ramon that Martin and his three friends were now in the archeological site with the English-speaking guide. They hurried onwards, oblivious of the three men following them as fast as they could cover the ground.

"Remember compadres, Martin is mine, just cover me from any outside interference", he snarled. "You've flown far my little martin", he panted to himself.

This was a young man's job, he thought, now recognising that he'd been sitting at desks for far too long. He was glad when the gates to the site finally came into view. Taking in the archeological site with one long sweeping glance, Philippe directed his men towards Ramon who was gesticulating from behind one of the rows of stone columns.

"Where is he?" Jorgé gasped. Where's Martin?"

"Parides has gone after him. They've disappeared down the trail at the other side of the sacrificial altar", responded Ramon. "He said that he'd flush him back towards us and to wait here".

"Si esta es perfecto, Parides conoce el problema", said Philippe, recognising that his lieutenant would guide Martin to his doom at his own, Jorgé's hands. Philippe was glad of the respite and leaning against one of the pillars, signalled his men to take cover behind the columns. And here they come he thought, as he saw Martin with another male racing towards them. Just like driven vicuña, he smiled in bloodthirsty anticipation, remembering hunts that he'd enjoyed in the Andean foothills many years previously. His breathing was becoming less laboured now as Ramon floored Martin and then immediately tackled the other man.

He leant forward, saw the amazed recognition in Martin's eyes as he said smugly,

"Buenos tardes Señor Martin. We meet for the last time".

A violent pain passed through his left side as he squeezed the trigger of his.38 and he wondered vaguely about the pleasurable hurt that finally killing Martin was giving him. Philippe didn't hear the other shots nor did he recognise that he, himself, was dead on his feet. His now sightless eyes did not see Ramon's body cartwheel backwards off the other stranger's prone form. Nor was he aware of the men who appeared magically in their midst and he did not witness his other three operatives surrendering. It was over.

Jim Turner had got off a shot fractionally before Philippe's one, followed by another from Hank. Both of them had cut down the other armed hood who had tackled McAllister and who was now sitting up rather groggily.

"God they got Bernie!" His exclamation of sorrow carried grief and affection for his friend.

Caroline and Sally were being helped down the final few steps from the pyramid by Chuck Hanson. Sally, already in tears and rushing to her beloved Bernard's motionless body. "Darling, darling I'm sorry, why does it have to be this way!"

Her sobbing frame was gently raised from Bernard's body by Jack and Jim Turner together, when with a loud groan his body moved and a loud exhalation of breath made them all start. "He's alive!" shouted Sally. "Get a doctor!".

Hank was checking for physical damage and a pulse, "He's O.K. Mrs Martin, his heart's playing the stars and stripes. He's just unconscious. All these hundred dollar bills you see covering the ground must have deflected the bullet. I think that he's only slightly injured. Possibly a broken collar bone and a flesh wound, I reckon".

Sally sank weakly to the ground, Carolyn patting her hand.

Jack said, "Always said that Bernie could fall down a sewer and come out smelling of aftershave, but this time he's been saved by the almighty dollar".

Sirens announced the arrival of ambulances and police cars, the carabineri had arrived in large numbers, just in case.

"Bernie's coming round", observed Jack who was aiding Hank's search for damage, "And you're right, it is only a flesh wound, although by the shape of his shoulder there's more than a broken collar-bone. He's one lucky son-of-a-gun though!"

"You'd all better go with him", Jim Turner said as the medics loaded Bernard into the ambulance. "I'll catch-up with you later. And don't leave town".

The Mexican Commissioner was descending from a large black Mercedes, his beam summed up Jim's feelings.

"Todo es satisfacione, eh!, Senor Turner?".

"Si Todo es magnifico Comisionado, muchas gracias por todo su ayuda".

Jim Turner had phoned Nick Vyon on the return journey to Cancun. "You can let the Bureau know boss, their friend can rest in peace, yes no-one else other than Martin injured and he should be walking wounded in the morning. The Mexican Police Commissioner arrived in the final moments to check that all was satisfactory and I thanked him very much for his help. No news of the Venus? O.K. we'll hear in due course from the DEA if they're tracking it. We'll be heading home tomorrow afternoon after I've seen the hero and his friends. I've got the full transcripts and they're mighty interesting. I feel that we should give Martin a little time with his wife and friends and will ask him to call on us in ten days from now, by that time we'll know what other questions we have to ask. Oh yeah boss!, and I have to extend the Commissioner's thanks to you, also from me and my guys. The local surveillance was a great help. I'm off to buy the guys a slap-up meal and a big drink, does it go on the expense account? Mean bugger!", he said aloud to no-one in particular as he replaced the mobile in his pocket. "Sorry guys, I tried", he added.

I was released from hospital next morning and I joined Sal, Jack and Carolyn back at the Condessa for a few days before we returned to New York and then travelling onwards to Penn Yan. My shoulder had taken the impact of Philippe's bullet, but Sally's presence and my friends' company aided the healing process both physically and mentally. Comfortable and luxurious accommodation also helped.

Sally's comment of, "Even the straws for the cool drinks have their little dust-caps", had us all amused at her own obvious enjoyment.

I'd been fully forgiven, I thought. It was now time to keep all those promises I had made when on the run. The future of this planet is now firmly in others' hands, I decided. It was no longer my problem. My own credit card had now expired and I had to ask Sally to settle our hotel bill, as all my remaining dollar bills would need exchanging before I could use them again. The currency now being either torn, dirty or blood-covered. It was an even greater pleasure to be informed by reception that the Cancun Commissioner of Police had paid our bill.

The receipt had a note of his good wishes for a safe and pleasant journey home and a guaranteed future welcome to his country from his people. All of us agreed that the Yucatan Peninsula had much to offer. Our taxi-ride to the airport was conducted in much bonhomie and in high good humour. Only twinges from my shoulder reminded me of something that already appeared somewhat unreal. Jim Turner and his team would await further instructions as to where the other Chief Executive Officers had gone before they too would leave Cancun.

He was at the airport to wish us a safe trip and remind me to keep an appointment with the Agency, in ten days from then, for a full debriefing.

His assurance that it was just a matter of time before they collared all the other dangerous participants involved with the Top Ten's world domination and control, was of great comfort to Sally and myself. Depending on where Jefferson surfaced, he reckoned that Jefferson would be another team's problem from that point on. The Venus was under surveillance night and day by the DEA who would have a reception committee awaiting its arrival at any port of call.

Suddenly I felt very tired and was happy to be told what to do by Sally and Jack, I hardly noticed our journey back to Penn Yan.

Twenty-one

Jefferson had transferred to the limousine before the Lear had taxied to its allocated parking, he was in a hurry to reach the Venus. Even his secretary Ardeth had deserted him. The final faxes from his New York office had confirmed that a temporary secretary had taken her place. Ardeth's own resignation letter having also been faxed to him. Only when he'd reached the commercial port, and boarded the Venus had he relaxed a little in his stateroom suite.

Captain Schiffé had been given his sailing orders and they'd left harbour within fifteen minutes of his boarding. Ordering his favourite tipple of Bacardi and Cola he sat back in the armchair studying large scale maps of the Caribbean and of Brasil. For the second time in the period of a few days he experienced the thoughts of the hunted instead of the hunter. Yes salesman, he thought. Both of us are survivors, but I may have to disappear completely. Money wouldn't be a problem; his numbered account in Switzerland had more than a billion dollars in it and this was increasing daily. He'd better live to enjoy it, he thought, or that particular Swiss Bank would be constructing another edifice, courtesy of yours truly, outwith anyone else's knowledge except the immediate banking circles. Banks, insurance companies and pension funds, they can't go wrong, he deliberated, unless they had rogue traders. Larry smiled wryly to himself. Up to this point he'd felt himself to be above and beyond the reach of the laws that most others had to observe. The enormous multi-national company that he'd headed, had mega-strength, both in the economic and political arena. Now, because of a precipitate action that would probably become a necessity within the next two decades, he had to forsake his power and position and find somewhere to hide. He'd have to assume a new identity, probably undergo some painful plastic surgery and start again in something that wouldn't draw attention to himself.

Travel would be out for some years, at least until the world's law enforcement agencies lost interest, and that would depend on how much public pressure there was likely to be. He would be a pariah amongst the other Nine, but they would have to save their own skins, he considered. It would depend on how much of a general cover-up there was.

It wasn't often that he'd considered his other half during his business career, his wife had faithfully supported him throughout their marriage, but in many ways she had also gone her own way in life. Her circle of friends had been different to his and he'd been very generous over her allowances and she was now independently wealthy. There was little doubt in his own mind that she would survive and probably continue to enjoy the lifestyle that she'd become accustomed to. It would be the explanations that she would be asked about that would be most annoying for her and, depending on how much was revealed, the necessary answers. However, she hated the tropics, wasn't privy to his business deals, and having enjoyed her own social circles would cope well with the future by herself. As they'd made a conscious decision not to have any family before their marriage, there were no complications.

He was carrying over $100,000 in a specially fitted security vest that had been made for him many years previously. That should keep the wolf from the door until I can arrange things, he decided. There were also various currencies in the yacht's vault and some Bearer Bonds; he'd remember to take these with him. He rang the galley for another Bacardi and Cola. Where do I start?, he pondered, poring over the maps. Larry had little intention of entering Brasil via Rio de Janeiro. The yacht even at full speed would take almost three weeks to get there and he'd little doubt about the reception committee. In the full glare of International publicity, the Brazilian authorities would have no alternative, but acquiesce to any requests for justice. A knock on the door heralded Captain Schiffé 's entry with a number of faxes for his attention.

"Come in and close the door would you Schiffé", he said, indicating that the Captain should take a seat. "Just give me a moment to scan these faxes first and then I'll be with you". None of them was good news. Four were from other Top Ten CEO's with confirmation that his neck was on the block and that they were quite literally saving themselves and admitting all to their various Governments. It was to be fully expected and much as he would have done in the same position. A reflex nod of his head was accompanied by a bitter smile. The other business faxes indicated concerns about the early whispers and knowing gossip. It wouldn't be long before a US coastguard cutter or other naval ship was dispatched to escort his return to the States.

Another knock at his stateroom's door had Captain André open it to reveal a steward with Jefferson's drink.

"Will you join me Captain? I have a few things to discuss with you and it may require a little time".

"Thank you sir, but only in a soda. I run a strict discipline while we're at sea".

"Yes Captain, I forget. Then steward bring us a selection of sodas".

Larry topped-up his large Bacardi with care from the can. The code lettering grabbed his attention. He stiffened and asked André "Where did you load this batch of soft-drinks from Captain? This can shows that it was produced in Mexico, the date of manufacture being just six weeks ago. I thought that I'd given strict instructions that all our soft drinks had to be taken from our home base and not to be purchased elsewhere".

"That's correct sir, but we cleaned our store-room while in port at Cancun and some of the outdated supplies were exchanged I believe", replied André.

Another knock had the steward entering with a tray of cold cans and Jefferson said.

"Right Captain, give me five minutes and perhaps you could find out how long it will take us to reach Trinidad before you return".

"Yes sir, I'll see to it this instant", and André closed the door behind him and made for the Bridge. My God, he thought. He's not going to nit-pick over the damned supplies of his soft drinks. And now he wants to go to Trinidad, I wonder why? Captain André hadn't read his boss's faxes. He had paused only to identify the recipient, but couldn't avoid grasping the rough content. Trouble was in the wind, he thought.

Jefferson was studying the varied cans of soft drinks, the dates of manufacture and which cannery had filled them. All were from the batch with the second ingredient added. There couldn't have been that amount of old stock aboard could there? Hell and damnation, he thought. He'd already drunk some of it. What if the Venus had been stocked with the first recipe also? — And where would the final batch be? He rummaged in his briefcase. There had been faxes from New York to the Lear that hadn't made a lot of sense, and he'd left those for later as there were more important things to deal with. Yes, here it was! A late confirmation about the cancellation of the addition of the third ingredient by both canneries in Central America. They'd produced only a test batch for delivery to Jefferson aboard the Venus! The words almost leapt off the page at him. This stuff's aboard! Steady, I have to think this out. His mind was wind-milling —— Calm down! Think this through!

Well I've already drunk some of it, he considered, as he took another sip of his drink. It's not going to make any difference, but I must trace and dispose of the third batch. He decided it must be in the storeroom, but he'd have to be careful not to alert Captain André or any of the crew. An idea was forming in his mind, this might be helpful after all, a gift from the Gods. Studying his maps he came to a decision. He would get off at Port of Spain in Trinidad, then cross into Venezuela or Guyana; it should be relatively easy to gain entry to Brasil from either country, and if it worked; there would be no-one around to pin-point where he'd gone; it was the perfect solution.

His musings were interrupted by another knock. Captain Schiffé had returned with the necessary information and also wished to know when dinner was to be served. The chef would be preparing it shortly and had asked the captain for an exact time.

"Yes Schiffé, eight-thirty will be fine. Give the galley a call will you", and calmly added. "By the way Captain, I should like to examine your manifest and the storeroom before dinner. But first at what time do we reach Trinidad?"

"Tomorrow morning sir, around ten or thereby we should enter the Port of Spain", Captain André replied.

"Good, good, good Schiffé. I think that I'll fly from there catch up with you in Rio three weeks from now. I've a lot of things to attend to and I can get better and more secure communications ashore".

André was puzzled. The secure communications aboard couldn't be improved upon, but he wouldn't look this gift-horse in the mouth or tempt the gods by pointing this out to his boss. It was a major relief to him that Jefferson was considering leaving the yacht for the present, although he had to admit that the boss hadn't been his customary, arrogant and demanding self. There must be some major deal in the air. He snapped to attention as his boss said.

"Let's go and inspect the stores and the manifests shall we?".

Jefferson's trained eye for different writing on his special mixtures over the years identified the pallet almost as soon as he entered the store, but he made a point of checking all the stores for his Captain's benefit. They returned to the Bridge where André laid out all the store's manifests, which were categorised and itemised with exact dates of purchase.

"All is in order Schiffé", said Jefferson. "But I noticed a new batch of mixed soft drinks that I think were destined for test by myself. Their date of manufacture is less than three weeks ago. Have the stewards replace those in the deck saloon with them, so that I can taste them before I leave".

"Yes sir. Will we be tying-up for long in Port of Spain sir?"

"No Schiffé. In fact you won't enter port; the chopper will take me ashore from a safe anchorage. Then you can make a faster passage to Rio in case I need you there".

Captain Schiffé spoke out. "Sir, on behalf of the crew may I say that they haven't had much of a break since we left Fort Lauderdale. The loss of the cruise with your friends and now this fast continuous trip to Rio do not make for a happy ship. Could I not arrange a delegated day-off for the crew to take a break prior to our voyage to Rio".

It was just what Jefferson needed for his plans. He had skilfully manoeuvred Schiffé into making the request through the removal of docking at Trinidad.

Now he replied. "Yes, all right Schiffé. One day more won't make much difference, I suppose. You can take a day off when you are in Brazilian waters, say in Belém or maybe Fortaleza, and I'll donate a case of my Bacardi for the crew's enjoyment".

Pigs will fly one of these days, thought André, adding aloud. "Thank you sir. With your permission I'll inform the crew right now of your generosity".

With that, he flipped the Tannoy switch and broadcast the news. Faint cheers could be heard from all sectors of the yacht. And that makes certain you can't renege on that promise, André thought. The opportunity to blow off a little steam in another eight days or so should remove any future tensions and trouble.

Jefferson spent his time shredding documents and surreptitiously dumping the contents of a few cans of each type of drink from the deck saloon's refrigerator over the side. He confined his own consumption to those from his stateroom, making fully certain of the date before pouring. The extra currencies were transferred to his vest, the Bearer bonds to his briefcase. An early night was called for, he decided. The next few days could be very tiring.

Anchoring offshore amongst the commercial ships awaiting discharge or loading facilities at the Port of Spain, Captain André called the port authorities informing them that they were in transit, but had a passenger to deliver to the International airport by chopper.

As the helicopter lifted off, Jefferson was amazed to see a number of the crew actually wave. Amazing the effect a day off and some free booze will do, he reflected. His own calculations were that the third ingredient stocks in the saloon's refrigerator would remain fully intact until the crew party in Fortaleza or Belém. With a bit of luck there would be no trail for any outside authorities to follow. They would surmise that he'd fallen overboard. He had taken the precaution of removing the Log and had explained to Schiffé that he wished to check the year's details to date and that André should start a fresh Log from the following morning.

The Captain's notations about his own generosity with the provision of a case of spirits and also his departure from the yacht by chopper had already been written up. It would have been very inconvenient for his own planning to have such clear pointers as to where he'd gone. He was off to start a new life and build another empire. Already he was in his full planning mode. Name change and some plastic surgery would be required before a new identity could be constructed that would be impenetrable to even the most exhaustive of investigations. He reached into an inside pocket in his briefcase and extracted a Brazilian Passport made out in a different name, but carrying his photograph. It was one of many that he'd collected at his stopover in Zurich.

Yes salesman, he considered idly, as the chopper landed. You taught me a lot!

Epilogue

The six friends were enjoying a celebration meal in the Red Fox Inn, Myron and Gerald were being regaled by first, Jack, then Carolyn and eventually Sally with finally Bernie adding to the story.

"God, I don't believe you guys, do you Gerald? To think that I've sweated over a hot stove for days just to show you how much I care about you all !"

Myron's expression of total disbelief sought agreement from his partner. Gerald agreed, but his eyes were dancing with mischief.

"Anyway guys", continued Myron. "I give you a toast, to the good old CIA".

The others looked askance. "I got a check this morning, I billed them for the Sobatsu couple's stay. God bless them!".

"By the way Bernie", said Jack. "Those wrought-iron chains that you once mentioned. They're now a fact". He placed his hand gently around Carolyn's.

"Glad to hear it Jack. Congratulations both of you", I said.

"Let's listen to the news then", said Gerald, "while I organise the coffee and brandies".

"And no colas!", we all replied together.

"This is a CNN broadcast".

"The Mexican Government has announced that another drug-gang has been successfully broken up in Cancun. The Mexican Government had been working in harness with both the CIA and the DEA to put an end to this menace. A number of the gang were killed in the final shoot-out. The Mexican Government has been highly praised for their help and co-operation in the matter by the US administration. British Intelligence was also singled out for especial praise over their people's involvement and for supplying the information that aided the US security services to bring the drug-dealers to justice.

A modern-day Marie Celesté was found drifting off the coast of Brasil this morning by Brazilian coast guards.

The Motor Yacht Venus, owned by Planet Ales Incorporated of the United States was found drifting in the southern current off Recifé Brasil. Its engines were still running, but all the crew were found dead aboard at their stations. Early investigations have not revealed any foul play, but the US coastguard is sending a forensic team to Recifé later today and will also send a work-crew to recover the yacht for a fuller examination. A member of the Brazilian coastguard boarding party said that the yacht's crew appeared to have fallen asleep, like some Rip-van-Winkle effect. There was nothing untoward except that the owner, Mr Laurence C. Jefferson, who was known to have been aboard, had vanished. The Federal Bureau of Investigation would like to interview Mr Jefferson in connection with breaches of the US anti-trust laws and they know that he left Cancun Mexico some two weeks ago. They think that there could be some connection with the earlier disappearance of Mr Jefferson's senior chemist at Planet Ales' laboratories in New York. They would also like to interview him. The Venus which sailed from Cancun was en route to its next destination, that of Rio de Janeiro".

"The British Parliament continues to block the import of all genetically modified foodstuffs from America. They are seeking assurances from the US that the two companies who control the genetics and chemicals for the growth of these foods do not hold the world to ransom with the pricing of them. While the new terminator gene has ben put on hold at present, financial experts acting on behalf of the UK Government argue that new seed will be required every season thereafter and that all the patents, supply and marketing lies within too few hands, thus creating a monopoly of all agrarian production around the globe. British commercial bodies are also expressing concern at the number of patents being applied to genetic material by huge American companies. They state that it will be little short of blackmail when many of the new generation drugs and advances in medical science have to be purchased, thereby obtaining the technology and information necessary for a vibrant, cutting-edge, Health Service. The US is threatening a trade war with Europe if Britain and its European allies do not make immediate, positive arrangements to allow the importation and use of all such products.

An American study group has been studying the increases in feminism, lesbianism and homosexuality. They propound the theory that the rising percentages of all three groups, taken together with other indicators, that this could be a direct form of the earth protecting itself from overpopulation and by reducing any future population increases by other means. The leader of the group was quoted as saying, "What man himself will not undertake, in the necessary form of controlling his numbers; be certain that nature will oblige."

Global warming continues to have a severe effect on the climate changes experienced around the world. Scientists are demanding immediate action to reverse the pollution that is exacerbating this problem. The El Niño effect is being followed by the equally devastating climatic aberrations of La Niña.

Volcanologists are predicting a period of extreme volcanic activity within the Pacific ring-of-fire. Theories are being mooted that the removal of the cooling influence of underground water supplies from ancient aquifers for irrigation, and possibly that of ever increasing oil extraction, that this is destabilising the earth's magma and allowing the earth's core to overheat. Violent movement of the earth's tectonic plates is expected to follow. This will result in numerous and recurring earthquakes of devastating dimension around the globe. Together with already rising sea levels, now being experienced worldwide, greater areas of coastline will be at risk and the danger of more frequent and larger tsunamis in the Pacific region are expected.

An august body of European scientists who have been researching the conflicting theories and reasoning on why the Dinosaurs became extinct have now published their findings. The theory of a gigantic meteor being responsible for an instant and violent climate change is now being replaced by the possibility that extreme volcanic activity spewed out sufficient toxic gases to wipe them out in a very short period of time.

Jack said. "These newscasts are all concerning you Bernie, so much so, you could have written the script! But you're right. It's up to others now; it's not your problem any longer".

"You're wrong Jack", I replied. Even more, I realise now - that it's everyone's problem".